QUEEN OF A DISTANT HIVE

ISBN 978-1-912145-10-2

www.acorndigitalpress.com

Dedication

To Anthea Dove –
with many thanks for excellent editorial advice and kind
encouragement

QUEEN
OF A DISTANT
HIVE

THERESA TOMLINSON

CONTENTS

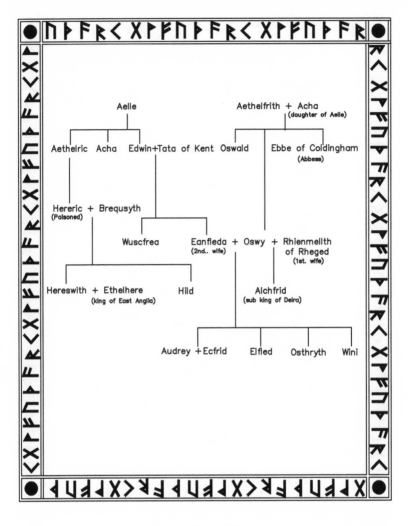

Family Tree

King Oswy's Northumbria

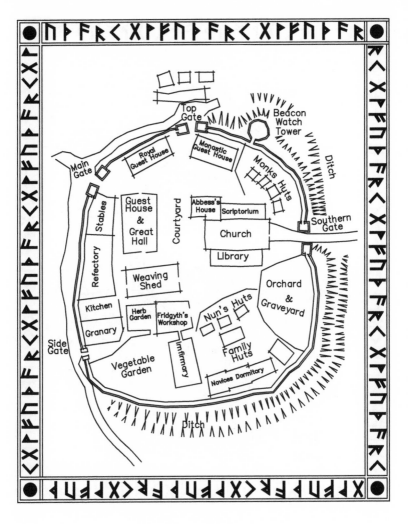

Hild's Monastery

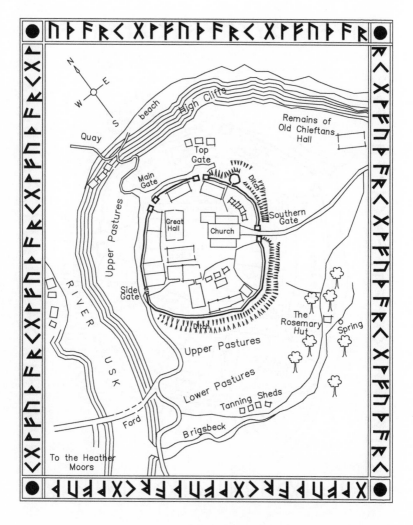

Streonshalh

LIST OF THE MAIN CHARACTERS

King Oswy – overlord of most of the northern lands, since he killed King Penda of Mercia at the battle of the Winwaed. His main residence is Bebbanburgh.

Queen Eanfleda – Oswy's Queen. The daughter of King Edwin of Northumbria and the mother of King Ecfrid, Princess Elfled and Princess Osthryth. Her main residence is Bebbanburgh.

Hild – a royal abbess who rules a double monastery of monks and nuns at Streonshalh (Whitby) and Hartlepool. Her father Hereric (who had a claim to the throne of Deira) was poisoned when she was a young child.

Elfled – the daughter of King Oswy and Queen Eanfleda. She was 'given to God' to be raised as a nun when she was a baby, in thanks for her father's victory against King Penda at the Battle of the Winwaed. She was put into the care of Abbess Hild, who became her foster mother.

Ecfrid – son of King Oswy and Queen Eanfleda, he was raised as a child hostage at the court of Queen Cynewise of Mercia. He was recently appointed sub-king of Deira and married to a much older widow, Queen Audrey.

Irminburgh – a beautiful and ambitious Kentish noblewoman, related to Queen Eanfleda. She was raised as a foster daughter to Queen Cynewise.

Caedmon – once the cowherd at Hild's monastery; his gift for singing and poetry has been discovered and he now resides in the monastery, where he is training to be a monk.

Cynewise – the ageing widow of King Penda of Mercia. She was put in charge of Ecfrid when he was a child-hostage. Following her husband's death she was kept a prisoner by King Oswy, for fear she would stir up rebellion if allowed to return to Mercia

Wulfhere – the older son of King Penda and Cynewise, now King of Mercia.

Prince Aethelred – the younger son of King Penda and Cynewise, raised in Deira as a Christian by his foster father, Siward of Dreng, on the orders of King Oswy.

Fridgyth – pagan wise-woman, appointed by Hild as monastery herb-wife.

Sister Lindi – Elfled's new tutor, a young nun, lately arrived from Hartlepool.

Cwen – the Chief Webster in charge of the weaving hut.

Wulfrun – Cwen's daughter, appointed by Hild as Elfled's companion and bodyguard. (See my Young Adult novel *Wolf Girl*)

Ketel – once the main boat-builder in Streonshalh, lately appointed monastery reeve by Abbess Hild.

Edric – the tanner who lives in Brigsbeck Valley, where he conducts his trade away from the main habitations, due to the offensive nature of the process.

Muriel – the tanner's wife.

Godric – the tanner's oldest son, who has learnt the process of vellum-making.

Ralf – the tanner's younger son, a tanner and shoemaker.

Herrig – a young orphan boy who works for the tanners.

Siward of Dreng – Prince Aethelred's Christian foster father, appointed by Oswy.

HISTORICAL NOTE

The Kingdom of Northumbria was made up of two ancient kingdoms – Bernicia to the North, which stretched roughly from the River Tees, to what is now the Scottish Borders and Deira to the South, which stretched from the River Humber to the Tees.

In the earlier part of the 7th century Northumbria was constantly at war with Mercia, a vast kingdom that stretched south from the Humber to Wessex and to the Welsh borders in the west. In 642 AD Penda, the fierce pagan King of Mercia, killed King Oswald, who ruled the whole of Northumbria, at the battle of Maserfield. Following Oswald's death, his younger brother Oswy became ruler of Bernicia only, as a vassal of King Penda, while his young cousin Oswin was chosen by the local Witan (council) to rule Deira in the southern half of Northumbria. Resentful that he only had half the land that his older brother Oswald had once ruled, Oswy challenged his cousin to do battle for Deira, but seeing the vast size of the forces against him, Oswin refused to fight. He dispersed his army and sought shelter in the hall of Hunwald, who he believed to be his friend, but he was betrayed there and murdered by Oswy's men. Still Deira resisted Oswy's rule and accepted Oswald's son Ethelwald as their king. It was only in 655 AD, when Oswy killed Penda at the battle of the Winwaed, that he eventually succeeded in ruling the whole of Northumbria. Oswy then became the powerful overlord of most of northern Britain. Following a Mercian rebellion, he allowed Wulfhere, King Penda's Christian son, to rule in Mercia and in 666 AD he appointed his son, Ecfrid to rule as Sub-king of Deira.

NAMES OF THE MONTHS

After-Yule-month – January
Mudmonth – February
Hreda's-month – March
Eastermonth – April
Threemilkingmonth – May
First Gentlemonth – June
Second Gentlemonth – July
Weedmonth – August
Offeringsmonth – September
Winterfullmoon – October
Bloodmonth – November
Yulemonth – December

"A small society comprising systems worthy of your high esteem. Its leaders great of heart, its customs, character, and conflicts – these I'll report, bit by bit, as is appropriate."

Virgil Georgics (on bees)
- A new translation by Peter Fallon.
Oxford World's Classics

CHAPTER 1

AN EXCELLENT EXCHANGE

"Make sure you have at hand clear springs and pools with moss-fringed rims, a rippling stream that rambles through the grass."

Virgil – Georgics. A new translation by Peter Fallon,
Oxford World's Classics

Fridgyth walked at an ambling pace as the light began to fade. She led Drogo the mule uphill away from Streonshalh towards the heather moors, having forded the River Usk while the tide was at its lowest.

"Easy does it, my darlings," she murmured, as they struggled on up the steep slope. "Worst bit over soon."

The ageing herb-wife kept up a constant stream of soothing conversation aimed not so much at the mule, though he flicked his ears pleasantly at the familiar sound of her voice, but at the valuable cargo he carried. Fridgyth needed to make this journey at dusk, in order to keep the tiny inhabitants of Drogo's panniers calm and not to disturb their daily pattern of work. Two double bee skeps were wrapped in fine linen and carefully placed into the mule's baskets. Drogo had been specially chosen for this task because, like the herb-wife, his pace had slowed. His steady, plodding movements made him just right for the job.

Towards the end of Weed-month, Fridgyth regularly transported two of her best hives in this way, out to the heather moors, where

1

they'd stay for a few weeks to feast on the powerful sweetness of the blooming heather. Over her many years of healing work for the monastery, the herb-wife had observed that honey from heather made the most potent ingredient for her medicines. The glorious deep pink and purple flowers that crept over the surrounding hills in late summer seemed to concentrate the last powerful gleams of the sun's warmth into the sweet, sticky, substance the bees produced. A wound dressed with heather honey rarely turned foul, and when mixed with thyme and blackberries, it made the most effective cure for a painful throat or racking cough. Such complaints were common in Streonshalh, for the monastery was situated on high, north-facing clifftops. However, the acquisition of this precious medicinal ingredient required two slow journeys back and forth to the wilderness of heather, and Fridgyth would entrust neither her bees, nor the supervision of the mule, to anyone else.

As she moved on, she became aware of the sound of hooves behind her. She stopped, curious to see who else was leaving Streonshalh at so late an hour. A loaded wagon headed steadily up the slope behind her, hauled by a fast pair of mules, and Fridgyth recognised the red-haired lad who drove it as Ralf, the Briggsbeck tanner's younger son. Even without the last rays of sunlight catching his fiery hair, she'd have known the waggon, for as it came closer, the reek of the tanning pits travelled ahead of the cart.

She held Drogo back and waved the waggon on. "Get past!" she cried. "Don't stop for old slow-bones here."

But instead of passing, as she'd expected him to do, Ralf drew his wagon to a halt. He didn't come close, for he'd seen the tops of the hives sticking out of the panniers and understood the importance of Fridgyth's mission.

"Who's the slow-bones, then," he called, "the herb-wife or the mule?"

"Get on your way, bold-face!" she retaliated cheerfully. "I daresay we're both slow-bones, if the truth be known."

Ralf lifted the reins to drive his beasts on, but then he seemed to change his mind and, for a moment or two, appeared strangely reluctant to set off again.

"It is just that…" he began. "I had it in mind to ask a favour… and when I saw you here…"

Fridgyth smiled. "Oh aye?" she said.

He fastened the reins of his waggon and climbed down to stand in front of her. The herb-wife patted her mule to keep him still and waited patiently, unsurprised by the sudden change in Ralf's behaviour.

"How can I help?" she asked gently, as the lad awkwardly shifted his weight from foot to foot.

Fridgyth was used to being approached in this uncertain manner. Love potions were her stock in trade, as was knowledge of certain lovemaking tricks, which might prevent conception and the burden of too many mouths to feed.

A bashful enquirer might need encouragement before he was able to fully state his business, but the herb-wife always cheerfully shared her knowledge without passing judgement. Over the years her reputation for sense and kindness in these matters had travelled around.

She thoughtfully looked the lad up and down. Though not as handsome as his older brother Godric, Ralf was still a strong, healthy lad. The tanners' trade had thrived since Abbess Hild had founded the monastery on the cliffs, for boots, shoes, bags and saddles were everyday requirements. The scriptorium too now made demands on certain branches of the trade and Fridgyth had heard that Ralf's brother had recently been studying to learn the skill of curing calfskins, in order to supply the monastery school with parchment. Both the tanner brothers would make attractive husbands. No lass who married a tanner would go hungry, cold, or short of decent clothing, though she'd be expected to turn her hand to a few unpleasant and stinking tasks from time to time. These reflections whisked through the herb-wife's mind, while Ralf still hesitated, uncertain how to frame his question.

"Is it a lass?" Fridgyth asked at last.

He heaved a sigh. "Aye, a lass… a lady far above me in station… and I cannot name her. She is kind to me, but…"

"What's the problem then?" Fridgyth asked.

"This." He waved his hand at the wagon. "The damned stench of the tanning pits, which follows me everywhere. My lady hides her distaste, but I know that she shrinks from the very stench of me."

Fridgyth nodded sagely; she could see the problem, she would not deny it.

Ralf managed at last to get to the nub of his request. "I have heard, that you brew a potion, that smells so sharp and so sweet, that it cuts through any foul odour."

Fridgyth chuckled. "You must mean my lavender brew," she said. "Yes, lavender might well work for you. Some say it's a love potion too, but I'd not vouch for that. I know it can heal skin sores. You have to wash in clean water and then rub a small amount on your hands neck and hair. It makes you smell like a bed of sweet herbs... but only for a little while. You have to wash and apply it again each time you wished..."

"I thank you," he said and he began to look cheerful again. "I can wash in Brigsbeck near the spring, before the tanning work fouls the water."

"Well... as luck would have it..." Fridgyth said and she began to fiddle with some small containers that swung from her girdle. "I have a small vial about my person. I always carry it with me."

"Bless you, herb-wife! How can I pay you?" Ralf asked, for he knew that Fridgyth would expect a fair exchange for the many hours of chopping, pounding and seething, involved in the making of her lavender brew.

"Well... I have no need of parchment, leather purse or pouch," she began.

The lad suddenly turned to his wagon with a smile.

"I think I have the very thing," he said. "Shoes! I've many pairs in this wagon, but they are spoken for, and none of these would fit women's feet, but I could make you a strong pair of turnshoes for winter. I'd stitch them firmly and add a second sole inside, lined with lambs' fleece. They could be finished with an ankle strap to secure them and ready to wear before the bitter-months arrive."

"Oh yes," Fridgyth immediately agreed with enthusiasm. "Our deal is done! An excellent exchange."

New leather turnshoes would be a blessing as winter approached and rather more than she'd have expected to barter for a small container of lavender brew.

"You shall have two vials of lavender for a pair of turnshoes," she offered fairly, "one for each shoe. If it does the trick with your lass, come back for more! Take this for now. The top is plugged with beeswax, so you can warm it and reseal it. You won't need much, but remember, wash first!"

He took the small container from her and sniffed it. "I can scent it through the beeswax – a good, clean smell," he said.

"Get on with you then," Fridgyth said "And may Freya smile on you and your lass."

When they had completed the transaction to their mutual satisfaction, Ralf turned to go, but before he'd had time to climb back onto his wagon, they both heard the sound of hooves ahead. The rhythmic thudding was faint at first, but quickly grew louder.

"Who's this?" Fridgyth asked.

"Someone travelling fast," Ralf commented.

"And I thought I was to have a quiet journey," Fridgyth complained.

Two riders appeared over the brow of the hill ahead and Fridgyth sighed, for they advanced at a furious pace and she feared that the speed and noise of their passing would upset her bees. She moved at once to pull Drogo off the pathway and haul him and his burden onto the rougher ground at the side of the track. It was clear that these riders, well mounted and armed, would take little heed of an old woman and her mule.

Ralf leapt back onto his wagon and moved it forward and to the side a little. He halted it protectively between the herb-wife's mule and the advancing party. The riders thundered by without giving them a second glance, but they raised a considerable cloud of dust as they passed.

"No thought or care for locals," Fridgyth grumbled, as a fine spray of dirt settled around her. She cleared her throat, spat, and brushed herself down.

"No," Ralf agreed. "But it looks as though the abbess is expecting guests?"

"Not that I'd heard of," Fridgyth said. "But I'm grateful that you and your waggon were there between us. Now, you get on your way, the light is almost gone, and you let me know how my potion works. I'm interested to know."

Ralf whipped up his mules and set off, a smile on his face. Fridgyth took up Drogo's reins and urged him forward again, at a steadier pace.

It was well past midnight when Fridgyth reached the pleasant, sheltered spot by the stream that in previous years she'd judged to be perfect for her bees. The scent of the heather, even in the moonlight, was redolent of the honey the bees would produce. Though exhausted, the herb-wife stumbled through the essential tasks; she unloaded the hives and provided Drogo with fresh water and oats. She too was hungry, but tiredness overruled her need and she simply took a sip of mead from her drink-horn, wrapped herself in her cloak and settled to sleep until sun-up, on a bed of springy turf.

The following morning she woke early and made a good breakfast of bread and goats' cheese. Having made sure that the bees were contentedly foraging, she bade them farewell with a gathering charm.

'Freya bless your feast, my darlings,
Search sweetness from the brightest blooms
Guard your queens and keep the peace
And I will fetch you home again.'

Then she set off back to Streonshalh with the mule.

CHAPTER 2

THE DRAGON-WIFE

The journey back was easier as it was mostly downhill. When they reached the ford, the tide was flowing, so the herb-wife clambered onto the mule's back in order to keep dry. Drogo, eager to return to his comfortable stable, did not complain at the extra weight. Once safely across, he set off with determination along the steep hillside path that led to the monastery, Fridgyth walking at his side. The monastery of Streonshalh had grown enormously since Abbess Hild had first been granted this piece of land. The settlement that had developed on this blustery hillside now consisted of a timber-built church, a school, a scriptorium, a monastic guest house and most magnificent of all a royal guest house. There were separate areas for the tiny cells for the dedicated monks and nuns, and family accommodation for those lay workers who chose not to be celebate. Weaving sheds on the landward side and a smoky, industrial area of metalwork hearths on the seaward side now made the settlement substancial. The whole place was surrounded by a high wooden palisade built on top of an earthwork. Fridgyth chose to enter the monastery by the small side gate, avoiding the cheerful enquiries and quips that usually came from the guards at the main gate. The side gate was just wide enough for a mule and his burden to slip through

Once Drogo was installed in the monastery stables again, she returned to her sturdy wattle and daub herb-wife's hut. At the sound of her approaching footsteps, her tabby cat Wyrdkin rushed to greet her with a mad fit of purring and head butting. Scooping the creature into her arms, she marched in through the open doorway and thumped herself wearily down upon a stool. Her young assistant Della, already at work chopping dried herbs, looked up and smiled.

"Welcome back," she said. "Have you managed it all?"

"Yes," Fridgyth said, struggling to calm the affectionate cat with a few firm strokes. "The bees are already a-foraging, bless them! But tell me what's new?"

Della shook her head and finished spooning the chopped herbs into the baked clay pots that were made especially for them.

"Not much," she said. "Tom Shepherd's wife birthed a boy last night. You should have heard him howl when he took breath. I told her it was a healthy sign." The girl put her work aside and got up. "Let me make a camomile simple for you and lace it with honey – I can see you are worn out!"

"I am," Fridgyth readily agreed. "But I'm curious too. Two riders, armed and in a hurry, galloped past me last night, heading this way. I was up above the ford and they covered me with dust!"

Della shook her head, as she scooped boiling water from the cauldron that swung from a hook above the hearth. "I've heard nothing, but I expect Father will soon be here. He'll know."

"Get down daft beast," Fridgyth said, setting the cat firmly on the floor.

She gratefully took the soothing brew and looked around her small domain with satisfaction as she sipped it. The air in the hut was pleasantly refreshed by the clean scents of sage, thyme, rosemary and lavender. Drying bunches of those herbs hung from every free spot on the wooden beams that supported the roof. The herb-wife watched as her capable helper made sure that all the pots and bottles were clean, tidy, and neatly in place again. They stood on shelves that had been provided by the girl's father, Ketel, once a boat builder, now the trusted monastery reeve.

She was just finishing her drink, when a young mother appeared, with a red-faced and miserable child in her arms.

"It's his teeth coming through," she began.

"Shall I…?" Della offered.

"No," Fridgyth struggled to her feet. "You've done very well, but I'm back now. Give him here!" she held out her arms to take the child. "Let's have a look at you, little man. We happen to have a little camomile and honey well cooled just here. It will serve fine to rub on those sore gums."

A few more anxious patients came and went, and the sun was low in the sky, by the time the reeve appeared in the herb-wife's doorway. He gave Fridgyth's waist a familiar squeeze, as he slid past her solid girth, to take his usual seat by the hearth.

Both women smiled, but said nothing, for they understood that as newly appointed reeve, Ketel took the responsibility the abbess had given him seriously. The need to slip away to the more relaxed domesticity of the herb-wife's hut had become a daily event.

"Do we have visitors?" Fridgyth asked impatiently, keen to know what was happening.

"Aye," he replied. "And I shouldn't be chatting here with you, but I wanted to make sure you were safely back. Two messengers arrived last night, from Bebbanburgh, and they announced that we're to have a rather surprising lady guest to stay."

Fridgyth looked up sharply. "They almost rode me down," she complained. "And they announced it, you say… not requested it?"

"The messengers came from Oswy and, as you know, our overlord does not make requests, he gives orders. The new young King of Deira is expected to come here too. This meeting is hastily arranged, and I think our poor abbess feels most put-upon, but she cannot refuse."

"Not another Synod!" Fridgyth said.

"No. No Synod, but this is a delicate and tricky business, for the future peace of both Northumbria and Mercia may depend on the outcome of this visit. The lady will arrive next week and King Ecfrid is due here at anytime. He is riding over from Eforwic to meet her."

"Who is it, Father?" Della asked, intrigued.

Fridgyth glared at him. "Surprising visitor! Lady guest! Stop speaking in riddles, you old fool and tell us who this visitor is!"

Ketel paused for effect, knowing the revelation he was about to make would startle them both. "We are to expect a visit from

Cynewise of the Mercians!" he announced. "Penda's widow will be brought in the abbess's barge from Handale Head."

Fridgyth was stunned. The very name he'd spoken, 'Cynewise of the Mercians' brought a thrill of terror with it.

"What?" she cried. "The dragon-wife is coming here... to Streonshalh? That vile woman! The widow of the man who caused the death of my husband and my little ones?"

Della was just as shocked. She clapped a hand to her mouth. "The dragon-wife," she whispered. "The one we once went to Handale to see?"

Ketel nodded; satisfied that he now had their full attention.

Fridgyth glanced from father to daughter. "And you say you've seen her?" she asked, her curiosity piqued, for she herself had never set eyes on the infamous Queen of Mercia.

"No," he said, and he chuckled. "I once took Della, when she was nowt but a lass, to visit my sister – the one who married a salt skimmer, and went to live in the valley below Handale Head. You will remember our Eileen?"

"Yes, of course I remember your Eileen," Fridgyth agreed impatiently.

"Well, we were curious to catch a glimpse of the Mercian Queen, while we were there, but we never set eyes on her. I'm sure you must know that Oswy imprisoned her in the hall he built on Handale Head, after he'd killed King Penda. He feared she'd stir up rebellion against him and try to put one of her sons on the throne if he allowed her to stay in Mercia, so he compelled her to stay here in Deira where he could keep a closer eye on her."

Fridgyth frowned, searching through vague memories of the aftermath of the fierce King of Mercia's death in battle against Oswy of Northumbria. "I knew that she was held captive, but it is long ago now. And you say she's still there at Handale Head?"

"Yes. Oswy has kept her in comfort mind, her and all her entourage."

"But her son did rebel, without his mother's aid," Fridgyth said. "Doesn't Wulfhere of Mercia rule his father's kingdom once again, now?"

"Yes," Ketel agreed. "Wulfhere rules Mercia, but as a Christian, and as Oswy's vassal, something I believe his mother thinks little of. Queen Cynewise has long been free to go where she wants, but she refuses to return to Mercia saying she's comfortable at Handale Head, so now she stays there at Oswy's expense... demanding the best wines, entertainments, expensive silks and furs... and for all the women that serve her too!"

"Huh!" Fridgyth shook her head at the stubbornness of the old woman.

"So why is she coming here?" Della asked, a faint tremor of excitement in her voice.

Ketel sighed. "Well... her youngest son, Prince Aethelred was taken from her when he was very young, and raised as a Christian at Oswy's command. He was put into the care of Siward of Dreng, who you will remember as one of Oswy's older thanes and a staunch believer in the Christ-God. Now, again at Oswy's command, Prince Aethelred comes to Streonshalh in the company of his foster father, to complete his studies. The King wishes mother and son to be reunited. The abbess thinks privately that Oswy wants Queen Cynewise to return to Mercia."

"He wants to wash his hands of her, now she'd old and powerless and simply an expense to him!"

"Aye, maybe!"

Fridgyth bridled. "And our abbess is to oversee this difficult reunion."

"You have the gist of it," Ketel agreed. "Whenever great tact and patience is required, Oswy turns to Hild."

"How old will Aethelred be now?" Fridgyth asked. She puckered her brow as she tried to make a calculation.

"About eighteen, or maybe nineteen. He will arrive in a few days' time. King Oswy wanted him to be raised as a Christian and it seems he's been very successful in that for Aethelred behaves almost as though he were a monk. Like Siward of Dreng, he is – very devout and wishes to stay in the monastic guest house, rather than the royal guest house."

"Poor Hild," Fridgyth murmured. "Another awkward task for her. So... Oswy wants to set the dragon-wife free... but she refuses to go?"

Ketel sighed. "Cynewise still has a bad reputation and she clings to the old beliefs. While King Penda led his deadly raids abroad, his Queen held court at Tamworth and kept his prisoners and hostages for him. Our guest-master refuses to accommodate her in the female side of the monastic guest house, for she claims still to be a priestess of Freya."

"Well... that is something I cannot blame her for!" Fridgyth quietly acknowledged.

"No," Della agreed. "None of us could blame her for that."

For along with many in Streonshalh, the three of them still celebrated the turn of the year and the seasons and festivals of the ancient gods.

"So, how is this problem of her accommodation to be resolved?" Fridgyth asked.

Ketel smiled. "We consulted Lady Hild... and, as ever, the abbess viewed it with practicality. It could be dangerous to offend Wulfhere of the Mercians by mistreating his mother in any way, and it would not help the purpose of the visit if any one of our guests feels dishonoured."

"Hmm! So, what is the answer?" Fridgyth asked.

"Well," he said gently, as though he knew that she might disapprove of the very idea. "The abbess suggests that we accommodate Cynewise in the royal guest house... and as Oswy has commanded this visit, she will be given Queen Eanfleda's chamber. It is the most prestigious accommodation that we can offer and of course, it is not a monastic building."

Fridgyth shook her head in disbelief. "That woman... the dragon-wife? The widow of the man who ravaged our lands and slaughtered so many of our people. I never thought to see the day she'd come here and be given royal accommodation. My husband died defending our lands against King Penda's warriors and my children starved because of him."

Ketel nodded in sympathy. "This is difficult for us all," he acknowledged. "But King Penda's raids were long ago... and this aged Queen was not responsible for those her husband killed. If we want this meeting to succeed between mother and son, we must try to forget the past."

Fridgyth threw him a furious glance. She wanted to scream at him that he'd feel differently if King Penda's raiders had slaughtered his wife, but... she knew that it wouldn't be fair, for poor Berta had died of the plague and suffered greatly in a different way. How could you compare one death to another? The deaths of their spouses had left them both equally broken-hearted.

Della looked anxiously from one to the other, disturbed by the tension the news had brought.

Fridgyth's anger subsided quickly. "You are right," she said, with some effort. "We must try to forget the past and let it go, but it will be difficult."

Ketel smiled gently and reached out to press her arm. "Some of the Mercian Queen's servants will be arriving soon to prepare the chamber for her. They say she will bring her own bed... a travelling bed."

Both Della and Fridgyth smiled at the very idea, and the anger that the news had brought faded a little.

"It seems it is the custom, amongst the wealthy women of Wessex," Ketel said. "And Wessex is where Cynewise came from, before she married Penda."

"A travelling bed... the very idea," Fridgyth murmured.

Della gave a gentle chuckle. "You could do with a travelling bed, Fridgyth, when you go to the heather moors again, to fetch back your bees."

The sound of the refectory bell rang out and Fridgyth realised that she was both tired and hungry. Though they could make small meals for themselves in the herbwife's hut, they often enjoyed the food that the monastic refectory served up three times a day, for the benefit of all who lived within the palisade, as well as a touch of gossip. The herbwife struggled to her feet with a sigh. "Let's go to supper," she said. "We may find out more while we are there."

CHAPTER 3

DISTURBING MEMORIES

The reeve, his daughter and the herb-wife trooped into the refectory. A wave of excited chatter and the appetising scent of warm bread and vegetable pottage greeted them.

No sooner had they appeared, than Princess Elfled stood up and waved them over to the high table, where she sat with her young, female bodyguard, Wulfrun, and her tutor, Sister Lindi. Fridgyth made her way through the timber hall that was crammed with monks, nuns, and craft-workers of many kinds, along with lay brothers and sisters and their families, who all sat at wooden trestles, waiting to be fed. Everyone sat in their designated places, but heads turned and bodies leaned across the isles, so that gossip was eagerly exchanged between the different groups.

"Sit here, Fridgyth," Elfled ordered, as the herb-wife arrived at the top table, which was slightly elevated by a wooden platform and comfortably close to the glowing hearth.

Elfled, daughter of the overlord Oswy, had been handed over to Abbess Hild as a baby, to be raised as a nun, though at this moment the young Princess was in a most un-nun-like state of excitement.

"My brother Ecfrid is coming here," she cried. "He will arrive at any moment. I've not seen him since the Synod… not since he became King in Deira."

Fridgyth nodded. She herself felt some concern at the thought of meeting him again. She'd quarrelled with Ecfrid long ago, when he was a wild and reckless boy of sixteen. Now aged twenty-one, he was still very young to be allowed to rule the wide stretch of land that made up the more southerly half of the kingdom of Northumbria, known as Deira. But because he was the grandson of the great King Edwin, he was at least popular with the people... more popular than his wily father, if the truth were told.

"I hope he doesn't bring Audrey with him," Elfled added with a wry face.

"Queen Audrey deserves your respect," Sister Lindi scolded, but she turned to Fridgyth with a knowing smile and patted the empty space on the bench beside her in a welcoming manner.

Lindi had recently arrived from Hartlepool, to replace Brother Eadfrid, as the Princess's teacher, for the young monk had been invited to join the monastery on Lindisfarne, in order to further develop his extraordinary talent for the illumination of manuscripts.

"Queen Audrey is always kind to you, Princess," Fridgyth said reprovingly as she sat down. She felt that she should support Lindi's efforts to instil tact and courtesy into her young charge.

Elfled struggled to come to terms with the pious role her father had forced on her and privately the herb-wife had much sympathy. Oswy ruthlessly used his children to further his own ambitions, by dedicating them to God, or marrying them wherever he saw an opportunity to gain more power or land.

"But Audrey's so serious," Elfled insisted. "And Ecfrid always used to make me laugh, but that was before he married an old widow. She'd better not come here with him, I say!"

Fridgyth and Lindi exchanged a swift glance of amused and tolerant sympathy.

"Your brother has much to do and think about," Lindi said. "But I'm sure he will find time to cheer his sister while he is here," she added kindly. "Won't he?" she asked and she nudged the Princess gently with her elbow. "Won't he?"

A smile appeared on Elfled's face as she nudged her clever tutor back. "He'd better," she said.

"Eat up. You'll need your energy when he comes," Fridgyth added. "I daresay he'll ride out with you and Wulfrun. It's a shame you can't ride with them too Lindi."

"Yes," Lindi smiled sadly. "But then, I did choose freely to become a nun."

Fridgyth appreciated the touch of liveliness that Sister Lindi had brought with her. A female tutor had been judged to be more suitable for the Princess as she grew to womanhood. Sister Lindi had been recommended as the brightest of the young female scribes from the monastery on the Island of the Hart, which lay to the north of Streonshalh and still took its rule from Hild. The abbess had quickly seen that Lindi was ready to laugh, as well as teach, and Elfled appeared to be happy under her tuition.

Fridgyth glanced about her to assess the gossip that was rife on every table. Knowing glances were exchanged between the scholars, spinners, weavers and metal workers, then onwards to the beast-herders and back again. News of new visitors always travelled fast.

Sister Mildred, the food-wife, who rarely deigned to serve in person, leant over Fridgyth to place a bowl of plums in front of the Princess.

"That woman, coming here!" she hissed. "Is Oswy coming as well?"

"No," Fridgyth told her firmly with a shake of the head.

"Good," she whispered, giving a nod of approval. "Just Ecfrid then! The Princess will be pleased to see her brother."

"Yes," Fridgyth said. "And you too, I suppose!" she added, for the food-wife's devotion to the new, young King of Deira was well known.

"Bless him," Mildred said with a smile, "But Mercians! Why are Mercians coming here? They'd better watch out, that's all I can say?'"

"Be careful what you say," Fridgyth warned glancing about her in case any unfriendly ears picked up their words. "And don't you know that they come for your good food? It's all your fault, you spoil our visitors when they come!"

"True enough, I do," the quick reply came. "Now tell the truth!"

Fridgyth shook her head and spoke more seriously, leaning close. "I know little more than you. It seems they want our abbess to act as peacemaker yet again. Oswy angers everyone, then he sends the parties to Hild, with orders for her to make peace between them."

16

"Aye," Mildred agreed with a sigh. "And she usually manages to do it, somehow. But it's visitors… always visitors! Extra mouths to feed! And does the King ever send extra rations along with them? No, he does not!"

"Of course not," Fridgyth agreed.

"Well, at least he's not coming himself."

"You should remember that it's at his bidding we've got Ecfrid ruling us now."

"True enough," Mildred sighed. "That's one good thing he's done. Ecfrid can come to Streonshalh any time he wants."

"Hmm! But King of Deira or not, he still has to do what his father decrees," Fridgyth pointed out.

"I know," Mildred, acknowledged quietly. "But one day…" she raised her eyebrows in a meaningful manner.

"Be careful," Fridgyth warned. "The wrong company might interpret that as treason."

Mildred replied, with a brief cackle and a slap on the back. "I only say it to you," she said. "Anyway, you'd best make the most of the food while they are here. We've plenty at the moment, but we'll be on sparse rations when the weather turns cool. Get a bit of fat on you, to keep you warm for the winter."

"I've plenty of fat," Fridgyth told her.

Mildred went on her grumbling way and the herb-wife turned back to the Princess. She observed that Elfled's companion and bodyguard, Wulfrun, was unusually quiet and she wondered if the girl was missing the Frankish goldsmith who had been sent away to Eforwic, to train with a master craftsmen there. Fridgyth narrowed her eyes in thought, for she believed she'd glimpsed another lad with his arms around Wulfrun, just a few nights ago, in the upper pasture, at dusk. She'd thought nothing of it for they were not the only young people who gathered out there when the evenings were warm. Perhaps Wulfrun's troubled look indicated that the girl was torn between two sweethearts, but then she recalled that Elfled's young bodyguard might also have some similar concerns about meeting the young King of Deira, just as she did. She resolved to speak to her about it when the opportunity arose.

A hush descended on the refectory briefly, when the diminutive figure of the abbess appeared, but Hild failed to join any of the tables, and paused only to catch Fridgyth's eye, then vanished again.

The herb-wife understood perfectly. She rather rushed through the rest of her meal and then quietly left the refectory, to hurry across the courtyard. As she passed the largest of the weaving sheds, she stopped for a moment and stood there listening to the faint rhythmic clacking sounds of a loom. Someone was working late, and missing their supper; she suspected she knew who.

Instead of going directly to the abbess's house, Fridgyth strode towards the long, low timber shed, patterned down both sides with wooden shutters to make the most of the available light. The boards on the north-western side of the building were propped up to catch the last gleams of the evening sun. The door of the shed stood open too and Fridgyth stepped inside.

Wulfrun's mother Cwen stood alone in front of one of the heavy warp-weighted looms that were propped up against the timber wall. As she pulled the single heddle rod, it swung towards her with a soft clack and she began to beat the weft into place with a pointed weaving batten. Sensing that she was being watched, she paused, but then recognised the herb-wife and carried on.

"Ah – it's you," she said softly.

"Aye it's me, Cwen. What glorious shades of gold and garnet you produce," Fridgyth said admiringly as she moved forward. "This is a wall hanging fit for a king!"

"Or a queen," Cwen corrected her. "This one is to refurbish Queen Eanfleda's chamber, in the royal guest house."

"Gold from weld, madder for red, but how do you achieve that deep shade of red? No madder I've known would give that depth of colour."

Cwen chuckled. "This is Frankish madder, sent by Queen Eanfleda herself. Each time the trading boat arrives from Bebbanburgh, small packages appear for me," she said and she followed her words with a small satisfied sigh.

"Yes... she will never forget what you did for her," Fridgyth said. "But I guessed it might be you, choosing to work here alone so late, rather than come to the refectory. The son may not be as friendly as the mother. You've heard that Ecfrid is coming to visit us?"

Cwen stopped her work and let her hand fall to her side. "Yes," she said. "And… more surprising guests too. This is another reason why I'm still here and working late… I must try to finish this hanging by tomorrow, so that it can be placed in the visiting Queen's chamber."

"Who'd ever have thought it?" Fridgyth said. "But I believe we've nought to fear from the young King. We enjoy the abbess's protection here and you especially have found favour with Queen Eanfleda. Ecfrid would never risk his mother's displeasure again – or even more, his father's. After all, he came to the great Synod… and gave us no trouble then."

The anxious wrinkle was not completely banished from the webster's brow. "He wasn't King of Deira then…" she said, but suddenly she smiled and nodded. "I don't fear anyone these days, Fridgyth… it is just that his visit brings back memories I'd rather forget, that's all."

"Yes," Fridgyth agreed. "That's how I feel too, and I wanted to be sure that his visit didn't come as a shock to you."

"I appreciate that, herbwife," Cwen said.

"Princess Elfled can't wait to see her brother," Fridgyth added. "And I thought I'd speak to Wulfrun, when I get the chance to speak alone. She too may fear Ecfrid's anger, for her past actions put paid to his youthful rebellion, but even he must see that things have worked out well for him, now that he rules Deira with Oswy's wholehearted consent."

Cwen nodded. "That's kind of you," she said. "The lass might listen to you, she doesn't listen to me." She lifted the weaving batten and began to beat the weft energetically into place again.

"Of course not… you're her mother. They never listen to their mother," Fridgyth said.

She left the weaving shed and went to look for Hild.

CHAPTER 4

BLOOD-FEUD

The abbess's house stood close to the main preaching cross, which was adjacent to the church. Fridgyth entered without pausing to announce herself, such was the privileged position she enjoyed as the abbess's confidant. She found Hild hunched over an unfurled manuscript. The abbess straightened herself painfully at her friend's approach and rubbed her shoulders, looking guilty.

"I told you not to sit scrunched up like that," Fridgyth said, though she quickly remembered to straighten herself, for she too was stooping too much of late.

Hild suffered from a common disease that came with age, and one that Fridgyth recognised and referred to as 'the aching disease', but she could do little to bring relief. The symptoms were fevers, swollen, stiff and painful joints – much worse in winter than in summer. The abbess's powerful sense of discipline kept her upright and moving, but she struggled constantly with pain.

"I suppose you've heard?" Hild said. "Did Ketel tell you?"

"Yes. Oswy wants the youngest Mercian Prince to finish his education here at Streonshalh, there's small surprise in that, but what astounds us is that his mother, the much feared dragon-wife comes to meet him."

Hild frowned. "Do not say dragon-wife," she reproved. "Is that how they name her then? Queen Cynewise must be treated with the utmost courtesy."

"Nobody would be foolish enough to say it to her face," Fridgyth allowed. "But even you must acknowledge that this visit could be difficult to host. She is the most notorious woman in these lands."

Hild heaved a great sigh. "Yes," she admitted. "And Queen Cynewise has not seen her son since King Penda died. The boy was just three years old when he was taken from her."

Fridgyth shook her head. "Oswy took her child away to punish her, and now you are expected to heal the wounds. I've little love for Penda's widow, but I can imagine the resentment she must feel… and you are expected to dredge up peace once again from another mess of Oswy's creation."

"At least he allowed the boy to live," Hild said. "Victors so often slaughter the young of their enemy! That is why these terrible blood-feuds continue for so long. You will remember that King Penda killed King Edwin's son, and he was my young cousin."

"Yes," Fridgyth acknowledged. "You are right. Perhaps this boy is lucky to be alive."

Hild shrugged. "Prince Althelred has received a Christian education and he now comes to Streonshalh with Siward of Dreng, his foster father, in order to ensure that Christian principles are firmly entrenched in him. I have Brother Bossa in mind as his tutor!"

Fridgyth nodded. "Even if King Penda had survived, I expect the boy would eventually have been sent to a foster father."

"Yes," Hild agreed. "But it would have been a foster father of his parents choosing, and regular visits would have been maintained."

"To me it feels wrong," Fridgyth said. "To send a child away from home, so young."

"Elfled, might say the same," Hild added, with a faint, smile.

"But Elfled was given into *your* care," Fridgyth replied warmly. "That is a different matter entirely. Nobody could be a better mother to the Princess, than you."

Hild lifted an amused eyebrow. "The Princess might not appreciate that!"

Their eyes met and they both chuckled.

"Well... keeping a sharp eye on them... that's what being a mother, really means," Fridgyth said. "And I expect we'll manage this visit as we always do!"

"I understand," Hild said with a meaningful glance, "that Oswy offered Cynewise the option of keeping her boy, if she converted to Christianity."

Fridgyth stared in disbelief. "So Cynewise chose Freya, over her own child?" she said. "How astonishing! I could never have done that, and I wouldn't have thought that *you'd* approve such pressured means of conversion either."

"No, I do not," Hild agreed, with an ironic smile. "Forced conversion to Christianity was never my way, but unfortunately Oswy didn't consult *me* when he made his decision!"

Fridgyth grinned.

"As you say, we will do our best," Hild went on. "And speaking of smoothing things over... you know that Ecfrid is coming too?"

Fridgyth nodded.

"That business with Irminburgh is long ago," Hild assured her.

"Yes, best forgotten!" Fridgyth agreed at once.

"And," Hild added. "I think he may help with the Mercian Queen!"

Fridgyth frowned at that, puzzled.

Hild raised an eyebrow, quizzically. "Do you not remember what happened to Ecfrid as a child?"

Then something stirred in Fridgyth's memory. "Ah... yes, " she murmured. "I do recall that Ecfrid was kept as a hostage by Penda's Queen. He grew up in her court at Tamworth and was raised by her... he must know her well."

Hild nodded. "Now the boot is on the other foot."

Fridgyth saw the irony. "Oh yes! I see... now Cynewise is kept as a hostage in Ecfrid's kingdom, but I wouldn't have thought the Prince would want to have anything to do with his old jailor, let alone help her."

Hild smiled. "Well, that's where you are wrong, dear friend. You see, by those same ancient laws of blood-feud that we spoke of just now, Cynewise *should* have had the boy slaughtered. She could have had him killed when Oswy ambushed King Penda by the flooding

22

River Winwaed. As soon as she heard of her husband's death, she ought to have taken her revenge, it was her duty as a loyal wife."

"But she didn't," Fridgyth said thoughtfully.

"Maybe *that*'s why Oswy allowed Prince Aethelred to live too," Hild offered in explanation.

Fridgyth glimpsed something unexpected in the dragon-like image that had grown in her mind of the Mercian Queen. "Freya loves birth and growth... not death!" she murmured, but then remembered that she was in the presence of the abbess. "Oh, I'm sorry, I should not be saying that to you."

Hild smiled warmly. "You forget, I was once a child of Freya too, and I think it was an honourable thing for the Mercian Queen to do. Cynewise delivered him back to his parents after King Penda died and made herself vulnerable by bringing him herself."

"That was how she came to be Oswy's prisoner?"

The abbess nodded. "Ecfrid came back to us an angry, resentful, eleven-year-old. I've sometimes wondered whether he would have preferred to stay with Cynewise, for I understand that she treated him more as a foster child, than a hostage."

"Perhaps we judge this dragon-wife too harshly," Fridgyth admitted.

"Well, you will be able to make your own judgement soon, for she has been sick of late, and your reputation as a healer has travelled to Handale Head."

"My reputation? You mean... I'm to attend her when she comes here?"

"Yes."

Fridgyth was stunned at the thought.

"Was I not correct to offer your services?" Hild asked, surprised at her uncommon silence.

Fridgyth swallowed hard. She'd never refused her skills to anyone and could think of no good reason to withhold them now, though the thought of treating King Penda's formidable widow was daunting.

"No... you were correct to offer... of course you were," she managed to say. "But I'd best go to check my stock of herbs and make sure that I'm ready for this consultation… and I must fetch my hives back from the heather, before she comes."

"Good,' Hild said.

The abbess struggled to her feet to see Fridgyth out.

"Will Oswy not send a famous healer or leech to her?" she asked.

Hild smiled. "He provides her with anything she wants… and she wants you."

Fridgyth shook her head in astonishment and hurried outside.

Once alone, the herb-wife headed not to her hut, but through the side gate in the wooden palisade and out into the darkening upper pasture. The prospect of treating the Mercian Queen made her feel that she needed time to take it all in. Luckily her herbs were well stocked and organised, but she needed to think and adjust to the astounding prospect that lay before her.

"I must tell the bees," she murmured.

She wandered out into the meadow, heading towards the remaining three hives. The sun was setting behind the western hills, as Fridgyth lifted one by one, the loose, woven skeps that covered the hives. The bees that had remained behind in the upper pasture appeared to be content, for the grassy field was still full of daisies and buttercups.

"Now then my darlings," she murmured. "You will never believe what I have to tell you."

And she began to croon:

"The widow comes, the dragon-wife.
Her fierce mate killed my man.
But he in turn was slain, and still
she saved the victor's whelp.

Fridgyth lowered her tone until her voice almost blended with the bees' deep hum. As she chanted her song to the bees, she began to feel her fear and anger ease a little.

"Now we are widows, both."

"We suffer the same loss and the longing,
Her hurt is no less than mine.

I will tend her as I would another,
with mercy! And kindness
As best I can."

Soothed by the buzzing of the bees and the more settled course her own thoughts took; she replaced the tops of the skeps. The bees understood the situation… it was always wise to tell the bees.

CHAPTER 5

A WOLF FOR WULFRUN

The light was fading fast by the time Fridgyth turned back towards the side gate, but the distant sound of voices made her look down from the steep hillside towards the ford. She couldn't see clearly in the thickening dusk, but it seemed that a large party of riders had approached the river crossing.

Who could this be, arriving so late?

Outriders set about wading through the water, even though the ford was no longer shallow. Undeterred and mounted on good horses, they reached the abbey side safely and began to ascend the steep hill to the monastery.

Fridgyth drew back behind the hives again as the main party followed across the ford and up the hill. She began to recognise the Roman Eagle standard that King Edwin had once used. *This must be Ecfrid arriving – the child hostage who the dragon-wife had saved; now no longer a child!* Grandson of great Edwin and brother to Princess Elfled.

Fridgyth watched quietly as the cavalcade advanced up the slope. The outrider's horns blared as the main gates of Streonshalh monastery were thrown open.

There was no mistaking Deira's new King, even in the dusk. Ecfrid rode a black stallion, caparisoned with a gleaming, ornamental bridle. Fridgyth could see that he had grown to be a handsome man, his hair darker than his father's, but he had the same hollow cheeks. He sat easy in the saddle, with the same upright posture that Oswy bore.

She waited quietly behind the hives until the last of the baggage mules had disappeared inside the gate. Only then did she set out again, but she stopped as she noticed a faint, sliding movement in the corner of her eye and realised that she was not alone in the upper pasture.

"Who's there?" she called.

"It's me," a soft voice replied.

A slight figure moved cautiously from behind an elder bush that flanked the outer well and she saw that it was Wulfrun. The girl strode forward and stopped to wait for the herb-wife. She had a guilty look about her, as if she was embarrassed to be caught out there.

"I see that Ecfrid has come," Wulfrun whispered. "I needed a little cool air to think and calm my fears."

"I knew that something troubled you at supper," Fridgyth said. "And it crossed my mind that it might be this visit…"

They fell into step together, avoiding the main gate and walking instinctively towards the side gate set in the monastic palisade.

"I thought at first that perhaps you yearned after a certain handsome, Frankish goldsmith," Fridgyth went on teasingly, "but then I seemed to remember getting a glimpse of you in the arms of one of the young tanners."

Wulfrun regarded her sharply. "You see everything, herb-wife. Yes… I miss the goldsmith, but he was wild with excitement when they invited him to go to Eforwic to train with the best man there, so I am pleased for him. He made me a parting gift!"

The girl drew a knife from a leather sheath that swung from her belt and Fridgyth's eyes widened as the handle was presented to her for inspection.

"What do you think of that?" Wulfrun asked.

It was a meat knife, but it was like no meat-knife the herb-wife had ever seen.

Fridgyth caught her breath. "Astonishing!"

The handle was wrought in a dark, gleaming metal that reflected the flickering flames of the torch that had been set in a sconce to light the side gate. The knife handle was shaped like a wolf's head, with tiny glittering garnets for the eyes.

"He made a wolf for Wulfrun," Fridgyth said.

It was a stunning gift. An ordinary meat knife would be an acceptable gift for any young woman, but this knife was much more… a thing of beauty, but also a weapon in the right hands.

Wulfrun was more than capable of using a weapon; she had been trained in the use of arms for her role as Princess Elfled's bodyguard. Hild had perceived, as the years went by, that a strong and capable young woman might be the most unexpected and effective bodyguard for King Oswy's spirited daughter. Over the years, Wulfrun had become much more than a bodyguard, she'd turned out to be a kind and loving companion to the Princess too.

"This knife is a tribute to your courage," Fridgyth said, still admiring the craftsmanship.

"But, I fear my courage is lacking of late," Wulfrun admitted.

"And what has brought this loss of certainty?"

Wulfrun glanced towards the main gates, where the cavalcade had passed through. "Fridgyth… you of all people know! Will Ecfrid remember the part we played in separating him from Irminburgh?"

The herb-wife shrugged. "Much has happened since then… he's a married man now and he's been given a kingdom to rule, though he is still so very young."

"Married or not… I don't think he will have forgotten Irminburgh," Wulfrun said quietly. "She was his first love, though she brought us so much trouble, and I don't think he will have forgotten the part I played in her banishment, but my mother's life was at stake. I could not stand by and allow her to be hanged."

"No you could not," Fridgyth told her firmly. "And I played a part in preventing their rebellion too, and so did Sister Begu. We must just hope that, with maturity, Ecfrid has come to understand that we had no choice but to act on your mother's behalf. Since his brother died of the plague last year, Ecfrid has been given the kingdom that he always wanted, without ever having to fight for it. He should be content with that. I have worries too, for the abbess wants me to treat the Mercian Queen, when she comes, for her health fails her!"

"I don't envy you that," Wulfrun said.

They reached the side gate and it was almost dark, but for the flames of the torch.

"You are quite right," Wulfrun acknowledged thoughtfully. "I will try to treat our new King as respectfully as I can, and hope that he has forgiven me."

"Go inside and stop worrying!" Fridgyth told her. "I doubt that our new young King will even give us a thought!"

The side gate allowed them to avoid the stables, and the fuss and bustle that Ecfrid's arrival had set in motion.

With a small smile, Wulfrun left the herb-wife and headed to the abbess's house.

The next few days passed in a rush of preparation for the arrival of the Mercian Queen. Cattle were slaughtered. Steam poured out from the kitchens as venison, hares, and fowls were prepared and stuffed. Some of the dedicated monks and nuns were called away from their tiny cells to help in the bakery and brewery. The royal guest house was scrubbed from top to bottom, and refurbished with every new rug and wall hanging available.

Two days before the expected arrival of the Queen, the abbess's barge, the *Royal Edwin* was sent north to fetch some of the servants from Handale Head. When the strangers appeared in the refectory, that evening, a sudden quiet fell over the gathering. They were mainly women, with a few older men, all expensively dressed in richly embroidered clothing embellished with the symbol of the golden boar. They strode into the hall and waited expectantly.

King Ecfrid, who sat by his sister on the high table, rose from his seat to beckon them forward.

"Welcome Lady Helga," he said, as an older woman led the way and dropped him a condescending curtsey.

"Mercian hogs!" There came a whispered, resentful, hiss from one of the metal hearth workers' tables.

Ketel rose from his seat and with a sharp, disapproving, sideways glance quelled any further ideas of discourtesy. Ecfrid strode forward to meet them and, with a bow and a flourish, escorted them to a table that had been prepared for them. Many covert glances flew in their direction, but gradually the buzz of conversation resumed. Fridgyth, relegated now to one of the lower tables sat beside her old friend Sister Begu, observing it all.

"If the attendants are so proud and imperious, I shudder to think what the dragon-wife must be like," Begu whispered.

Sister Begu had acted, as nursemaid to Princess Elfled when she was an infant and, now in old age, the elderly nun was something of a law unto herself.

Fridgyth nodded, with a chuckle. "The abbess insists that we must behave with courtesy and I'd hesitate to insult the Mercian emblem of the boar. It is believed to bring courage in battle and whatever you may say of King Penda, he was fearless in his fights. How do you think Wulfrun fares in all of this?"

They both glanced towards the high table, where Wulfrun and Sister Lindi both stood in attendance, behind the Princess, whereas they normally sat at her side.

"She's doing well for she appears to be quiet and calm," the old nun said. "And I have heard that King Ecfrid has presented her with a silver ring."

"Who, Wulfrun?" Fridgyth asked amazed.

"Yes," Begu said. "Lindi told me that. It seems he wishes to make amends for what happened long ago, though I think both Elfled's tutor and her bodyguard will be glad when this visit is over."

"I'm sure they will," Fridgyth agreed. "Maybe all of us will."

Fridgyth found it hard to settle to sleep that night, even the cat restlessly patrolled about the hut, refusing to curl up. At last she got up and forcefully put Wyrdkin out, then tried to sleep again. She'd been pleased to hear that Wulfrun was being treated well by the Prince, but apprehensive still of the part she herself must play, when the Mercian Queen arrived.

She woke next morning before it was light, and quickly realised that it was the sound of a voice that had disturbed her.

"Someone is shouting," Della mumbled sleepily. The girl rolled over on her straw stuffed mattress, and then sat up and struggled to her feet. She staggered over to the door and lifted the wooden latch.

The cat shot into the hut and Fridgyth sat up on her low, wooden pallet bed and swung her feet onto the floor; she sighed, trying hard to bring to mind the name of the woman who was next expected to give birth.

"Is it Fritha?" she asked.

"It's coming from outside," Della said.

"Of course it is," Fridgyth agreed, with a yawn.

"No. I mean it's coming from outside the palisade."

Fridgyth reached for her girdle with all its useful hangers, smoothed her hair a little and slipped her feet into her boots. She followed Della outside and they both headed for the side gate but even before they got through it, they understood that they were needed.

"The herb-wife, I need the herb-wife!"

Fridgyth touched Della's arm. "You go back inside, I'll see to this."

But the girl hovered by the side gate, concerned at the growing sounds of distress as a man approached.

"I'm here," Fridgyth cried.

She recognised once again the stench of the tanning pits, for this was Edric, Ralf's father, and he was in a state of great distress.

"Herb-wife we need you, and the reeve too!" he cried. "You must both see how he is!"

"Who are you talking about?" she asked.

The tanner stumbled towards her and grabbed Fridgyth's arm.

"It's my son! We have just found him!"

"But I saw him only a few days since, heading out onto the heather moors with a cart full of shoes to sell."

"Not Ralf," he cried. "Our oldest boy, Godric… he's dead, drowned in the top tanning pit. He didn't come home last night and then this morning… my wife went out to look for him and…" His voice broke down and he could not stop shuddering.

For a moment, Fridgyth stared in disbelief, but then she realised that if what he said was true, they did indeed need the reeve. "I'll come with you at once," she said. "Della, run to find your father! He may be sleeping still, but this could be important. Tell him to come to the tanning pits... now quickly, go!"

Della took two strides back inside the gate and then turned to run.

CHAPTER 6

A ROPE OF ROSEMARY

Edric clapped his hands to his head in an agony of distress. "Too late I fear, for your help, herb-wife," he cried. "Ah, forgive me, I cannot think straight, but still you should perhaps see how he is! A terrible sight!"

"Let's go," Fridgyth said. "The reeve will come as soon as he can."

She took the tanner by the arm and steered him back in the direction he'd come from, all other concerns had fled from her mind.

They headed fast down the steep path, towards the valley of Brigsbeck, where hidden within a fold of land, well suited to the nature of the tanning trade, a spring bubbled down from higher woodland to form a useful beck.

They hurried past huts and hovels, halfmade fishing nets, pots, and spindles. A few curious inhabitants who had been disturbed by the noise rose from their beds to see what was happening.

Fridgyth braced herself for what lay ahead, knowing this was not going to be pleasant. A drowning was common enough in the river or the sea, but drowning in a tanning pit must be foul, for some of the pits contained stale human urine as part of the vital mixture, and animal dung. Godric was a lad much loved in Brigsbeck.

They arrived at a convergence of paths, where the beck flowed into the River Usk and there they turned uphill toward the rocky, woodland slope where the stream came tumbling down. They strode on past the main tanning yards and Edric's hut, where the family lived surrounded by stretching frames and piles of pelts. Onwards and upwards they went, toward the most distant of the steeping pits, which was somewhat more isolated amongst the thickening woodland. The pits had been placed in this isolated area partly for the convenience of their closeness to the beck, but also so that the dreadful stench they created might not trouble too many folk. When they arrived at the farthest pit they found the tanners' closest neighbours had gathered there in a troubled huddle. They stood in such a murmuring, tightknit group, that Fridgyth could see nothing beyond them.

"Get back," Edric shouted as they approached. "Do not look at him, do not look, it's a sight not fit to look on!"

The people shifted a little, their expressions shocked.

Fridgyth turned at the sound of hooves approaching on the path behind her, and was relieved to see that it was Ketel on his dappled gelding. As he slowed his horse and swung down from the saddle, the sight of him there, with the monastery badge of office fastened to his cloak, made the onlookers back away somewhat. They shuffled aside to reveal a heart-breaking sight, for despite the dreadful stench, the mother fiercely guarded the body of her son. Godric was laid out upon the trodden earth.

"It is truly a sight not fit to be seen," Edric repeated, "but I told my wife not to move him... for the reeve must see... he *must* see how he lies!"

"Hush now," Fridgyth said firmly. "We've both looked on many a poor drowned, corpse before... and maybe I can help your wife, if not the lad."

But despite her familiarity with death, Fridgyth *did* find it hard to look, for the morning light lit the once handsome face, that was now horribly bloated, the features gorged with odorous fluids from the tanning pit – and it was clear there was no hope of revival. Godric lay on his back, his hands drawn back behind him. His mother, Muriel crouched over the body, repeatedly stroking his clammy brow, as though she thought she might still stroke life back into him.

Ketel bent over the body and noted at once the way the lad's shoulders were pulled back. "His hands are tied!" he said.

"This is what I mean," Edric said. "I needed you to see the way he is trussed. Our Godric would never be so careless as to fall into the steeping pit."

Ketel stooped over the corpse and moved as though to turn the body over, but the mother stopped him. "Let me do it," she insisted, quietly. "I brought him into this world… I fed and clothed him… and I shall do this for him."

Edric went to help his wife and Fridgyth swallowed hard, as she watched the tender way they turned the lad, as though he were still their babe and might be hurt if handled roughly. His hands appeared to be fastened tightly behind him with what looked like seaweed.

Ketel was visibly shocked. "This is no accidental drowning; the lad's been done to death."

Fridgyth bent down to touch the bonds. "Rope," she said. "He's tied with rope… and what is this… a stick!"

"Why?" Muriel whispered as she crouched there in the mud. "What harm has my lad ever done to anyone?"

None could give her an answer.

"Did anyone see what happened?" Ketel turned to address those who still hung around.

They shook their heads.

"He'd been working on parchment for the monastery," his mother said. "And was praised for the vellum he made. Even brother Bossa…"

"Hold that torch closer?" Fridgyth ordered, as she bent to touch the ties that held the boys wrists. The rope was tied tightly, but it was also slippery with slime from the tanning pit, but something else was there too, something with narrow green pointed leaves. It was a herb she recognised.

"I'd almost think that looked like…" she murmured.

"What?" Ketel asked.

Fridgyth rubbed her fingers to disperse the coating of slime and discovered that beneath it were twisted sprays of leaves. She pinched some of them out and sniffed cautiously, only to find that despite the stinking tanning liquid, there was also the faint familiar hint of a clean, medicinal smell.

"Not lavender," she said frowning. "But rosemary!"

Ketel knitted his brows. "What strangeness is this?"

Fridgyth crushed the sprig between her fingers and held it up to the reeve's nose. He looked surprised as the same sharp scent broke through, and then he looked at her and frowned. "In the woods," he said. "Yes, there was always rosemary in Brigsbeck woods... and a twined rope made of it used to mean something...?"

Fridgyth shook her head, frustrated that she could not remember what the ancient significance of a rosemary rope might mean. She had the feeling that her mother had spoken of it long ago, but then she saw something else that took her attention. She reached down once more to pull a flat wooden tablet from between the lad's tied wrists. When she ran her finger across the smooth, sanded surface to clear the slime she saw, as did everyone else, an arrowhead mark.

"The rune of Tyr," Ketel said, his voice shocked.

"No... no," Muriel cried. "Not against my lad!"

An audible gasp came from those who still hovered around them. They exchanged fearful glances and, one by one, began to slip away to their homes, for though most of those who lived in Streonshalh were now Christian in name, the meaning of that ancient mark was clear to them all. Tyr was the rune of justice... the rune of retribution... the rune of revenge.

Edric covered his eyes with his hand and stood with his head bowed in shame. Muriel staggered to her feet, but then seemed suddenly to struggle for breath.

Fridgyth thrust the wooden tablet into Ketel's hands and grabbed the grieving mother, fearful that she'd fall. "We'll find out who has done this dreadful thing," she promised.

She had little understanding of what had happened, but felt only at that moment, that Muriel should be comforted.

Muriel gasped for breath. "Why.... why?" she panted.

She turned to her husband as though he might have an answer, but all he could do was look away from her, shake his head and cover his eyes again. Ketel frowned down at the rune-marked tablet. It had the shape of a flat square, with four small holes set in it, each one close to a squared off corner.

Ketel held it out for Fridgyth to examine again. "You know what this is?"

"Of course," she replied. "It's a weaving tablet, every home in Streonshalh has a stack of them."

Ketel looked once again at the swollen corpse. "We'll do all we can to bring the killer to justice," he promised quietly. "But for now we must think what is best to do. I'll send a cart from the monastery to take him to the mortuary there. Would you like him to be buried in the abbess's holy ground?"

The bereaved parents glanced at each other uncertainly, but after a few moments of hesitation Muriel nodded. "Yes," she said. "The monastery bought his vellum and he has had much to do with them of late, so I think it only right that we should go with their ways."

Edric pointed with a shaking finger to the rune-marked tablet and his voice shook with anger. "Whoever placed that sign upon our boy, they must hold to the old gods. Revenge… retribution! I turn the rune against the one who cast it!"

His lips twisted with bitterness. Muriel pulled away from Fridgyth and went back to stroke her son's lank hair.

Ketel exchanged a troubled glance with Fridgyth. "You must not cleanse him," he said gently.

"Why?" Muriel cried.

He understood well the mother's instinct to care for the body, for he'd lost most of his family during the plague that had swept the land, but as reeve he now had other concerns.

"There are knowledgeable men at the monastery and we should allow them to see Godric as he is. They may be able to tell much from their observations."

Fridgyth frowned at those words, wishing to remind him that there were many knowledgeable women in the monastery too. However, this was not the moment for her to challenge his authority.

"We'll carry him back to your home, and then I'll send the cart for him," Ketel said. "You may prepare him for burial as soon as they've looked at him and discovered all they can."

They nodded unhappily, accepting the sense of his decision.

Ketel removed his own good woollen cloak and without hesitation spread it on the ground beside the body. The kindness in his action caught at Fridgyth's heart, and all irritation with him vanished. Momentarily, she saw again the strong, young man he'd once been and the thought came again of rosemary and a memory long forgotten. She almost wanted to smile, but quickly suppressed the impulse, for this was not the time or the place for gentle reminiscing.

The reeve and Edric carefully lifted Godric's body onto the cloak and carried him back to his home, with Muriel walking at their side, still clinging to her son's slimy jacket. Fridgyth caught Ketel's horse by the bridal and led the beast, in sad procession, after them.

When they arrived at the tanners' dwelling, they laid Godric's body on the wooden bench, which stood in the spot where the family would sit on a warm summer's evening.

"Will you ride back with me…?" Ketel asked, as he reclaimed his horse from Fridgyth.

"No," she said. "I'll stay here with them until the cart arrives."

CHAPTER 7

A LOVELY BAIRN

As Ketel rode away, two of the closest neighbours emerged from their hut to offer help, but it was politely refused, and they went back inside, accepting that the grieving couple wished to be alone.

Fridgyth too, felt that she intruded. "You sit with your poor boy awhile," she said, pulling a small vial from her girdle. "I'll make a drink that will bring you sleep and soothe the pain of loss for a while."

"No, I need to feel the pain," Muriel insisted.

"Then I shall simply make you a warming drink," Fridgyth insisted.

The herb-wife boldly entered the tanners' home and set about feeding their dwindling fire with sticks, which were plentiful. She set a small cauldron above the hearth to boil and unfastened a bundle of camomile from her girdle along with a vial of honey. When she emerged again with two steaming mugs, she found that they had not moved.

"He's so cold," the Muriel murmured at last.

"And you are growing cold too," Fridgyth said. "This will warm you a little, but I see no harm in you laying more covers over him, if you wish to do so."

Edric nodded approval and Muriel got up and went inside. She reappeared with a soft rug made of stitched lambskins, which she lovingly laid over her son. Then she went back inside and this time she brought out a cushion to place beneath his head, so that he eventually looked almost as though he slept, tucked up in bed. His features too seemed a little less bloated than before.

"He was…" Muriel began, but her voice failed. Then at last she forced out the words with harsh determination. "He was… a lovely bairn."

Fridgyth nodded. "I don't remember his birth, not one of mine, I think, for I'd have remembered him if he had been. He certainly grew to be a handsome lad."

Muriel shuddered and tears came. "Born with a golden fuzz of hair," she murmured.

"Aye," Fridgyth agreed. "All the lasses loved his hair…"

"Do not mention lasses," Edric cut in fiercely.

Fridgyth looked up, rather taken aback by the sudden sharpness of his words. At her husband's outburst, more tears welled up in Muriel's eyes and poured down her cheeks.

"I won't mention lasses, then," Fridgyth said. "I won't speak of them if it distresses you so much Edric, but I cannot help but wonder whether he had a girl… a lover?"

Edric gave an angry shrug. "Best left alone," he growled, but all of a sudden, tears swam in his eyes too.

Fridgyth looked with interest from one to the other, for she sensed that there might be something important behind the supressed anger of his words.

"But," she added with gentle determination. "If the reeve is to discover who has killed your boy, he will need to know everything you can tell him."

Muriel knuckled the tears from her eyes and looked at her husband with a new sense of resolve. "The herb-wife is right," she said. "That rune… the rune of retribution, says it all. I think we should tell Fridgyth what we know. She will understand it, better than most. That is the rune of justice… but our boy shall have no justice if we keep quiet."

Edric still sat in grim silence.

A troubling feeling of responsibility crept over Fridgyth, for she sensed that she must play this just right, if they were to find out who had trussed the boy and left him to die in so disgusting a manner.

"If you speak to the reeve, he will try to keep confidence with you," she said, but then added "wherever possible."

She knew she must not make a promise on Ketel's behalf that he could never keep.

But after a further tense and miserable silence, Edric at last nodded at his wife. "You tell her," he said.

Fridgyth waited in silence, hardly daring to breathe for fear they might change their minds.

"He'd been seeing a lass," Muriel began, still looking down lovingly at her son, "a woman. He told us nothing about her, but we knew."

Fridgyth looked up surprised. "Godric was seeing a woman... not Ralf?" she asked.

"Yes Godric..." Muriel replied, sounding slightly irritated that the herb-wife might question her words, when she was struggling so hard to impart such difficult information. "Ralf knew of it," she went on, speaking with reluctance. "We dragged it out of him, for we saw that Godric was troubled and always up in the woods near Brig's Spring. Well, we feared... that she might be married, but Ralf became tight-lipped and would tell us no more about it, for he felt that he'd betray his brother..."

"Ah yes, I see." Fridgyth perceived at once that a possible explanation for the boy's savage death might lie herein. Retribution and revenge, justice... the rune placed on Godric's body.

"We are so shamed by this," Muriel said and her hands clasped and unclasped in an agony of humiliation. "But... I see that the reeve will have to make enquiries and I think that, in the end, we will not be able to hide from it! Our Ralf may not be the only one to have seen them together."

"You are right to tell me," Fridgyth said. "And I will pass this information on to the reeve, in as discreet a way as I can. I shall beg him too, to be tactful in his inquiries, but if an angry husband has taken revenge..."

"Our lad had no right to take a man's wife," Edric cut in bitterly, "but to kill him..."

"No indeed," Fridgyth said firmly. "However, the lad had offended… this is murder and it must be punished. The abbess has fairer ways of settling disputes. Nobody had the right to kill Godric."

They sat again in thoughtful silence and, as this information sank into her mind, Fridgyth found another question forming, but she'd given her word in confidence. At last she spoke.

"I met your Ralf," she said carefully. "I passed him last week, as he drove his mule cart out towards the heather moors?"

"Aye," Muriel said, bitterly. "He'll know nothing of what's happened here and we cannot get a message to him. What will we say to him? He will be devastated to hear of his brother's death, for they were close."

"Yes, close," Fridgyth agreed.

But with an unsettling degree of discomfort, she also began to recognise that his older sibling's untimely death must leave Ralf the sole inheritor of a growing, profitable business.

"He offered to make a pair of turnshoes for me," Fridgyth said.

Both parents looked up, a little surprised by the trivial nature of this remark.

"Then he will certainly do as he promised," Edric said sadly. "He is a good worker and… he is all we have left now."

Fridgyth tried to supress the unworthy thought that Ralf might benefit from his brother's death. It wasn't fair; she'd always liked the lad. He was far away selling his wares, and could not have anything to do with this death. When at last they heard the rumbling of the monastery cart, she was somewhat relieved.

Having stayed only to see the body carefully stowed and instructions issued to the driver, Fridgyth chose to walk back up the hill alone. As she retraced her steps, she realised that despite the initial revulsion she'd felt at the sight of the poor boy's body, she was now growing hungry and she'd had no chance to eat. The sun was high in the sky and she was expected to be ready to meet the old Mercian Queen the following day, and there was still her hives to bring back from the heather.

She knew she must pass the information about Godric onto Ketel and the abbess too, though they'd both got much else to trouble them. To some the death of a young tanner might not seem important, but Hild treated her visitors, workers, monks and nuns with equal concern. She realised that she hadn't even asked where Ralf had been going with such a well-stacked cartful of leather satchels, shoes and vellum. Surely the two brothers couldn't have fallen out over the same woman. From what she knew of them, their parents were right; the brothers had been close.

Fridgyth stopped for a moment at the edge of the upper pasture.

"So much to do," she muttered. "The bees must stay in the heather for a few more days, I fear."

She heaved a heavy sigh, tempted to go in and sit for a while in order to think more clearly, for the meadow afforded a wonderful, wide view over the sea. Too much was happening all at once, not one problem developing, but one on top of another. Why did life seem to have a habit of doing this? And rosemary? She smiled softly, the thought was ill-timed, but somehow the thought of rosemary had made her see Ketel as young and handsome, once again.

Fridgyth gave a small, dismissive shake of the head. She turned in through the side gate and headed straight to the refectory, where she joined Della and Begu on one of the lower tables.

"What kept you so long?" the girl asked. "Father would talk to nobody when he came back and he is speaking with the abbess now."

Sister Begu raised her brows and leant forward. "Rumour has it that there's been a murder at the tanning pits!"

"Aye," Fridgyth heaved herself wearily onto the bench beside them. "You will all know soon enough. Poor Godric Tanner was found drowned… you know the lad… drowned in his own steeping pit."

Della looked aghast.

"It seems from the way his hands were tied that someone drowned him on purpose. There's little point in me keeping it quiet, Ketel will need to call for witnesses or anyone with any knowledge of it."

"Heaven help us!" Begu murmured.

"No," Della sounded devastated. "Not Godric," she murmured.

Fridgyth glanced at her assistant in concern. "You were not sweet on him, were you?" she asked softly.

Della shook her head. "Me? A lad like Godric? He'd have no interest in me."

Fridgyth frowned at her. "Why not?"

"When would I have time for such things, all my day is taken up with helping you," Della said honestly. "I wasn't sweet on him, but he was fair-faced, and he was kind and I liked him... and to put him in a steeping pit!" she added with a shudder. "It is terrible... terrible!"

Fridgyth reached forward and squeezed her hand. "Forgive me for even suggesting it, honey. Yes, it is utterly foul," she said. "I'm tired and hungry and you'll not be the only lass distraught to hear of his fate."

A hunk of fresh bread and a bowl of warm pottage was put in front of the herb-wife and she nodded gratefully. Memory of what she'd seen made her stomach briefly rebel, but then the hunger returned and she set about eating the food.

As she finished her meal, she looked thoughtfully over at Della again. "If you loved a lad, would it trouble you that he smelt of the tanning pits?" she asked.

The girl looked surprised by the question, but then her expression turned soft and sad. "If it were someone as kind-hearted and fine-looking as Godric," she said sadly. "I wouldn't let anything put me off."

CHAPTER 8

DISCRETION

When she'd finished eating, Fridgyth got up from her bench and set off again to see Hild. She found the abbess and her reeve sitting together in quiet consternation.

Hild looked up as the herb-wife walked in. "How could such a thing have happened?" she whispered, her expression shocked. "That poor boy."

"Well… I have a little more information now," Fridgyth said quietly. "And perhaps it does explain it, though it is still terribly wrong to my way of thinking."

She sat down with them and related what the tanners had revealed. They listened carefully, their faces tense with concern. "The parents are deeply ashamed," she said. "And they cannot think why the lad would be so secretive about meeting a woman, unless she was married to another. I told them that we would try to make enquiries tactfully. I hope I was right to do that."

"Oh yes," Hild agreed sadly. "This makes the death no less shocking, but if Godric was secretly meeting with a married woman, it would at least seem to provide an explanation. I am the King's representative in Streonshalh and won't tolerate anyone taking the law into his or her own hands like this. What do you think?" She turned to Ketel.

Ketel glanced at Fridgyth and shifted his feet with a slight touch of discomfort. "No man or woman should be above the law," he agreed. "But at least this might provide a motive and not… as I'd feared a

45

crazed madman who might strike again. That would be something we'd all dread."

Fridgyth bridled a little. "To drown a young man in a stinking, steeping pit indicates both madness and rage to me," she protested. "Godric was strong and I cannot see how he could have allowed himself to be trussed like that."

"Do you mean that there could have been more than one attacker?" Hild asked.

Fridgyth shrugged. "An angry man may have brothers," she said.

"Well," the abbess said, "I think it right that we pursue inquiries on this matter, as and when we can, but with discretion too, in respect of the shame the boy's poor parents feel."

"Yes, lady," Ketel said. "And to make this information known abroad would warn the culprit too, I think."

"You too, Fridgyth," Hild said, with just the slight touch of a smile. "You must use discretion, for I know that telling you to refrain from inquiring will do no good. You see and hear more than most of us."

The herb-wife's eyebrows lifted in surprise at this small acknowledgement.

"I am always discreet," she said. "But now I need to make sure that I am ready to attend Queen Cynewise; it would never do to mix my healing herbs with my poisons, would it?"

Hild shook her head, smiling a little as the herb-wife got up from her seat, bowed to them both and left the abbess's parlour.

Fridgyth returned to her hut, where she fussed over her salves and herbs, while Della went off to see Wulfrun and the Princess. The girls wanted to discuss what should be worn for the arrival of the important guest, the following day. At the sound of footsteps outside, Fridgyth threw open her door expecting that Ketel had followed her, but she found her old friend, Caedmon standing there.

"What are you doing?" she greeted him brusquely. "I thought it was… never mind."

"I don't know where to go," he admitted. "The monastery is all hustle and bustle and they want me to sing for the Mercian Queen tomorrow night… and I don't know what to sing. Something to please our guests, the abbess says, but… that is not easy to think up."

"Come inside," Fridgyth said. "I'll make us a camomile brew. I'm in just the same sort of stew. I have to attend Queen Cynewise when she arrives and try to heal her ills – though how I shall manage to do it, I don't know – and there's much else to think about too. Have you heard about Godric?"

"Yes," he said sadly.

"Poor fool! Poor handsome Godric! Whoever killed him, marked him with the rune of revenge. As if we haven't enough to worry about."

"I'd rather make a song in Godric's honour," Caedmon confided.

He took the harp from his shoulder and sat down by the hearth. The two were old friends and had known each other since Caedmon had been the monastery cowherd. Though shy and hesitant, his fine singing voice and talent for creating songs had eventually been discovered by the abbess. He was now an honorary monastic oblate, though he missed the company of the beasts he used to care for.

Fridgyth spooned camomile and honey into a jug of boiled water and soon the grassy scent of the herb filled the hut. "Aye, sing, to me!" she said as she poured them both a steaming drink. "That'll soothe me."

But when the cowherd's fingers touched the strings, the sound he made was discordant. He began to chant in an angry voice, until he was almost shouting.

"*The old one comes, the ancient enemy*
The dragon-wife, mate of the fierce one…"

He stopped with another jarring twang and glared at her. "That's all that comes to mind," he said. "And I can't sing that to Penda's widow!"

Fridgyth threw up her head, leaned back in her chair and began to laugh. It began as a gentle chuckle, but then it turned into a full-throated belly laugh. Caedmon smiled sheepishly, rather shocked at the effect his wild singing had had on her, but then he too began to laugh.

"No, don't you start too!" Fridgyth howled and she wagged a shaking finger in his direction.

They both rocked with laughter for a while and tears ran down their cheeks, but then eventually they managed to quieten down.

"Eeh dear!" Fridgyth gulped. "Well, that's somehow made me feel better." She wiped her eyes. "Your words uttered perfectly what I feel about it all. What is she doing here… the dragon-wife? Shall I get my poisons down? I have been thinking of it."

She pointed wildly above her to the highest shelf where she kept a small stock of the more dangerous herbs: foxglove, monkshood and deadly nightshade.

Caedmon chuckled again. "Yes, do that!" he said.

Fridgyth looked at him with approval. Gone were the rough beast-herder's clothes that he once wore. Instead, he presented himself to all appearances as a cultured man of mature years, clean and tonsured as the other monks, in his un-dyed, flaxen habit. Caedmon could still neither read nor write and yet, with the abbess's encouragement, he composed and performed the most beautiful songs. He'd discovered too, that if he appeared briefly in the upper pasture just before vespers, to check on the welfare of his calves – nobody chided him.

"And you," he said, as he rested his harp on his knees. "I remember that you lost your family in Penda's raids, and now you say they bring his widow for you to treat. They ask too much I think."

She nodded, but tried to respond with fairness. "The raids that took my man were led by the Welsh King, not King Penda himself, though they were allies at the time. Mercia and Gwynedd were determined to destroy both our crops and our people. They burnt our fields and killed everyone they could, but that was war… and it was long ago."

There was silence for a moment, and then Fridgyth spoke again. "I loved your fierce words… but you are right, you cannot call the Mercian Queen a dragon-wife, not to her face. What's needed is an image that we can all accept."

"Yes," he agreed.

Fridgyth looked pensive for a moment. "I told my bees," she said. "I told them that the widow was coming and somehow they made me see her a little differently... she is just another queen bee, the Queen of a distant hive."

Caedmon looked thoughtful as he rippled the strings of his harp more gently, then set up a thrumming rhythm that sounded familiar.

Fridgyth smiled. "You make your harp sound like my bees."

His face grew animated and he spoke over the rhythmic hum.

"The Queen of a distant hive, she comes,
And we, the angry workers, fear her
Will she steal away our sweetness?
Or does she come to us, fierce and protesting?"

Fridgyth nodded. "I suppose you may be right in that," she admitted. "These Mercians may be as reluctant to come here, as we are to have them. King Oswy has willed it and what our overlord wills must be done, but maybe... if like good beekeepers, we settle their Queen and put her at her ease, all will be well. I know that is what the abbess hopes for."

Caedmon sighed. He nodded. "And our abbess treats us all with such kind concern. It is for her, if for no other reason, that we should try our best."

Fridgyth nodded. "Yes, we must try."

He suddenly smiled as new inspiration came to him. "A powerful queen," he said. "Like the Queen of Sheba!"

"Sheba?" Fridgyth said with a frown. "Where is Sheba...? I never heard of Sheba."

"Some distant place," Caedmon replied with a shrug. "I don't think it matters where. They tell me stories from their holy book; so that I might make use of them to make songs and some of them are not so very different from our own old tales. The Christ-God hung on a tree to save the world, just as Woden hung on the tree that we might learn wisdom! But one of their older stories tells of a mighty queen who came to visit the wise King Solomon, and she was the Queen of Sheba."

He rippled the strings again.

"She comes, decked in gold and garnets

49

Cynewise, Queen of a distant hive
Splendid as the Queen of Sheba
When she visited the valiant Solomon!
She comes to greet our wise, young King
Exalted Ecfrid, son of Eanfleda,
Grandson of our great Edwin."

He stopped and looked uncertain. "Will she be decked with gold and garnets?"

"Oh yes," Fridgyth said. "I'd expect her to be magnificently dressed. This is an excellent song, I might worry more that you credit Ecfrid with wisdom, but we can only hope that you are right about him."

But Caedmon still frowned. "I've made no mention of the abbess, and she has more wisdom than any," he said, fretting again.

"That's no problem," Fridgyth told him smartly. "Our abbess is truly wise, so she will understand your intention and approve it."

He lowered his harp. "They say Hild's name means 'battle', a strange name for such a peace-loving woman."

"Don't be deceived," Fridgyth told him. "Hild does battle every day. She battles with the ruthlessness of those set above her... and with the poverty of those in need, and with the pain she suffers, though she ignores it."

"Yes!" he agreed as he rose to his feet. "That is a song for another day. I have found my song for today, I think, and I must go away to refine it a little."

He moved to the door, looking more cheerful than when he'd arrived.

"I'm glad," Fridgyth said, as she patted his shoulder.

Once he'd gone she returned to her hearth and sipped the rest of her mug of sweetened camomile, with a wistful smile on her face. "There were rosemary bushes all around," she murmured as her mind drifted to distant memories. "And a clear spring that bubbled from the ground."

CHAPTER 9

WHAT IS SHE DOING HERE?

Late that night, Ketel appeared in the herb-wife's hut. He sat down wearily beside the fire. "What a day!" he said, with a heartfelt sigh.

"Yes, what a day!" Fridgyth agreed. "Is everything ready for this visit?"

He nodded. "We are as ready as we possibly can be, the royal guest house has been scrubbed with sand and strewn with herbs. Cwen has put two new wall hangings in the Queen's chamber, and even the Mercian servants seem impressed by them. But poor Godric, I don't know what to make of that. He seemed too honourable a lad, too…"

"Ah yes, but he was handsome enough to steal anyone's heart," Fridgyth said. She glanced at Della, who sat quietly by the fire making faint clacking sounds as she worked away steadily at a length of tablet braid that she was weaving.

Her father looked over too, and suddenly leant forward to point to her work. "You have those wooden tablets, daughter," he said sharply. "The rune of revenge was marked on one of those things."

Della stopped her work and looked at her tablet weaving in dismay.

"Every home in Streonshalh has them," Fridgyth protested. "You'll have to take on the whole of the town if you're to go looking to link weaving tablets with the killer."

Ketel sat back looking pensive, as his daughter resumed her work. "And a rope twined with rosemary," he added softly, looking over at Fridgyth.

"Aye, rosemary," she said, and she gave him a smile that was full of softness and meaning. "We remember where the rosemary grew, don't we?"

He smiled back at her. "We do," he said.

One of the monastery's sturdiest boats arrived from Handale on the early morning tide, well before most people were awake. It was laden with pieces of finely carved wood and iron fittings, all part of Queen Cynewise's famous travelling bed. The reeve and a group of early rising lay brothers went down to meet the boat. They carried the sections of the bed up the hill and into the royal guest house.

Della rose early as she was excited about watching proceedings. She returned to the herb-wife's hut to report her findings. "They are setting the bed up in the Queen's chamber," she told Fridgyth breathlessly. "The carpenters are helping with it and the Queen's barge is expected soon. It must get here before the tide turns. Prince Aethelred and Siward of Dreng have arrived, though the Prince doesn't look at all like a prince ought to look."

"What does he look like?" Fridgyth asked.

"Tall, very thin, more like a monk than many of the brothers we have here. His foster father is very thin too; I don't think they will spoil our food supplies. Shall I tell you when the barge is spotted? The children are already on the look-out from the clifftops."

"Yes," Fridgyth agreed.

The herb-wife checked and re-checked her herbs and potions, anxiously anticipating the Queen's arrival, but soon after Della had gone, Edric and Muriel appeared at her door.

"We have been to see our boy," the tanner said. "The abbess has given permission for him to be laid in the new burial ground, just outside the monastic boundary. It is reserved for those who are connected to the monastery, but not religious. In time, important people will be buried in that ground, maybe even royalty and we see that this is the way things are going. The abbess says we may be buried there too, alongside him, when our time comes."

The herb-wife reached out to hug them both. "Anything that makes you feel a little better must be good," she said.

"Aye," Muriel said, with a sigh. "You tell what else they found," she said with a sorrowful glance at her husband.

Edric nodded and continued reluctantly. "Brother Bossa has examined his body along with two more of the monks. They have discovered a small wound and deep bruising on the back of his head. They think our son must have been knocked senseless first, before…" And he found himself unable to go on.

Muriel began to weep quietly again. "I pray that he was caught unawares," she said. "The thought of him suffering…"

"It explains it," Edric managed to continue. "For how else would it have been possible? Our boy was strong and I think it must have taken someone with strength to do the deed."

"We won't let this lie," Fridgyth assured them. "The reeve will make many discreet inquiries, and I will too."

They stood there for a few more moments, looking pale-faced and heartbroken. Then Edric took his wife's hand to lead her home. "It's maybe best to let it lie, herb-wife," he said. "Yes, best to let it lie."

Fridgyth said no more, but reached out to give them both a comforting pat on the shoulders. They nodded in response and wandered away.

The sun was high in the sky when Della arrived with the news that the *Royal Edwin* had been seen in the distance. The herb-wife and her assistant set out together and met Ketel at the top of the steep path that led down to the wooden quayside. The barge could be seen to the northwest, although it was still a small speck in the distance.

As she approached, Fridgyth saw that Ketel hovered at the top of the pathway looking anxious, as well he might, with so much responsibility on his shoulders.

"Come, we'll manage this," she said and took his arm.

They set off together down the steep winding path that led from the monastery to the quayside. It was generally acknowledged in Streonshalh that the reeve and the herb-wife had a close and intimate friendship. Ketel had begged Fridgyth to marry him, several times, but so far she'd refused. As reeve's wife, she'd be expected to act as the monastery's hostess. Though the status of reeve's wife was usually higher than that of herb-wife, she was unwilling to give up her role. The job of healer suited her well as it allowed her extraordinary freedom of movement and independence. She worried at times that one of the many young widows in Streonshalh might set her cap at Ketel instead, and while she acknowledged the unfairness of these feelings, she was clear that she didn't want another to take her place at his side. Until recently, Hild herself had fulfilled the position of hostess, and she'd done it with vigour and tact, but the fevers and pains that she now suffered made it difficult.

"I can't get that poor foolish boy, Godric out of my mind," Fridgyth confessed as they walked down the hill.

"The abbess is eager for justice to be seen to be done," Ketel said. "If only we had some evidence, then a hearing could be called and judgement made, by right of The King's Law. Godric's wergild at least should be paid to his parents, for it was a disgusting and brutal murder. Such payment will not bring him back, but it would help to compensate them a little. We cannot have such goings on in Streonshalh, but… there are now so many other things to do!"

"His parents have said to let it lie," Fridgyth acknowledged, "but that would not be right. I'll ask around and it will be interesting to hear what his brother has got to say when he gets back from his travels."

"It is mainly my job to make enquiries," Ketel said rather sharply.

"But the abbess gave me permission to enquire," she answered, just as smartly. She slipped her hand coolly out of the crook of his arm just as they reached the quayside.

They found the abbess already there, diminutive beside King Ecfrid and Princess Elfled, who had already grown taller than her foster mother. Another lanky youth and an older man, both dressed in good but sober, dark brown cloth, stood behind them. Fridgyth guessed this must be the Mercian Prince, Aethelred, with his foster father. She glanced back at Della, and gave a swift nod, for she too agreed that they both looked more like monks.

The quayside was crammed with curious Streonshalh inhabitants, who were eager to set eyes on the disreputable dragon-wife. There was some danger of people falling into the deep harbour water as parents became distracted and excited children clambered everywhere. People stood back to allow the herb-wife to join the abbess. At her approach, Princess Elfled clutched her brother's embroidered sleeve and gave a mischievous smile. "You remember our herb-wife, brother," she said.

Ecfrid turned and gave a condescending nod. "I remember," he said.

Fridgyth bowed her head and dropped a small curtsy, but as she looked up, she thought she caught a spark of amusement in Ecfrid's eye. Wulfrun, who'd been hovering behind the Princess, edged her way to Fridgyth's side and, without saying another word, they both drew further back so that they could whisper together.

"Is all going well?" Fridgyth asked.

"Yes. The Prince is friendly enough," Wulfrun quietly replied.

There was no time to exchange further confidences, for an excited child shouted from his lookout spot, high on the bankside. "It's here, it's here!"

All heads lifted, straining to see as the abbess's barge swung suddenly into sight, as it rounded the jutting headland. The elegant twin prowed vessel moved fast towards them, carried onward by the wing-like lift and dip of ten pairs of oars. Thrilled whispers skimmed through the crowd.

"They say she was beautiful once!"

"But wicked… and a pagan still! The dragon-wife!"

"Aye, she will bring a curse on us all! Not right to bring her here."

"But the King has commanded it!"

"Which King? Father or son? Oswy or Ecfrid?"

"Both… they say! They have agreed that this meeting must take place."

The barge came closer, until it was near enough to be moored. At the captain's shout, the oars were lifted and hauled in. The quayside buzzed with curiosity. It was only due to the enormous respect that Hild commanded, that the abbess was able to move forward to greet her guests.

The oarsmen, all hefty lay brothers, leapt ashore and set about hauling the mooring lines. They pulled the boat up against the wooden jetty and fastened it securely.

The expectant crowd fell strangely silent, as the gangplank was set up, for King Penda's fierce reputation had not softened with the passage of time, rather the opposite. Visitors to Streonshalh were normally welcomed with a resounding cheer as they disembarked, but it seemed that in these strange circumstances, such a response might appear inappropriate. Instead all eyes searched amongst the group of women passengers that were still hidden in the shelter of a tent of stretched skins, which had been constructed on the deck. At last there was some movement as cloaked and hooded figures emerged. There were a few elderly men aboard, but mostly Cynewise's courtiers were women, dressed so warmly against the cold that it was impossible to identify the Queen.

"Which one?" Della whispered. "So many! Who are they all?"

Fridgyth shook her head, unsure. "I suppose they are the widows of King Penda's warlords, the remainder of her famous court. Most of them look to be as ancient as I am."

"They are not all old," Della pointed out. "I can see one who…"

At last a tall, thin, silver-haired woman threw back her hood, and straightened with some difficulty, but the proud lift of her chin and the glint of a golden circlet on her brow announced for certain that she was Cynewise, once Queen of all the Mercians.

Fridgyth glanced only briefly at the most important visitor, for a much younger woman, who rose to help her mistress, immediately grabbed her attention.

Wulfrun's mouth dropped open too. "Ah no," she whispered.

Fridgyth and Wulfrun exchanged a horrified glance. They had both recognised the clear features and creamy complexion of the younger woman, as did the Princess.

"Irminburgh!" Elfled cried. "They have brought Irminburgh with them! What is she doing here?"

Irminburgh pushed back a fur-trimmed hood and many more of those gathered at the quayside recognised her striking features and her thick dark braids of hair. The young Kentish noblewoman, who was a distant cousin to Queen Eanfleda, had lost none of her beauty. She'd once lived in Streonshalh and been left in charge of Princess Elfled while the abbess visited the King at Bebbanburgh. Irminburgh's outrageous conduct had resulted in her being packed off to a far distant nunnery in the north as soon as the abbess returned.

Shocked whispers fled through the crowd.

"Is she the one who wanted to marry Ecfrid?" Della asked.

"Yes, she is Irminburgh!" Fridgyth said faintly.

"I thought I knew her," Della said. "But isn't she also the one who accused Wulfrun's mother of theft?"

"Yes," Wulfrun answered, her voice gone hard. "She is the one."

CHAPTER 10

TROUBLE

Irminburgh led the Mercian Queen towards the gangplank where the young King of Deira waited, at the abbess's side.

It was Elfled, who dared to ask the question that had risen in everyone's minds. "Did my brother know that Irminburgh was coming here?"

The Princess received no answer. Everyone watched breathlessly to see what would happen next. Fridgyth thought she glimpsed again the spark of amusement there in Ecfrid's glance. The abbess must have been as shocked as any to be faced with Irminburgh, but she did not change her expression by the slightest flicker of an eyelid or portray her disquiet. The Mercian Queen stepped onto the gangplank, and Ecfrid himself moved forward to offer his hand and help her step ashore.

"Welcome to Streonshalh, Queen of the Mercians," he said formally, but then they smiled warmly and embraced each other with what appeared to be genuine warmth and affection.

"I see you've not forgotten your old foster ma," Cynewise said with a knowing smile.

"Never," he replied and he kissed her hand.

The abbess moved forward to greet her visitor by kissing her formally on both cheeks, and the Mercian Queen accepted this, though she stooped rather awkwardly to allow it.

Cynewise then turned to present Irminburgh. "And my youngest lady in waiting," she said, "I think you already know."

"Yes, the Lady Irminburgh is known to us here in Streonshalh," Hild said drily.

"I knew you'd be pleased to see me," Irminburgh said as she stepped ashore.

With a radiant smile, she sank into a graceful curtsey, aimed mainly at Ecfrid. He gallantly stepped forward once again to help her up.

Rather than letting her gaze linger on Ecfrid's pleasing features, Irminburgh moved surprisingly fast in a different direction. "My little friend," she cried and she moved quickly along the line of waiting people to fling her arms around Elfled, who looked stunned.

There was an awkward silence for a moment, for somehow Irminburgh had succeeded in making herself the focus of this reception, rather than the important Mercian Queen. Recollecting the official purpose for this gathering, Hild moved to correct the discourtesy, by ushering forward Prince Aethelred, to greet the mother he'd not seen since he was four years old. Mother and son came face to face. The young man bowed with cool and rigid formality. Cynewise did little to ease the situation, for she gave only the slightest nod of her head in acknowledgement of her son, appearing to regard him with disinterest.

Hild, with her usual sense of timing, filled another uncomfortable pause by ordering the waiting line of litters to be brought forward. Curious whispers rose from the crowd as they watched the newcomers climb aboard. A rather ragged procession formed, to follow the cavalcade up the steep hillside.

Fridgyth did not rush after them, but hovered at the quayside, trying to gather her thoughts. Elfled and Wulfrun, now briefly released from their more formal duties, made their way towards her, followed by their tutor.

"What is *she* doing here?" Elfled asked. "How has *she* somehow managed to wheedle her way back to Streonshalh?"

"I'm as stunned as you are," Fridgyth said, as they turned to walk slowly up the hill together. Della and Sister Lindi followed behind them.

"I'm sure Mother Hild did not expect *her*," Elfled said.

"No," Fridgyth agreed. "The last we knew of Irminburgh, she'd been sent to Coldingham, to live with Oswy's sister, Princess Ebba, who is the abbess of the monastery there. They say that Ebba allows her nuns more luxury... small indulgences."

"Irminburgh was supposed to become a nun," Elfled said with something of a sense of resentment. "I thought she was given to a monastery by her father, just as I was. How has she managed to become the Mercian Queen's lady instead?"

"Becoming a nun is not so bad a thing, Princess," Sister Lindi reminded her.

Wulfrun's hand strayed to the carved handle of her knife. "And what kind of a nun would Irminburgh make?" she asked. "I fear she may have come here to take revenge on us, because we stopped her plans and got her sent away from Streonshalh. What do you think, Fridgyth?"

"Don't see trouble before it comes," the herb-wife advised, but then she stopped for a moment and sighed, for she had suddenly realised that she'd have to come face to face with Irminburgh again when she attended the widowed Queen.

"What?" Della asked. "What troubles you?"

Fridgyth shook her head. "Never mind, never mind," she said and moved on.

"I will never trust her," Wulfrun said.

"No," Elfled agreed. "But... I have sometimes thought that Ecfrid might still love her..."

"She is so very beautiful," Della added, breathlessly.

"Yes, she is beautiful, and she seemed very pleased to see you Princess," Sister Lindi said. "She certainly drew everyone's attention, especially the King's."

"Yes, but you don't know what we know," Elfled told her with meaning. "I will tell you about it later."

A troubled look passed between Fridgyth and Wulfrun, but they said no more and carried on up the hill.

"Can Della come with us?" Elfled begged, as they reached the top. "We will go to the royal guest house and keep an eye on Irminburgh. We'll let you know what happens there."

Fridgyth looked to Lindi for agreement.

The young nun smiled tolerantly. "Let her come," she agreed.

They went off together, the girl's voices shrill with concern and excitement.

Fridgyth wandered back to her hut feeling more troubled than ever by this unexpected turn of events. Once again she set out her basket and checked her selection of herbs. She put on a clean apron, but then took it off again, unsure as to whether one should attend the Queen wearing such a practical garment.

The bell rang out announcing the noontide meal and Fridgyth went to the kitchens to help herself to bread and goats' cheese, which she carried back to her hut, feeling that she'd better remain there in case she was called. She had just finished her small meal and taken a sip or two of her own elderberry wine, to calm her anxiety, when fast footsteps sounded outside the door.

Della burst in, her cheeks flushed with running. "The abbess is asking for you," she announced breathlessly. "You're to go to the royal guest house as soon as you can."

Fridgyth picked up her apron, frowned and put it on again. "It is clean and suited to my task," she muttered.

She clipped back her sleeves and picked up the basket of herbs and potions that she'd prepared so meticulously.

"I'll stay here, in case anyone needs a herb-wife's help," Della assured her.

Fridgyth grimaced. "No excuses then, no avoiding it."

One of the Mercian ladies was waiting for her at the main entrance to the royal guest house. She looked the herb-wife up and down with disapproval, her eyes lingering on the undyed linen apron. "Who are you?" she asked.

"I'm Fridgyth, the herb-wife your mistress has requested. Who are you?"

"I'm Helga, the Queen's doorkeeper," she said. "Well, you'd better come this way. The abbess is with our Queen."

Fridgyth was somewhat relieved to hear that.

No expense or convenience had been spared in the furnishing of the Queen's chamber. Fridgyth recognised one of Cwen's rich coloured wall hangings, tactfully patterned not with the usual Christian images, but with flowers and the curled snake-stones that could be found all over the surrounding cliffs. The room was crammed with chattering women, some sitting on stools, others awkwardly hovering. Cynewise was sitting by the hearth, warming her swollen hands over a brazier. A goblet of Hild's best wine was set out on a small table at her side. Irminburgh perched on a low stool at her feet.

Fridgyth bobbed a curtsey, unsure of the correct approach to a widowed queen, who'd spent many years as a hostage.

"So – this is the famous herb-wife," Cynewise said, and she too frowned a little as she scrutinised Fridgyth. "I hadn't expected her to be quite so round and homely."

Irminburgh smiled sweetly up at Fridgyth. "The herb-wife and I met long ago," she said. "We know each other well.

A bubble of resentment rose in the herb-wife and burst through the tight knot of anxiety that had been gathering in her stomach. "The lady Irminburgh and I are well acquainted," she agreed "And as for my homely appearance, well… I could rattle a few bones, wave a rowan wand and rant a little if you would like, but I've come here to help and I see at once what ails our royal visitor."

Cynewise dropped her hands and looked deeply shocked, as too did her ladies, while Irminburgh dipped her head to hide the smile that came to her lips. Everyone then turned to the abbess to see whether she would be as appalled as they were.

Hild sent a wry glance in Fridgyth's direction, but made no apology for her. "Our herb-wife is somewhat forthright in her manner of address," she said. "But I can assure you that I have benefited greatly from her care myself. I also recognise your symptoms, for I suffer them too."

Hild held out her hands, to show Cynewise that the joints of her fingers were just as inflamed, swollen and knotted as hers. "You have the aching disease, which comes with age," she said. "A painful burden that comes to many of us who are lucky to live to be so old."

There was a moment of tense silence, then Cynewise's shoulders drooped, and her haughty expression fled, her still fine-boned face was suddenly drawn with misery.

Fridgyth was startled to experience a flash of pity. "Would it be possible for our royal visitor to consult with me in private?" she asked quietly.

Cynewise nodded wearily.

"I will take the ladies to the women's bower," Hild said. "And I hope you will join us in the great hall tonight, our food-wife has prepared a feast in your honour and our monastic bard has prepared a song for you."

Cynewise sighed, as though she'd prefer to dine alone, but she nodded, indicating that she'd make the effort to join them.

The women all rose to leave, save Irminburgh. "The Queen always requires my presence," she announced with the glimmer of another smile.

"No," Hild said firmly. "I require *your* presence, Irminburgh!"

Cynewise looked a little surprised by the abbess's firm tone, but she gave another slight nod of agreement. Irminburgh reluctantly got up and left the room.

CHAPTER 11

STINGING NETTLE

Once they were alone, Fridgyth asked the Mercian Queen if she could examine her hands. Cynewise complied in silence, and allowed the herb-wife to kneel before her and gently examine the swollen joints. She tensed a little and flinched when the tender areas were touched, but no complaint betrayed the pain she felt.

"How does it feel when you walk?" Fridgyth asked.

"Well enough, once I've got going," Cynewise replied. "It is getting going that's the problem. The first few steps are very hard and then it eases a little."

Fridgyth nodded. "It is as I thought."

"Well, can you cure it?"

Fridgyth shook her head. "Nothing can cure it, but I can ease the pain a little and maybe soothe the joints. While you are here I can come daily to work on your hands, but much of it is up to you. You must work through the pain and move, however hard it feels. Stinging nettle balm can help and I have some here."

Cynewise pulled back. "I think you jest!" she said, a touch of angry humour in her voice. "Is this some strange form of revenge? Stinging nettle!"

Fridgyth chuckled. "This ailment can be helped with nettle balm and also bitter teas, made from nettle, dandelion and white willow."

"Disgusting!" Penda's widow cried. "I think you try to make a fool of me."

"I will sweeten the herbs with my best heather honey, which will make the medicine both taste and work better. I have two good hives almost ready for the gathering."

Cynewise examined Fridgyth's expression for mockery, but could find nothing there other than plain speaking. "Nought else seems to help," she admitted, with a shrug.

"We'll start with teas, broth and some gentle rubbing," Fridgyth said, as she struggled awkwardly to her own feet and gave a small grunt. "As you see – I too have a touch of stiffness in my knees. We'll leave beating you with stinging nettles as the last resort."

Cynewise looked up sharply uncertain whether she jested or not.

"It is a true remedy," Fridgyth assured her with a wry smile. "But one for the most courageous… or the most desperate."

"Do you accuse me of lacking courage?"

"No," Fridgyth said firmly. "I do not."

She fished in her basket and brought out a stoppered horn bottle. A pungent smell spread around them as she eased the beeswax plug out of the top with the point of her meat knife.

"What is this?" the Queen demanded.

"It is stinging nettle balm, with marigold, flax oil and beeswax. I shall start your treatment right away… if you are ready?"

"Stinging-nettle again?" she queried warily. "You seem over fond of the vicious weeds."

"This balm is a gentler way of making the application," Fridgyth said as she knelt again in front of the Queen.

"Very well," Cynewise held out her hands. "Nought can be worse than the stiffness and the aching pain."

Fridgyth tipped a little of the greenish coloured liquid into her palm and set about massaging the swollen finger joints, gently at first and then with more vigour.

Cynewise caught her breath and held it for a moment or two, but then she let it out gently and her whole demeanour began to ease a little. "It tingles," she said, "but the sensation is not unpleasant."

Fridgyth smiled. "You see… this is not revenge."

The aged Queen allowed her to continue to work steadily on the swollen joints. "I cannot trust easily," Cynewise said at last, her tone a little more gentle and confiding. "Everyone wants revenge. And yet I could demand revenge of those who have injured me."

"Aye," Fridgyth said, her voice suddenly a little harder. "Many people wish for revenge."

"You too?" She said, sensing the different tone of voice. "What did my husband ever do to you?"

Fridgyth let go of the Queen's hands and her reply came fast as a striking hammer. "He rode with the Welsh King, who killed my husband and burnt our crops, so that my children starved to death. I was burnt too," she said lifting her chin a little and gently touching the scarred skin that now showed. "I got this trying to put out our blazing barley."

They both stared angrily at each other for a moment.

"Then why did you not starve?" Cynewise asked.

Fridgyth paused and sighed, she answered more gently. "A good woman helped me," she said. "She fed me, though she had little love for me. Now, like her, I offer my services, though I have little love for you."

Cynewise frowned furiously and a moment of tense silence followed. Fridgyth feared she'd gone too far, but then the Mercian Queen suddenly gave a quiet chuckle. "At least you are honest," she said relaxing into a smile. "And my hands feel warm and comfortable."

Fridgyth scrambled to her feet and gave a small bob of a curtsey. "I will instruct your serving women in the making of teas and send some honey round, but it will take me a while before I can gather the heather honey, which is the most powerful medicine I can offer."

Cynewise nodded and Fridgyth thought she was dismissed, but then just as she picked up her basket the widowed Queen of Mercia, turned a little awkwardly towards her and spoke again. "I thank you," she said.

Fridgyth hurried back to her hut, her feelings jumbled.

"Now where are my honey stealing clouts?" she muttered. She began searching in her clothes chest.

"Well… how did it go?" Della asked, avid to know.

"Not as bad as I feared," Fridgyth admitted. "I gave as good as I got… and we parted on fair terms. As you'd expect, King Penda's widow is proud and unbending."

"And is she sick?"

"Yes, but it is simply the aching sickness, like the abbess, though I fancy she is going to be much harder to treat. I shall do my best."

Della looked thoughtful. "I know that Penda was a fearful warrior and that he tore our lands apart, but... it seems to me that the old woman is not to blame for that. She has suffered too, with her husband killed and her youngest son stolen from her. She stays loyal to her husband's memory and her beliefs and our abbess tolerates such things in you... and plenty of others who live round here."

Fridgyth stared at her, astonished that this long speech should come from her biddable assistant. "You speak true, my lass," she admitted. "Those things happened long ago. It seems like another life... but the sadness lingers and I cannot scour it from my memory. I only lived because someone brought me food and left it at my door and something the Mercian woman said tonight reminded me of it. I only discovered it after she died, but it was your mother who brought me food and it was very generous of her."

Della nodded sadly. "And it was not the old woman in the royal guest house who killed your man and fired your fields," she added.

"You are quite right," Fridgyth was forced to admit. "Who taught you to see both sides so clearly, lass?"

Della grinned. "I think it was you," she replied.

Fridgyth got up and gave her a warm hug and they sat in thoughtful silence for a while.

"But what of Irminburgh?" Della asked at last. "Was Irminburgh there in the royal guest house with the Mercian Queen?"

"Ah... Irminburgh is quite another matter," Fridgyth said. "But Hild took Irminburgh away with her, and I'd give much to be party to what will pass between those two. Now I cannot think where I put my honey-stealing clouts? I must tell the bees all that has happened and take a little more honey from the meadow hives. I shall need to make another trip with the mule to fetch the heather honey too, for that is what that woman needs more than anything."

Della reached up to a hook near the doorway and held two ragged strips of cloth out to her.

"What would I do without you?" Fridgyth said with a smile. "Perhaps the honey will sweeten Penda's widow, and make her fold her dragon wings. Aye, and I must hurry and seize my chance while most of the bees are out foraging."

Having tied one clout about her forehead and tucked the other into the neck of her gown, she smeared a thin coating of older honey onto her face and fingers.

Della passed her a basket that contained a thin, smooth sanded slat of wood and two clean scrubbed honey tubs. With tongs Fridgyth picked up a lump of burning charcoal from the hearth and dropped it into a small metal dish. Still using the tongs to carry the hot dish, she picked up the basket and set off for the upper pasture.

The young cowherds ignored the herb-wife, as she put down her basket near the hives and then trudged through the cropped grass looking to select a sliver of dried cow dung. Once she'd found what she needed, she dropped it onto the charcoal so that it began to smoke and headed back towards her hives, which were set in a fenced off area beyond the grazing beasts. Fridgyth approached her bees quietly and gently blew a light stream of smoke into the upper part of the first skep. This treatment encouraged the bees still in residence to drop drowsily down into the lower skep. These double skeps were Fridgyth's own creation and, though other beekeepers scoffed, she persisted with them. She would not cheerfully drown her bees or smoke them to death as most of the other beekeepers did, in order to take the honey.

She began to chatter gently as she worked, confiding to the bees all the details of the surprising visitors to the monastery. The sound of her voice seemed to reassure the creatures. When she was satisfied that most of them had moved down into the lower skep, she lifted the heavy upper skep, which was packed with dripping honeycomb and slid a wooden slat between the two halves to separate them.

"Freya bless you, my darlings," she murmured as she eased the honeycomb out into a clean tub.

Pleased beyond measure with her haul, she reassembled the skeps and repeated the process with the second hive.

CHAPTER 12

THE QUEEN OF SHEBA

When Fridgyth returned to her hut with two weighty tubs of honey, she found Ketel sitting by her hearth, sipping a blackberry brew that his daughter had made for him.

"I'd have thought you would be too busy to be resting here," Fridgyth said at once.

"Thank you for your friendly greeting," he replied. "I am busy, but I want to be clear with you about the poor drowned lad before I set that bad business aside. I've been thinking about what his parents said this morning, and how they admitted that they think a jealous husband was most likely the cause of his death. After much thought and soul-searching, they say that they are not moved to press for blood-money, and I'm inclined to respect their wishes in this."

"So you will let this murder go unpunished?"

"I don't like it much," he said. "But the future peace of the whole of Mercia and Northumbria depends on the outcome of this meeting of kings, queens and princes and to spend my time questioning all the locals about Godric, would be very difficult just now."

Fridgyth set her tubs carefully down on the trestle and started unwinding her neck clout. "If Hild says 'let it be', of course I agree," she said. "I can see you have much else to concern you at the moment."

He looked worried still. "But if Streonshalh's sense of law and safety is threatened by this oversight…"

Fridgyth sighed. "No… no, leave be," she advised.

Ketel swallowed the last drops of his drink, replaced the mug on the table and got up. He dropped a kiss on his daughter's head, squeezed Fridgyth's waist and left quickly as she turned to slap him.

As he hurried away, Fridgyth sighed. "So much for poor Godric," she said.

"I'll never forget him," Della said sadly.

"No, nor will I," Fridgyth agreed.

The herb-wife and Della prepared medicines and salves with some of the honey that she had gathered until the light began to fade and the bell rang to announce the evening feast. They both set their work aside and straightened their clothing and combed their hair. This was to be an important occasion, and at least the food was likely to be excellent. They set off together for the great hall with good appetites and a degree of curiosity.

They were relieved that they were not expected to sit at the top table that night, for though the table groaned with horns of mead, platters of venison, roast fowl, and fishes of all kinds, anyone could see that the atmosphere amongst the most important guests was tense and formal. Cynewise had been placed between Ecfrid and Aethelred, while Irminburgh, dressed like a princess in a delicate rose madder gown, had been invited by the young King to sit at his left hand. For most of the meal, Cynewise ignored her estranged son and turned towards Ecfrid and Irminburgh, making it clear where her interest lay. Abbess Hild had tactfully placed herself between Aethelred and Siward of Dreng, where she struggled to converse for they were both solemn and ate little, seeming rather to disapprove of the lavish feast. It was with relief that the whole hall turned to Caedmon and his harp. His carefully worded song was much appreciated by everyone.

"She comes to us,
Splendid as the Queen of Sheba,
Cynewise, Queen of a distant hive,
Wonderful as when she visited Solomon the wise!
Cynewise meets with our sage, young master
Ecfrid, son of Eanfleda, grandson of great Edwin.
Fame to his foster mother,
As Solomon greeted Sheba,

With precious gifts of gold."

Cynewise listened, attentively and bowed in a dignified manner, then she sent Irminburgh to deliver a thin gold ring to Caedmon. He looked stunned and tried to refuse it, but Hild nodded with approval, so that he knew that he should accept it.

The Mercian Queen then rose from her seat and excused herself rather early from the feast. The herb-wife saw the effort she made to stand straight and begin to move gracefully towards the door, but Cynewise was made of stern stuff and she did not allow herself to limp or hobble. Ecfrid himself escorted her to the entrance of the great hall, to say goodnight. Her women all dutifully followed after her, though some of them looked a little reluctant to leave the feast. Ecfrid bent close to kiss his foster mother and whisper softly in her ear and they both glanced towards Irminburgh, who had got up to follow the Queen. Cynewise gave a sly smile and nod, and then suddenly she was gone and Irminburgh returned to enjoy the feast for a little longer, on Ecfrid's arm.

Rather shocked whispers ran around the feasting hall, but Hild managed to remain expressionless. Fridgyth got up, intending to gather what she needed, and then go to the royal guest house to make the Queen as comfortable as she could, before she retired for the night.

As she passed the weaving shed, once again she saw candlelight and heard the rhythmic clack as a heddle bar was dropped. She turned and made her way into the barnlike building, where she found Cwen working away.

"You must stop this," she said. "I wondered if you had heard the latest. You will harm your eyes and make yourself sick if you work like this… you are not a slave."

Cwen lifted the heddle bar up with a resounding crack and then she stopped and sighed. "Working stops me thinking… and worrying," Cwen said. "First Ecfrid and now Irminburgh. Ecfrid is our King now, even the abbess could not protect us from his wrath if he is bent on some revenge. Wulfrun came to tell me that Irminburgh wishes to see us both tomorrow morning and I fear…"

"Yes. I don't know what their game is, I admit," Fridgyth told her. "But they will have the abbess and all of Streonshalh to deal with if they mean any harm to you or your daughter."

Cwen rubbed her eyes. "I'm weary," she admitted.

"Go to your bed," Fridgyth advised. "All will become clear in time."

When Fridgyth at last got back to her hut, she gathered into her basket the ingredients she would need. "Stinging nettle, dandelion and willow bark," she murmured, "and a small flask of honey."

She pounded the willow bark to a fine powder, for fear there would be complaints of fibrous strands and paused a moment for thought. She remembered that the recipient of these medicines clung more strongly to the old beliefs than she did herself and so she chanted a charm.

"*Freya of the midnight cats,*
Give power to this potion.
Stinging nettle, pierce pain,
Willow bark soothe swelling,
Dandelion make her battle-brave,
For she is your own,
I thank you.

She smoothed her hair and muttered. "Well, I have done my best," before setting off for the royal guest house.

Helga opened the door again appearing extremely agitated. "Was it you that upset our Queen?" she demanded, accusingly. "Did you say something to offend her earlier?"

"No," Fridgyth replied rather defensively. "Why? What has happened?"

"Our Queen is furious and we don't know why, but since we came back from the feast, she is almost too angry to speak."

Fridgyth's spirits sank at this news. "Does she complain about the food?" she asked.

"No. The food," Helga admitted grudgingly, "was excellent. And we have tried so hard to prepare this place and make everything comfortable for her."

"What ails her then?" Fridgyth asked.

"I don't know. You had better come," she said.

Fridgyth followed her to the Queen's Chamber, to find it filled with women, all murmuring and upset, while Cynewise herself hauled on one of the wooden window shutters, trying to close it. "Bring more lights," she shouted. "I trust nobody here! I want these shutters closed for fear they spy on me. I need Irminburgh? Fetch Irminburgh!"

"She's with the King," Fridgyth reminded her.

"Oh yes," Cynewise recalled. "No don't fetch her then, but bring more lights! I need to see clearly what is happening here!"

Two of the women hurried away in search of more candles or lamps.

Fridgyth tried to stay calm and steady in all the chaos. "What makes you think you are spied upon?" she asked firmly.

"They are all around me," Cynewise cried. "I should have known it and never agreed to come here. They have induced my son to abandon his beliefs and now this…"

"What has happened?" Fridgyth asked steadily.

"A threat! It could be you… you were here."

"What threat? Do you wish to speak to the abbess?"

"No. You Christians will never understand."

Fridgyth put down her basket and went to the window. "Let me fasten this shutter for you," she said. "Then let us sit down. You must tell me what has brought this distress to you. I am no Christian, so you need not fear that I'll bring the Christ-God's curse on you."

Cynewise stared, aghast. "You are no Christian?" she murmured.

"No," Fridgyth told her firmly and she barred the shutter.

"You are not a Christian… and yet they keep you here preparing medicines for them?"

"Yes," Fridgyth said. "Sometimes I add a brief prayer to the Christ-God if the patient is Christian, but today I have chanted Freya's charm over the herbs I prepared for you. Now please, sit down and tell me what has happened to upset you so and I think it would be better if there were not so many people here."

Still trembling, the Queen allowed herself to be guided back to the cushioned chair that had been set by the glowing brazier. She looked round at her distressed women and dismissed them with a nod. "Go to the bower," she said. "And settle for the night. We will go back to Handale in the morning."

They rustled away leaving only Helga behind. Fridgyth pulled up a stool and sat herself down by the warmth.

"What is it?" she asked quietly.

The Mercian Queen glanced over to the darkest corner of the room, far away from the light and warmth of the lamp and the brazier. "It is there," she said. "I threw it over there. You will find it if you look… and if you understand such things as you say you do, you will know what it means."

Fridgyth got up and wandered over to the corner, uncertain as to what she might be looking for. Helga picked up the lamp and followed her, holding it high to give light. It was only when Fridgyth bent down and looked closely that she saw that something was there, for the small object was almost the same colour as the wooden floor of the chamber. She stooped to pick it up and as she did a touch of ice rippled down her back, for she knew at once what it was; a smooth, planed, square of wood thick enough for a rune to be carved and blackened into the surface. She turned it to the light to confirm what she already suspected; it bore the same rune she'd held in her hand the morning that they'd discovered Godric. Here again was the rune of Tyr, the rune of revenge, with a tough spray of rosemary pushed through one of the small corner holes and tightly tied.

CHAPTER 13

WHAT WICKEDNESS

Helga gasped in horror when she understood what it was that Fridgyth held. "What wickedness is this?" she cried.

The herb-wife's own hands trembled a little as she gripped the small weaving tablet, an ordinary enough thing, used every day, but turned malevolent by the sign that marked it. She too felt as though she wanted to throw it as far away from herself as she could.

"Where did you find it?" she asked, trying to keep her voice calm and steady.

Cynewise simply pointed to her bed.

"I was tired," she said, "and drew back the covers myself and there it was… waiting for me."

"We must think who could have put it here?" Fridgyth said.

"A multitude has been in here," Cynewise cried, as she opened her arms wide to indicate a great number. "The abbess, her nuns, the King, the reeve, the Princess… all their servants and you. I am newly arrived and I know none of them, only my own women can I trust. You know the old ways… you have just admitted it, it could be you."

Fridgyth felt herself flush uncomfortably. The royal bed had travelled ahead of the Queen and been assembled by her servants and it was true that many people had been in the chamber during the day, helping to prepare it. The door opened and another of the women returned with two glowing lamps. Irminburgh followed carrying a mug of steaming mead.

"They fetched me from the feast," she cried. "They told me you were distressed." She placed the mug on a low table and went to Cynewise. "My poor, poor lady. What ails you? Let me soothe you, let me rub your back."

They set the lamps to fill the chamber with a warmer glow.

"You must drink this… it will warm you," Irminburgh said.

Still angry and upset, the Queen tried to explain to Irminburgh. She allowed herself to be cosseted by the young woman and Fridgyth watched them, still stunned herself.

"You must let me take this… this horrid thing to the reeve at once," she said. "He needs to know what has happened here. Believe me, lady, he will see that you are guarded well and do everything he can to keep you safe while you are here in Streonshalh. Our reeve is a good man and the abbess must be told too."

Cynewise looked up at her angrily. "Your abbess, what will she have to say about warning runes?"

"A great deal," Fridgyth told her. "Hild was raised as a child of Woden and Freya; she understands these runes well. A little more mead will do you no harm for now, but I shall go to see the abbess and the reeve and then return here to help you settle for the night."

The women watched her in grim silence, then at last the Queen spoke.

"Yes, very well, give me the mead… and take that foul thing away!" Cynewise agreed.

Fridgyth strode out of the royal guest house and marched across the courtyard, her heart thundering in her chest. Her steps slowed a little and almost stopped. What was she doing? A week ago, she would not have lifted a finger to help the dragon-wife of Handale Head. Why should she now be rushing to her aid?

She glanced down at the simple tablet.

"Just a queen from a distant hive," she murmured. "Not the Queen of Sheba!"

She set off again with determination and arrived in the great hall, only to find that most of the guests had gone to their beds and the tables were being cleared. A young oblate told her that he thought the reeve had gone to speak with the abbess. Her heart thumping faster than ever, Fridgyth hurried on to Hild's own house. She strode into the parlour unannounced, to find the reeve deep in discussion with the abbess and King Ecfrid too. They glanced up startled at her interruption.

"The death of Godric must not be ignored," she announced.

Hild and Ketel looked shocked that she would interrupt them so discourteously and it was Ecfrid who spoke first.

"Greetings to our bold herb-wife," he said, with a slightly amused lift of one eyebrow.

Fridgyth curtsied hastily. "I'm so sorry, my lord," she said. "But there is reason for this rude interruption."

She slapped the rune-tablet down on the table in front of them and Ketel and Hild both gasped, visibly disturbed. Fridgyth thought that Ecfrid paled a little too.

"But… but I thought we agreed this afternoon…" Ketel began.

"No, no." Fridgyth forestalled him, raising an admonishing finger. "This is not the tablet found on Godric, this one has just been found in the bed of our royal Mercian visitor."

"Ah, no," Hild whispered.

Ketel cursed beneath his breath, then apologised to the abbess.

Ecfrid spoke calmly and with foreboding. "So… they follow me here," he said.

They turned to him in surprise.

He nodded, frowning. "And I do not like it that my foster mother is threatened. Cynewise has suffered enough. No, I do not like it at all… and I thought these threats had ceased two years ago."

Hild signalled Fridgyth to pull up a stool, which she did. They turned back to Ecfrid.

"The rune of Tyr," he acknowledged.

"Aye, the rune of revenge," Ketel agreed.

"Such runes were sometimes found when I visited my brother at Eforwic," Ecfrid explained. "They were always placed where I would personally find them, beneath my food trays, beneath my bed and sometimes even slipped beneath the saddle of my horse. Those I trusted most watched me at every turn, but then since… since the plague – there has been nothing and I hoped that these threats had ceased!"

"The sight of this tablet is most troubling to us," Ketel explained. "For we found a young tanner drowned in his own tanning pit just yesterday with a rune-tablet tied to his back; the same marking and the same sized weaving tablet."

"As in Eforwic," Ecfrid acknowledged.

"We'd thought the tanner's death was the result of a private quarrel over a woman, but… this seems to make it something more… much more. And yet… I struggle to see how such a death could be linked to Queen Cynewise, or yourself…"

They sat in silent thought for a moment. The horror Fridgyth had felt as she picked up the second rune-tablet, still made her tremble a little.

Hild reached out and pressed her hand. "You did right to rush in here to tell us, Fridgyth," she acknowledged. "The boy was drowned before either the King or Queen Cynewise arrived here and so that must mean…"

Fridgyth looked up and finished the thought for her "…that someone here in Streonshalh was responsible, not a visitor. Though some of the Queen's waiting women had arrived to prepare her chamber."

They were quiet again, grim-faced.

"And we have visitors coming and going all the time," Hild said. "We are an open community here… we welcome any who come with good intent."

Ecfrid began to speak again, reluctantly. "And it may be that they do not work alone. I wonder… could this signify rebellion? An objection to the presence of King Penda's widow as our guest here in Streonshalh? I am her foster son and perhaps as such they do not want me as their King?"

"I think it unlikely," Ketel said.

Hild nodded. "The people of Streonshalh welcomed you as their King… rather more than your brother," she added frankly.

"Whatever the reason for this might be, surely a guard should be placed outside Queen Cynewise's door," Fridgyth said anxiously.

Ketel got up, saying, "I'll see to it at once."

Ecfrid too rose. "No. Let me set my men to guard Cynewise," he said, somewhat possessively. "And only *her* women must wait on her, for a while, at least."

They strode out together.

Hild turned to Fridgyth. "I'll not tell you to stay out of this," she said. "But… dear friend," she finished fiercely, "keep me informed and be careful. Poor Godric's death tells us that someone here in our settlement will not hesitate to kill. This could set us all at odds with each other again, and then Oswy's hopes for reconciliation will be lost."

"Could that be the purpose behind it, do you think?" Fridgyth asked. "To prevent this peace-making?"

"And Godric?" Hild asked.

They both shook their heads, perplexed. "Some kind of warning?" Fridgyth suggested. "And now we have Irminburgh here again. I don't know how you managed to keep a courteous smile on your face when she walked off the boat!"

Hild shook her head and smiled. "Nor, I! I knew nothing of it, but there have been times when I thought that Oswy had been too harsh with Ecfrid, when he made him marry a wealthy, older bride who really wished to be a nun!"

"Yes," Fridgyth agreed. "Irminburgh was quite wrong for him, and driven by ambition, but he is still young and she's still a beauty!"

"And Cynewise raised them both together, of course," Hild said. "They knew each other as child hostages at the Mercian Queen's court. I gather that Irminburgh was desperately unhappy at Coldingham and sent messages to Queen Cynewise pleading that she might share her exile."

"Ah," Fridgyth nodded, understanding more.

"I suppose it is no surprise that Cynewise might want her foster daughter at her side."

"No," Fridgyth agreed. "But it would have been better not to bring her here with her." The herb-wife got up. "I will keep you informed if I see anything that makes any sense of this shocking incident, but now I suppose I'd best continue with what I set out to do and help Penda's widow settle for the night."

CHAPTER 14

PENDA'S WIDOW

When Fridgyth got back to the royal guest house, she found that Ecfrid and the reeve were already there. The King's own bodyguards were stationed at the entrance to the elegant building and not knowing her, they challenged her right to go inside.

"Fetch the reeve to vouch for me," she insisted, struggling to keep her patience with them.

Ketel appeared and told them that the herb-wife at least must be allowed to come and go at will. When she was eventually allowed into the Queen's chamber, she found that Cynewise had recovered a good deal from her shock. The space was full of apprehensive women again, and Helga watched anxiously through the narrow openings in the shutters. Irminburgh was seated at the Queen's side holding her cup.

"There are guards at the back of the guest house now," Irminburgh announced soothingly. "They wear the King's livery! That is some comfort to us all."

"You acted quickly," Cynewise commented, when the herb-wife appeared. "I'll not let these cowards frighten me. I was Penda's wife and have survived much worse than this in my time!"

"You are well guarded, lady," Fridgyth reassured her. "And I have in my basket herbs that will help you to sleep. May I prepare another drink for you?"

Cynewise looked uncertain for a moment, but then she nodded. "Irminburgh will help you," she said.

Irminburgh rose with a teasing smile and led the way out of the chamber. Fridgyth followed her into a lamp-lit cubicle, where a brazier stood. A small cauldron had been suspended above it from the roof beams and two wooden lidded flagons of clean water had been placed on the floor. A wooden shelf had been fitted there, filled with drinking vessels.

"All newly fitted for the Queen's visit," Irminburgh pointed out. "No expense has been spared."

"No," Fridgyth agreed drily. "You would almost think that Cynewise was our Queen."

"Queens come and go," Irminburgh said lightly.

This private conversation in a corner of the royal guest house, was not how the herb-wife had envisaged her first meeting alone with this old enemy. However, she thought it best to approach it with practicality, so she reached out to take a medium sized clay jug from the shelf and a smaller mug.

"So, herb-wife," Irminburgh said conversationally. "Streonshalh is never boring."

"No," Fridgyth agreed guardedly. "Streonshalh is never boring!"

"And the abbess still rules."

Fridgyth dropped a careful amount of herbs into the jug and poured on boiling water. "Hild will always rule in Streonshalh," she said.

She scooped a generous spoonful of honey into the mug and stirred vigorously, then muttered a brief chant to Freya.

"The abbess allows you much leeway, still," Irminburgh commented.

"Oh yes. I stand high in the abbess's estimation," Fridgyth said, trying hard to sound calm and confident. "She knows I will always do my best for all who seek my help, and she accepts that I do it in my own way," she added tartly.

She used the spoon to strain the hot liquid, now redolent of a meadow in bloom, into the mug and returned to the Queen's chamber. Most of the women had gone off to their beds in the bower after helping the Queen into her bed, where she lay, propped up on pillows, beneath an elaborately carved bed head. The sides of the bed were linked with metal fixtures, shaped like shells. Now that calmness reigned, Fridgyth had the chance to see what an elaborate structure it was.

Cynewise took the offered mug and began to sip. She made a small noise of approval and sipped again. "This is more to my taste," she said.

"Good," Fridgyth agreed.

Cynewise scrutinized the herb-wife thoughtfully. "*You* were not surprised, when you picked up the rune-tablet, were you?" she said at last.

"No," Fridgyth admitted. "I have seen the same thing before."

"So, I hear," she said. "And have you made such things?" Cynewise asked searchingly.

"I have marked out healing runes," Fridgyth said defensively. "Healing runes only. Nothing of that foul nature."

"Irminburgh understands these things too," Cynewise said. "She grew up with the worship of Freya, when she was a child at my court."

"Oh lady, I know nothing of such things now," Irminburgh protested. "I am a Christian, like King Ecfrid… and his father."

"Like Ecfrid," Cynewise said. "Though he too was raised by me."

Fridgyth glanced from one to the other. *What was the girl really doing here?* Ecfrid was married to an important king's daughter and Deira could not afford to offend Queen Audrey's family by sending rumours flying around that he kept company with his old love. Might Irminburgh's presence just possibly herald the beginnings of some new plot, to unsettle Ecfrid in his marriage and perhaps even his throne? What a revenge that would be for Cynewise! After all they had only the Queen's word that the rune-tablet had been found in her bed. Cynewise now gave every appearance of being calm and confident again – and yet Fridgyth thought she'd witnessed real fear in the Queen's reaction to the rune of Tyr. Something in this situation made her feel like a small mouse, played with by two crafty cats, but she had her own methods of dealing with that.

"I thought the Lady Irminburgh was to be dedicated as a nun at Coldingham," she ventured innocently.

Cynewise and Irminburgh exchanged an amused glance.

"Abbess Ebba released me," Irminburgh said. "Queen Cynewise, begged me to share her exile at Handale and King Oswy agreed."

"Irminburgh amuses me," Cynewise said.

"I'm sure she does," Fridgyth said and she bobbed a curtsey. "I will leave you now and return in the morning to apply warm seaweed wrappings. I hope you sleep well."

"Seaweed," Cynewise pulled a face. "Stinging nettle and seaweed… I think you mean to punish me," she said, but the herb-wife sensed a touch of amusement in the comment.

"How do you feel now?" Fridgyth asked.

The Queen passed the mug to Irminburgh and lay back. "Sleepy," she admitted. She closed her eyes, a faint smile on her lips.

Fridgyth said no more; she simply left.

Though she was weary, the herb-wife struggled to get to sleep, for many questions whirled through her mind. She woke next morning to the sound of Della building up the fire and moving about the hut.

Fridgyth shook herself awake and got up hurriedly, yawning and smoothing her hair. "I must prepare a seaweed poultice for our royal visitor," she said and then, with a quiet laugh, she added, "the smell will challenge her senses, I think."

"But you must eat too," Della told her firmly and the girl placed fresh flatbread and a hunk of goats' cheese down in front of her.

Fridgyth smiled and ate obediently, then got to work. Having pounded dried kelp into a grainy powder, she was just about to ladle it into a wooden bucket, when Della gave a small gasp.

"What is it?" Fridgyth asked.

The girl had been glancing out through the open shutter. "The King," she murmured. "Our new, young King and a man servant."

"What? Coming here?"

They heard a man's voice giving a sharp order, but before Fridgyth had time to say more, the door of her hut swung open and Ecfrid walked in. He dropped a wooden tablet down on the table beside the herb-wife's mortar, a rune-tablet marked in the same way as the others.

"I come to you, herb-wife," he said. "As you seem to know more than most, about what goes on in Streonshalh."

Della nervously bobbed two quick curtseys, while Fridgyth stared open mouthed for a moment. "Where?" she murmured at last.

"In the stables! Fastened to my horse, tied to the saddle," he said. "I think someone is very angry that I honour my foster mother."

"In the stables?" she murmured. "Where everyone goes."

"Yes," Ecfrid said. "Everyone goes in there, half the monastery and all the servants and many of my own men too. They go in and out all the time."

"Does the reeve know?" she asked.

"No, but I shall tell him immediately. You have no idea who could have done this?"

"I have not," Fridgyth assured him.

Slightly distracted, he examined what she was doing. "What is this odorous mixture, that you grind?"

"Chopped seaweed. I mean to apply it to the Mercian Queen's aching joints, for it will help her."

He frowned and then laughed. "I think she may feel better when she is rid of you," he said.

"Aye, some would agree with that," Fridgyth conceded.

"Have a care, herb-wife," he said, as he turned to go. "You alone of those in Streonshalh have access to my foster mother now, and you may stand to be blamed if she is distressed or harmed in any way."

He picked the rune-tablet up again and left, as Della bobbed another nervous curtsey. They watched him go, uncertain as to whether he was amused, or quietly threatening.

"Say nothing to anyone," Fridgyth warned the girl. "I'm going to do my duty."

CHAPTER 15

HEALING RUNES

Helga opened the door to her when she arrived. "Prince Aethelred is with the Queen," she warned. "You must not speak to her until he has left."

Irminburgh appeared at her side. "It does not go well between them," she said.

Fridgyth shook her head. "He was taken from Cynewise as a child," she said. "I cannot imagine why anyone would expect such an encounter to go well?"

Irminburgh looked shocked. "You know about that?" she said.

"I make it my business to know such things," Fridgyth told her.

"Yes, I recall that you push your nose into many things," Irminburgh said. "You had better come with us."

She led the way to the Queen's chamber, where they found the Prince and his mother sitting formally, facing each other surrounded by an audience of waiting women. Cups of expensive Frankish wine and dainty honey cakes were set out on a low table between them, none of which had been touched.

Fridgyth bustled into the silence carrying her bucket, linen strips draped over her shoulder. "If my intrusion is badly timed, I will of course come back later," she announced.

Some of the women looked up at her and gasped, outraged, ready to object.

But the young Prince leapt to his feet. "No, no," he said. "I would not prevent my lady mother from receiving the good care of the herb-wife."

He bowed to Cynewise and hurried out, with barely concealed relief and Irminburgh went to escort him to the entrance.

"You made a timely entrance, herb-wife," Cynewise admitted.

Immediately the tension lifted and the women breathed out with relief, smiled at each other and picked up their embroidery or wandered off to do small tasks.

"He is my flesh and blood, but I do not trust him," Cynewise confided to Fridgyth. "They raised him in their beliefs, and now they want him to marry Oswy's daughter. I'd far rather he married Irminburgh, though she has different plans."

"Oswy's daughter?" Fridgyth stared. "But I understood that Princess Elfled was always destined to be a nun."

Irminburgh returned and smothered a laugh as she caught the end of the conversation. "Not Elfled, Fridgyth. There is another daughter reaching marriageable age very soon, Princess Osthryth. She is a most Christian princess and quite pretty I believe."

"Now, if Aethelred would marry Irminburgh, then at least I'd have a daughter-in-law that I could feel comfortable with," Cynewise said. She reached out as the younger woman came to her side and put her arm warmly about her shoulders. "In time she might even become Queen of Mercia, for my Wulfhere has no sons as yet."

"But lady, I am older than Aethelred," Irminburgh protested. "And we know that such marriages have their problems. Look at poor Ecfrid."

"Yes, poor Ecfrid," Cynewise agreed. "But *you* are cousin to Queen Eanfleda and of Kentish royal blood – and even though Aethelred is a now a Christian, he is handsome enough. He just needs feeding up a bit!"

Fridgyth observed that a fleeting expression of anger crossed Irminburgh's face. She sensed that she wanted to say more, but quickly thought better of it. What was she about, this ambitious young woman? Surely the possibility of becoming Queen of Mercia must be attractive to her.

Cynewise dragged the herb-wife's thoughts back to the task in hand.

"Yes, your interruption was timely, herb-wife," she repeated. "Though by the smell of your bucket, I may live to regret it. What have you brought to torment me with today?"

"The healing power of the sea," Fridgyth announced. "You will be most comfortable if you lie on your bed, I think. I shall cover it with rough sacking in order to keep the good linen clean. I'll need warm water, to mix my brew and privacy might be best for you will need to raise your skirt and roll up your sleeves."

Half fascinated, half appalled, Cynewise dismissed her women, save for Irminburgh. Fridgyth pulled a sacking sheet from her basket and spread it on the bed and then covered it with a fine linen sheet, which could be sacrificed to provide more comfort. Cynewise lay down gingerly on the prepared bed and sank back, propped up a little with pillows.

Fridgyth mixed the powdered kelp with water that had been heated on the brazier, until it took the consistency of warm mud. She pasted it onto the linen strips and, working quickly, bound them closely about the Queen's knotted knee joints, ankles, elbows and wrists.

"This stinks like the slop bucket," Cynewise commented, "but it is not unpleasant to the touch."

"Now we'll put a light cover over you, so you don't become chilled, and you should rest awhile. Tell us when the poultices turn cool!" Fridgyth said.

Cynewise closed her eyes and lay back.

Fridgyth took the opportunity to sit down on a stool. "A sip of mead would do the Queen good," she said and Irminburgh went off dutifully to fetch it.

The herb-wife sat in silence for a moment.

"*He* could have done it," Cynewise murmured.

Fridgyth turned to her and the Queen's eyelids flickered.

"Yes," she repeated. "He was here when we arrived… him and that man… Siward of Dreng, the one they call his foster father…

either of them could have placed the rune in my bed. He is no longer my son, and it seems this blood-feud will never end."

Fridgyth found herself strangely saddened to hear those words.

"Surely not. Not your own son," she said. "And he has had no choice at all in the way he was raised, just as Ecfrid was given no choice when he was sent to you as a small child. How could they send one so young as a hostage?"

"It is the way of things," Cynewise answered softly.

They sat in silence for a while and Cynewise continued to lie still, allowing the salty mash to sink into her joints. Eventually Fridgyth poured a small amount of flax oil into a metal basin and warmed it at the brazier with a few drops of lavender oil. At last Cynewise moved and said plaintively. "I grow a little cold."

"Now for the second stage,' Fridgyth announced.

She unwrapped the seaweed poultices and gently cleaned away the sludge, then began to massage the warm, sweet-scented lavender oil into the swollen joints.

"How's that?" she asked.

"Comforting," came the sleepy reply.

Cynewise lay very still and gradually her breathing slowed and deepened, until Fridgyth realised that she had fallen asleep, just as Irminburgh returned with a cup and a flask of mead, carried carefully on a trencher.

"Too late," Fridgyth told her.

The young woman looked offended for a moment, but seeing how peacefully Cynewise slept, her expression changed. "Asleep, and it's still morning," she said, her voice surprisingly soft. "I don't think our Queen has slept like that, since Penda died."

"Let her sleep then," Fridgyth said, "and I'll come back this evening. Give her a small amount of mead when she wakes. It will do her just as much good, then."

Fridgyth left the royal guest house and headed in the direction of her hut, just as the bell rang for the noontide meal. She was hungry now, but as she passed the refectory, she stopped for a moment in thought and instead of going to eat; she walked out through the side gate and took the steep downhill path towards Brigsbeck.

The stench of the tanning trade grew as she passed one steeping pit, then another. She caught glimpses of hide and skin as they broke the surface of the soaking mixture that consisted of water, wood ash and urine. As she approached the tanners' yard she passed open wooden sheds where piles of skins, which had been folded hair side in, lay sweating, to start the messy process of tanning. At last she stepped into the yard, to find many skins stretched over frames in the open air. Smoke smouldered out from a further shed where treated skins were being cured. One young lad worked in the yard. He clumsily scudded rotting flesh and fat from a frame-stretched calfskin, using a shaped bone scraper, set in a handle.

Fridgyth stopped to swallow hard. Her throat constricted and she feared for a moment that she might vomit. She understood more than ever why Ralf had requested her lavender brew.

The lad looked over at her and stopped his scraping.

"Where's Egric?" she asked.

The boy nodded towards the thatched dwelling. "In there," he said. "They have stayed by the hearth since Godric was buried. They speak to nobody. I am Egric's apprentice, so I'm still here. I'm trying to get on with the work and feed the fires and clean the skins."

"I know you," Fridgyth said. "You're one of mine. What's your name?"

"Herrig," the boy replied. "I go foraging for the kitchens up there," and he nodded towards the monastery.

"Aye, but that's not why I remember you," Fridgyth said. "I was there at your birth."

The boy's expression changed to one of surliness and Fridgyth recalled that both his parents had died in the recent plague. He turned away from her without saying more and set about his disgusting task again.

Fridgyth went on towards the hut and pushed the wooden door open. She stood for a moment and looked into gloom, while her eyes adjusted to the darkness. The central hearth was cold and empty, even though the day was cool and the shutters were closed. A slight movement drew her eyes and she began to make out the prone figure of the grieving mother lying on a mattress and the hunched shape of the father crouched beside her.

"This won't do," she muttered, as much to herself as to them.

She walked out again and shouted to the lad. "Herrig! Leave that skin for now, boy! Fetch kindling and a shovel of hot charcoal from the smoke shed."

The lad dropped the scraper he'd been using and ran to obey her.

CHAPTER 16

AT BRIGSBECK

Back inside the hut, Fridgyth pushed a wooden shutter open just a little way, so that a shaft of light fell into the dim interior. Edric made a sudden intake of breath and then exhaled noisily, but put up no resistance to this rude intrusion. His wife still lay inert.

Despite the difficulties of their work, the tanners' home-place was usually well kept and clean, but Frigyth looked around to discover recent neglect. She found a bundle of rather withered leeks hanging from a nail and suspiciously tested a mouthful of water from a clay pitcher, but found it fresh enough. She discarded two rounds of hard flat bread that stood on a table, by throwing them onto the midden outside.

Herrig returned with the requested shovel of glowing charcoal and kindling. She took it from him and sent him straight back out to the nearest neighbour again. "Beg fresh bread from them," she said. "Tell them the herb-wife says so."

Fridgyth set about making a fire on the hearthstone and at last the tanner spoke. "What are you doing?" he asked faintly.

"I'm sorting you out," she said. 'You two must go on living."

She got a blaze going and chopped the leeks, took a pinch of dried sage and thyme from the bundles on her girdle and threw them all into a small cauldron with some water. Searching again she took a pinch of salt from a crock on the wall and a handful of oats from a tied sack on a shelf and added them to the brew to make pottage. Having set the cauldron to simmer on the chain that was suspended above the hearth, she began to stir. The boy returned with warm, fresh bread and a troubled neighbour trailing after him.

"They refused all help," the woman protested, anxious not to be regarded as neglectful.

"I know, I know. Leave them be for now," Fridgyth advised. "I'll stay a while and tell you when I leave. Would you check on them tonight, perhaps?"

"I will," she said, and she wandered away again, somewhat relieved.

Fridgyth turned to the boy. "Now you get back to your work and don't you shirk, just because your master is troubled," she told him.

"I haven't shirked at all," he told her, though he went willingly away.

The small dwelling quickly filled with the more appetising scent of simmered leeks and fresh bread. The tanner, roused a little by Fridgyth's efforts, tried to haul his wife into a sitting position.

"Come now," he begged.

"Leave me," Muriel protested. "I want to die too."

Fridgyth placed a small stool in front of them and set two steaming bowls and a wedge of bread by each one.

"You have another son," she reminded them sharply. "He may be back at any time, and he'll need you when he finds out what has happened to his brother. Sit up and eat. Has a messenger been sent to find your Ralf?"

Muriel sighed, but she pulled herself up into a sitting position and wiped her eyes.

"No. A messenger would struggle to find him for we can't be certain where he'll be by now. He won't be back for days," Edric said quietly.

Fridgyth pulled up a stool for herself and sat down on it. She leant forward to place Muriel's thin hands around one of the warm bowls. "Sup," she ordered. "You too," she added, with a nod to the husband. "Here, take a spoon."

Slowly and shakily they obeyed.

Fridgyth watched them with some satisfaction and after they'd both taken a few mouthfuls she felt that she could question them.

"Where is it that your Ralf has gone?" she asked.

"To Gilling," Edric said. "He has an agreement with the prior there, that he alone will supply the monastery with turnshoes."

Fridgyth was somewhat surprised for she'd never been as far as Gilling herself, and she knew that it was quite a distance. Everyone knew the name of Gilling, for it was the monastery that Queen Eanfleda had insisted her husband should build in reparation for the treacherous murder of his young cousin, Oswin, King of Deira.

"Gilling," she repeated the name thoughtfully. "They say it is the grandest monastery in Northumbria, but built with blood-money."

Edric sighed. "That was a bad business, true enough, but kings will take what they want, and Oswy wanted Deira. He couldn't kill his cousin in battle, for the young man refused to fight."

"So, how did it happen?" Fridgyth frowned, trying to recall the sad story.

"Our young King took refuge in Hunwald's hall, for Oswin believed Hunwald to be his closest friend, but he wasn't, he was in Oswy's pay. The hall was attacked and burnt to the ground, with the young King of Deira in it. The Queen was appalled by such an act, and she swore that her husband would never be allowed into the Christian heaven, unless he made amends by building the finest monastery to the Christ-God. So Oswy built the monastery at Gilling, no gold was spared to pay for his wickedness."

Fridgyth nodded. "And now Oswy is overlord of all the northern lands. He got what he wanted, didn't he? Ecfrid is King of Deira in name, but he must still obey his father's wishes."

"That's the way of it," Edric agreed with a sigh.

Fridgyth remembered Ralf's cart piled high with leather goods. "Your son has won himself a profitable pact with Gilling," she could not refrain from commenting.

"Oh, yes," Edric agreed. "It is an excellent deal."

"Though it is a long way for him to go!" she added.

"It takes three days to get there," Edric acknowledged. "And then he will fit turnshoes for all who are in need of them. He can do alterations on the spot and he'll spend some time coming to an agreement about payment, for those monks are shrewd. On the way back he calls in at many of the villages to barter any leftover turnshoes. We never know when to expect his return when he sets off with a wagonload of goods for Gilling."

"How do they pay him?" Fridgyth asked.

Edric shrugged. "Rolls of linen, for flax grows well round Gilling, flaxseed, oats or barley if the harvest has been good and on his way back he exchanges some of the goods in the villages. He usually comes back with a wagon piled high with provisions and cloth."

Fridgyth wondered vaguely if she'd ever get her own promised pair of turnshoes, after this terrible family disaster, but she dragged her mind back to more immediate concerns. She struggled to see how there could possibly be a connection between the tanners and the latest discovery in the royal guest house, but the rune-tablet appeared to be exactly the same. Unsure as to whether it was wise to reveal what had happened, she enquired indirectly.

"Do you know that we have a royal visitor?" she ventured. "King Penda's widow. Have you seen her?"

Muriel who had finished her pottage suddenly spoke with feeling. "No, and I would not wish to," she said.

Fridgyth was glad that the woman was speaking again, and it seemed with some conviction too.

"Have either of your sons had ought to do with her?" she asked. "Has Ralf ever taken shoes to sell at Handale Head?"

Muriel looked offended at the very suggestion, but her husband thought carefully.

"I think not," he said cautiously. "In recent years Godric has dealt only with parchment for the monastery. Ralf has enough to do supplying Gilling, though I'd guess there'd be good pickings up at Handale Head. They say Oswy has kept the old woman in comfort all these years and a good number of servants with her, but I'd have thought..." he paused, distracted.

"Thought what?" Fridgyth prompted.

"I'd have thought he'd have mentioned it, if he'd been there."

"So it's possible?" she pressed.

"It's not impossible," Edric allowed.

They sat in silence for a short while, their thoughts following different paths and then Edric got up and wandered to the doorway, where he shouted a few instructions to Herrig. Moments later, Muriel too struggled to her feet, picked up a broom and began to sweep the muddy floor.

"Oh dear... what a mess, what a mess," she murmured.

Fridgyth got up, highly relieved to see that they seemed to have regained a touch of their usual purpose and energy. She took her leave of them and picked up her basket. "Send for me, if there is anything I can do to help," she said.

"You've helped us enough," Muriel told her firmly. "You are right herb-wife, we need to get on with our lives and be ready to look after our other son, when he returns."

Fridgyth gave the neighbour a nod as she passed their dwelling and left the tanneries to return to her other concerns.

CHAPTER 17

WATCH AND WAIT

When Fridgyth arrived back at her hut, she found Ketel there with his daughter, sipping ale by the hearth with the cat curled on his lap. He had a worried expression on his face. "I have been racking my brains," he said, without preamble as soon as the herb-wife appeared. "I have been asking myself what a young tanner, a pagan queen and a Christian king can have in common, but can make no sense of it."

Fridgyth shook her head. "Well, Ecfrid was raised by Cynewise," Fridgyth reminded him. "And I'm not sure how truly Christian he is now, for I doubt he has had much choice in the matter. Irminburgh too must have experienced many pagan rites as a child. And what of Prince Aethelred? What does he really think, reared as an exiled hostage and forced to take on this new religion? Child hostages, all of them, reared by their families' worst enemies... any one of them might hide the deepest resentment in their hearts."

Ketel frowned in thought. "How could any of them be responsible for Godric's death?"

Fridgyth sighed, for she had no answer to that, only a sense of confusion and duplicity. "I have been with the tanners," she said. "And something we talked about, reminded me how ruthless Oswy can be in his pursuit of power."

"You cannot think Oswy..." Ketel looked up appalled.

Fridgyth sighed. "Well, all these visitors are here at Oswy's behest and kings will do anything to gain more power. His arms reach far, and he has got others to do his dirty work before. I think it is far too simple to put Godric's death down to a jealous husband."

"I agree with you," Ketel said. "We can set that idea aside I think, there is much more to this.

"Irminburgh could have put that second rune-tablet in Cynewise's bed," Fridgyth suggested. "And we only have Ecfrid's word for it that he's been threatened too, while Cynewise seems to fear her own son Aethelred. Could he be angry enough to wish her ill? It's clear his mother thinks more kindly of her foster son, than she does of him?"

Ketel remained shocked, but he didn't pour scorn on her suggestions.

"But Godric?" Della asked. "Why kill poor Godric?"

Fridgyth sat down and shrugged. "Maybe a warning that they mean business, if, as Ecfrid thinks, these runes are a protest against the Mercian Queen." she said. "We know that Godric had been meeting a woman in the woods. Was he simply in the wrong place at the wrong time and killed as a warning?"

Ketel grasped his head in both hands and groaned, so that Wyrdkin got up offended and leapt onto the floor. "What now?" the reeve muttered.

"Watch and wait!" Fridgyth said.

"Yes, but discreet questioning would not go amiss," he said, looking up at her. "I can move freely amongst the King's men, and you may learn more from the Queen's attendants."

Fridgyth nodded. "That's true."

"Prince Aethelred dresses like a monk," he went on. "And Brother Bertram says he eats like a sparrow."

"He'll fit in here then," Fridgyth said drily, "especially through Lent. But I hear they wish to marry him off to another of Oswy's daughters."

"Yes," Ketel admitted.

"Hild didn't mention it to me," she added somewhat huffily. "Though of course there's no reason why she should."

"She didn't know about it until Ecfrid announced it yesterday," Ketel said. "More orders from Oswy it seems. If Wulfhere were to die still childless, Aethelred would then take the throne of Mercia, with Oswy's daughter at his side."

"In other words Oswy would have even greater power in Mercia again," Fridgyth commented. "No wonder Cynewise didn't like the sound of this proposed marriage... she wants her son to marry Irminburgh, that way she'd have influence again. Meanwhile Irminburgh addresses everyone as though she were already a queen, but queen of where?"

Ketel sighed, got up shaking his head, kissed them both and left.

Della watched her father go, but then turned back to Fridgyth. "You all seem to hate Irminburgh, and yet to me she has spoken kindly," she protested.

Fridgyth sighed.

"And she has been speaking kindly to Wulfrun too," Della went on.

"Well, I'm glad to hear that," Fridgyth admitted. "But, Irminburgh has a lot of making up to do."

"What was it that she accused Cwen of?" Della asked. "It happened before the plague ever came to us and mother died... I was still a child."

"A valuable necklace that had once belonged to Queen Eanfleda's mother came to light and Irminburgh accused Wulfrun's mother of the theft of it, so that Cwen was imprisoned and threatened with death."

"Ah no," Della was shocked.

"She almost persuaded Prince Ecfrid to rebel against his father too, nearly bringing us to war again. Many of us tried to defend Cwen and when the plot was uncovered, the abbess banished Irminburgh to Coldingham, but you cannot keep the Irminburgh down, it seems."

Della still shook her head. "I think she is trying to make amends..." she began.

"Nothing could make amends for what she did," Fridgyth said.

That evening at supper both Fridgyth and Della observed the top table from their more humble seats. Cynewise had chosen to take her meal in her chamber and Prince Aethelred was nowhere to be seen.

Irminburgh appeared dressed like a queen again and graciously accepted the place that Ecfrid offered her at his side, but it was clear that her presence made both Elfled and Wulfrun, who were seated close to them, feel uncomfortable. Sister Lindi, honoured to be seated alongside royalty and knowing little of what had happened in the past, made polite conversation as best she could.

Sister Begu hobbled over to take a seat beside Fridgyth. "Charming as ever, that one," she muttered, with a nod at Irminburgh. "But we remember, do we not?"

Fridgyth agreed. "We remember only too well."

"Hmm! I hear she presented Wulfrun with a silver ring today and a garnet studded bracelet for Cwen. She wishes to make amends, apparently."

"Did they accept these gifts?" Fridgyth asked

"How could they refuse?"

"I did tell you," Della protested. "But I've never seen anyone as lovely as Lady Irminburgh, not even the Queen," she added wistfully.

"Which queen?" Fridgyth asked sharply.

"I was thinking of Queen Eanfleda," Della said. "And with our young King there beside her... they make a handsome pair. And though they are served only with salmon and eels today, they eat as daintily as though it were a feast."

"Oswy should never have married his son to Audrey," Fridgyth admitted, finding a scrap of grudging sympathy.

"Yes," Sister Begu agreed. "But we'd all be wise to keep such observations to ourselves. And I hear that our overlord is now planning a pilgrimage to Rome."

"Oswy, going to Rome?" Fridgyth asked surprised.

"Yes. He's going with Bishop Wilfrid as his guide, now that the two are friends again."

Fridgyth looked amazed.

A monk who served in the monastic guest house hurried into the refectory, looking fraught. He bowed repeatedly and spoke to Ecfrid. Suddenly all faces turned in the direction of Fridgyth's table, and Princess Elfled rose to her feet, waving frantically. "Fridgyth, come here!" she shouted.

Ketel followed the monk into the hall, and also started waving urgently at the herb-wife, clearly in need of help.

Della got up and Fridgyth rose too. "No, my girl. You finish your meal," she said. "Enjoy your glimpse of the glittering ones, I'll send for you if I need you."

Ketel grabbed Fridgyth by the arm and hurried her outside.

"What is it?" she whispered.

"I cannot believe it," he hissed. "We must not start a panic, but I fear the worst – what will come next? It is Prince Aethelred! Come!"

They ran across the courtyard and found Brother Bertram, the guest-master waiting anxiously for them at the entrance to the building.

"We may be too late," he warned, his voice quavering and his hands shaking.

They hastened after him and were led into one of the larger cell-like rooms that had been specially provided for those religious visitors who chose the more ascetic life. Fridgyth remembered visiting Bishop Colman in the very same chamber, after the fateful Synod, when they'd feared for the bishop's life. Now she found it occupied by Prince Aethelred. Siward of Dreng was there already, urgently rubbing his hands.

"Wake, please wake," the old man cried.

"Let the herb-wife see him," Ketel said.

The older man moved back reluctantly. "Please save him… save him if you can," he cried.

Fridgyth saw at a glance the clammy skin, the lips turning blue, she knew the symptoms well.

"He's poisoned," she said. "What has he eaten?"

"Just a little mushroom broth," the man said. "He never eats meat on Fridays and he does not like fish. They sent this broth from the kitchens, prepared especially at his request."

A bowl stood half empty on the table beside the bed, the spoon had dropped onto the floor.

"I have periwinkle, somewhere here!" Fridgyth cried as she fumbled in amongst the bundles that she carried in her girdle. "Fetch me boiled water, a mug and a good sized basin!"

She found the bundle marked with the rune of ash. "This is the one."

Brother Bertram ran down the corridor calling for boiled water, while she teased open the knot that held the bundle tightly fastened, for periwinkle was a vomiting herb, not to be freely given. She then unhooked the small silver spoon that she always carried hanging from her girdle.

The guest-master returned puffing and pink cheeked with concern. "It's here."

As soon as a steaming mug appeared, she tipped the contents of the bag into the hot water and stirred it vigorously. Faintly purple tinged dried petals swirled around and swam to the surface.

"Sit him up," she ordered. "Slap his face, keep him with us."

Ketel hauled the Prince into a sitting position and the foster father shook him gently.

"Harder," Fridgyth cried. "Do not be dainty, though he is a prince you must slap him if you want him to live!"

The foster father hit the boy hard then. "Wake up Aethelred!" he ordered. "Don't you die, I will be held responsible!"

"We will all be answerable," Ketel cried.

CHAPTER 18

MUSHROOM BROTH

Fridgyth tested the heat of the periwinkle brew with her finger and satisfied that it was hot, but not scalding, she announced. "I'm ready! Hold the Prince now. We will need the large basin."

Ketel and Siward supported Aethelred between them, while Fridgyth tipped his head backwards and steadily began to force the liquid down his throat.

Brother Bertram snatched the basin up, rather too late, as the boy juddered back to life and vomited copiously, over the bed and Fridgyth.

"Blessed Freya," Fridgyth muttered gratefully, then she remembered where she was and added – "thanks be to the Christ-God!"

More violent vomiting followed and when it seemed that Aethelred had completely emptied his stomach, he gasped for breath. Fridgyth called for clean water and a goblet of the best Frankish wine.

"Bring pillows," she said, "proper down stuffed pillows. He needs to rest now."

The plainly appointed monastic cubicle provided only one small straw stuffed pillow, so Brother Bertram hurried away again to fetch something better.

Fridgyth exchanged a relieved but worried glance with Ketel. "What now?" she murmured. "We cannot have the kitchens serving up poisonous mushrooms in their broth."

Ketel looked grim and nodded.

Bertram reappeared with two soft, down-stuffed pillows, which Fridgyth set beneath Aethelred's head. They all watched anxiously, but the Prince seemed to be more comfortable and he now appeared to be breathing well.

Fridgyth picked up the rumpled, plain woollen bed cover that had been thrown back, for she meant to tuck it around him to make sure that he was warm enough, but she started in horror at what was then revealed at the Prince's feet.

"Ah no," she cried. "Not another!"

"What!" Ketel demanded.

There beneath the cover she had found another wooden weaving tablet, marked with the rune of Tyr and twisted again with dark green leaves. She picked it up and even though the small chamber now smelt of vomit, still the faint, clean scent of rosemary could be detected.

"This is no accidental poisoning," Ketel said. "And rosemary again… dear god! How has this happened?"

He picked up the half empty bowl and strode away without another word. Fridgyth followed him, knowing that he headed for the kitchens.

The bakehouse, brewhouse and kitchens were accommodated in a sturdy series of well-thatched buildings. They were separated from the great hall, for fear of fire spreading, but linked by a covered walkway, so that food could be carried from one to the other without the servers having to struggle with wind and rain.

The light had gone when the reeve arrived, but the kitchens were well lit with torches and the workers clearing up after the evening meal. Mildred the food-wife ruled her domain as strictly as the abbess ruled the whole monastery, and Fridgyth found her drawn up to her considerable height, her eyes blazing and her cheeks flushed.

"There is *no* poison in my kitchen," she said. "I've provided food for this community since the abbess came from the Bay of the Hart and in all that time there has never been poisonous mushrooms served."

"But it has happened tonight," Ketel insisted. "And I must know how it happened? Have a care how you answer me food-wife, for this prince is sent here by King Oswy himself."

Mildred gulped and stared wildly about at her helpers. "Who brought those mushrooms in?" she demanded.

"Just the usual lad," Sister Redburgh said.

She came to stand at Mildred's side, arms folded across her chest in defiance, all ready to defend the mistress she usually complained about. "Our food is second to none," she added. "That's why they all come here, and we go short ourselves each winter in order to feed so many visitors."

Fridgyth hurried forward to press a soothing hand on Ketel's shoulder, knowing how quick the food-wife and her workers would be to take offence. A slight suspicion came to her at the mention of a lad who brought mushrooms for them..

"Which lad is it that brings you mushrooms?" she asked.

Mildred turned to Redburgh, uncertainly.

"His name is Herrig," Redburgh told them, "and he has never failed us before. His father brought us mushrooms before him and taught the lad to recognise the good ones, though both parents died last summer of the plague."

Fridgyth nodded for Redburgh's words confirmed in her mind the image of a ragged, sullen, boy who scraped at a calfskin. .

"The lad struggles on alone doing many jobs," Redburgh said. "I keep a good watch on him though, for I have found him in the orchard, rather too close to my hives and warned him that stealing honey or apples would not be tolerated. There's a lose paling in there and I have asked one of the carpenter's to repair it for I don't want anyone sneaking in and taking my honey."

"As I thought," Fridgyth murmured. "I know Herrig!"

"Do you not check what he brings to you?" Ketel demanded.

Both women bridled again at that.

"We check as best we can," Mildred said. "But with all these sudden visitors, we've had little time to spare."

"No, we have to trust our pickers," Redburgh butted in. "Especially when we've half of Deira coming here for their meals!"

"This Herrig, where does he live?" Fridgyth asked.

"I suppose he must still live in the old hut that his parents left for him," Redburgh said. "And he works for the tanners too. Scavenging mushrooms is just his way of earning a little more, and we exchange a basket of them for bread, or stew."

Ketel turned and marched out of the kitchen and Fridgyth ran after him. "Wait," she cried. "Let me do this. You have far too much to do. He's a ragged little thing and awkward too, but I had him running to obey me when I visited the tanners this morning."

The reeve stopped, his face drawn with anxiety.

"At least some connection seems to emerge," he admitted. "A connection between Brigsbeck and our royal visitors, though I still fail to make much sense of it. I would have deemed it carelessness, were it not for the rune! Why would someone want to kill Prince Aethelred?"

Fridgyth shook her head. "I don't know, but I say that lad needs questioning carefully. I cannot believe that Mildred or her workers could have had a hand in this, the blame would so clearly fall on them, but nor can I see that pathetic boy making a plan to kill a Mercian Prince."

"I agree with you there," Ketel said. "He must be being used by someone and we need to know who. I could have him fetched here."

"No. Let me go to see him and question him?" she begged. "I think I'd be more likely to get the truth from him that way. If you bring him here he'll be petrified and you may not get a word out of him. His parents died of the plague. The lad may feel he has little to lose."

Ketel frowned, but he saw some sense in what she said. "Very well," he agreed reluctantly.

"I should really go to see Cynewise now," she said. "And I need to clean myself up first. It won't help to go flying down to Brigsbeck at this hour. I shall go tomorrow morning, just as though I were checking on the tanner's welfare again and speak to the boy."

Ketel agreed. "I'll set a guard on the monastic guest-house now," he said. "And I must tell the abbess what has happened. I fear she won't like it at all. At this rate we'll have guards everywhere and inside the monastic boundary too. The abbess believes we should all be able to trust each other."

"But that was before Oswy started sending visitors here." Fridgyth said. "And someone should tell Queen Cynewise too."

"Would you…?" Ketel began.

"What? Tell the Prince's mother? Tell her that her own son was poisoned?"

Ketel frowned. "I will leave it to your discretion," he said. "But I'll tell the abbess the truth."

CHAPTER 19

A SENSE OF CHAOS

It was quite dark by the time Fridgyth arrived at the royal guest house, having changed into her one best tunic and gown. Cynewise was already propped up on pillows and in her bed, alone in her chamber. "You're late," she said, when Fridgyth arrived.

"I'm very sorry for that," she said, "but there was good reason for my being late. I regret to have to tell you this, but your son was discovered to be very ill."

"My son?" Cynewise looked almost puzzled for a moment. "Oh, Aethelred. What ailed him?"

"Stomach trouble," Fridgyth replied, for she sensed that discretion as to the cause of the sickness might be best for the moment and that the mention of another rune might cause panic. "He is much better now," she added.

"I didn't think he ate enough to have stomach trouble," Cynewise commented. "And I've been in bed and waiting here for you. Irminburgh seems to have deserted me."

"Did the seaweed poultices help?" Fridgyth asked.

"Yes… and the lavender too. Will you massage my hands again?"

Fridgyth selected a small vial of lavender oil from amongst the many medicines that crammed her basket. Having unstoppered the container and poured a trickle of pungent oil into her palms, she seized the opportunity to question Cynewise, while she set about massaging the swollen joints of her hands.

"Yesterday, you spoke of a blood-feud, lady, when we found the rune-tablet. Why was that?" she asked, searching carefully for words that would bring the information that she needed, but not set off alarm.

Cynewise looked away into the distance, and just as Fridgyth thought she was refusing to answer, she murmured darkly. "He wants rid of me."

"Who?" Fridgyth asked, genuinely puzzled.

"Oswy of course," came the firm reply. "He has killed so many of my kin and he lives in fear of retribution. He knows that by the rules of blood-feud I have the right to demand that a member of his family should be killed in return."

Fridgyth was staggered at this frank admission, but it was not so far from the explanation for the rune tablets that her own mind began to seek. It was an effort to do it, but she made herself continue the gentle massage in a calm manner.

Cynewise looked thoughtful and spoke again. "Oswy fears that I'll demand revenge and there are still those who would move at my command if I gave the order."

"Revenge for the killing of Penda?" she asked.

Cynewise laughed, but it was a mirthless sound. "No. Penda died in battle, I do not consider that to be treacherous. He died with his sword in his hand and went to Woden's feasting hall; it was the death he wished for. No... that is not the offence that I speak of, but the murder of my oldest son, Peada."

"But I thought..." Fridgyth began.

"What! You thought he died of a mysterious sickness?"

The herb-wife nodded.

"I still have my spies," Cynewise said bitterly. "And they reported that my son was betrayed by his own wife, Alchfled and murdered in his bed."

Fridgyth was so shocked that she stopped her massaging.

"That is what I bitterly resent," Cynewise said. "Oswy insisted that Peada marry his daughter, as part of the peace treaty that was set up long ago between Mercia and Northumbria. I don't believe that either Oswy or Penda had any intention of keeping that peace, they just used their children as pawns to give them time, while they planned more warfare."

"You have suffered, lady," Fridgyth admitted.

"Now Oswy wants my youngest son to marry another of his daughters. He must think me a fool. I hear he had his young cousin Oswin murdered so that he could take Deira for himself. Is that not true?"

"I believe it to be true," Fridgyth acknowledged, though she also had to bite her tongue to prevent herself from reminding Cynewise that it was Penda who had started this blood-feud, when he'd killed Oswy's brother and set his dismembered body parts up on stakes in the battlefield to provide a raven feast.

"The man has no honour," Cynewise said, with quiet fury. "I will never trust him. Penda scorned Oswy's milksop Christianity. These Christians claim they don't fear death, but they do."

Fridgyth lifted her shoulders in a sympathetic gesture. "Don't we all fear death?" she asked.

Cynewise relaxed a little. "I am ready to return to the arms of Freya," she said wearily.

"Well, I hope you'll wait until I've finished treating you," Fridgyth said wryly.

"If Oswy really believes in the Christ-God, he *should* fear death," the Queen said cheerfully, "For he has lived a life of murder and treachery. He has suborned my youngest son and that is like another murder to me."

"So you pay Oswy back, by rejecting Aethelred?" Fridgyth suggested.

"No!" Cynewise said, offended.

"I'm sorry," Fridgyth said, with a sigh. "I'm just trying desperately to see what might lie behind these runes of revenge and prevent more tragedy."

Cynewise nodded, calmer again. "There has been too much death," she agreed. "And if, as you say, a young man who was merely a worker was killed, I'd suggest that it was a warning, that whoever it is, they mean business. And rosemary... rosemary signifies remembrance. It's all about something that happened long ago."

"Yes," Fridgyth said. "Of course. Rosemary sharpens the wits and aids the memory." She stared for a moment, feeling that something important hovered just out of mind. She'd almost grasped it before, but it had slipped away from her. "This is the trouble," she murmured. "When you get old, memories come and go."

"Yes," Cynewise agreed, bitterly. "And then sometimes they come back as plain as day, and you wish they'd stayed away."

Just at that moment Irminburgh appeared, flushed and smiling in the doorway.

"Where have you been?" Cynewise demanded.

Fridgyth wiped her hands on her apron and gathered her basket together. She snapped quickly back to practicality, but felt that she'd glimpsed something of what might be intended by the runes of revenge... a warning... a state of fear... an atmosphere of chaos.

"You may go now," Cynewise said imperiously to her, but as the herb-wife reached the chamber door, she added softly again. "I thank you for your care."

Fridgyth spent another restless night, her mind too busy to let her settle easily. Eventually sheer weariness of body allowed her to sleep, though she again woke early, impatient to set off for Brigsbeck.

Despite her sense of urgency, she made herself take time to prepare a few more useful medicines for the Mercian Queen, all the time racking her brains as to how best to approach young Herrig. It would be easy to put the boy into a state of panic and that would do no good.

Della rose too and made them both a breakfast of porridge. The sun was well up over the horizon, when the herb-wife at last set her jars and pots aside and headed downhill to the tanners' yard.

Fridgyth found Edric supervising the boy, as he stretched stinking calfskin, fresh from the steeping pit, onto a frame.

"That's it! Pull boy!" he ordered. "Now, fasten that side with sinew while I hold this one... aye, that's it, pull tight and steady," the older man instructed.

Now more used to the death-like stench of the place, Fridgyth greeted them in a casual manner and walked straight past them into the hut, where she found Muriel vigorously brushing down her best gown and Edric's cloak. The hut was immaculately clean and tidy.

"I'm glad," Fridgyth said, "glad to see you back to something like your old self."

Muriel stopped her brushing. "I'll never be back to my old self," she said. "But at least our place will look decent when Ralf comes home."

Fridgyth admired the scrubbed cauldron and commented on the wholesome scent of freshly baked oatcakes, and then she went on to the real purpose of her visit. She spoke with genuine reluctance. "I know I come at an awkward time," she began, "but I need to ask a favour of you."

"Anything," Muriel said, looking up with interest. "Anything. You did right to shake us out of our misery, herb-wife, and remind us that we have another son. I wanted never to get out of my bed again, but no good would ever have come of that. What is it that you want?"

"Could I borrow your lad Herrig for a bit? He knows the woods far better than I do and I need to do a little foraging. I'm sorry to take him from his work, but…"

"No, no. You're welcome to him. Edric often says he can get on better without him," Muriel assured her. She moved at once to the threshold. "Leave that skin," she called. "And send the lad here!"

Herrig arrived and looked warily from one woman to the other, uncertain as to what they wanted of him.

"You're to go with the herb-wife and do whatever she asks of you. Do you hear?" Muriel told him.

"Will I be paid?" he asked, after a moment of silence.

"Rude runt!" Muriel cried.

But Fridgyth chuckled. "You'll be paid, if you work well," she said. "But payment will depend on results."

Herrig looked thoughtful. "Fair enough," he said at last. "What have I got to do?"

"Just come with me," Fridgyth told him.

She left the tanners' yard and set off, walking beside the beck, up the sloping hillside and into the woods, with the boy trailing after her. They strode along in silence for a while, but once they were well out of earshot of the bereaved parents, Fridgyth slowed her steps and spoke to him. "I want some rosemary," she said. "Can you find some for me?"

Herrig frowned.

"You must know it. It's a plant with small blue flowers and many, tiny, pointed leaves. I know it grows somewhere in these woods, for I used to gather it here, long ago when I was young. It smells sharp and clean and it makes food taste good."

His eyebrows shot up. "Ah, you mean sea-rose," he said. "My dad called it sea-rose, even though it grew in the woods."

CHAPTER 20

SEA-ROSE

Herrig set off confidently leading the way. He walked a few steps in front of Fridgyth, but then after a while he stopped and looked back at her, suspicion on his face.

"Sea-rose is what they tied his hands with," he said.

Fridgyth nodded. "You're a sharp one aren't you?" she said. "Yes, Godric had his hands tied with rosemary and I want to know where that rosemary came from. It may help us find out what happened to him."

He frowned in thought and Fridgyth feared he'd refuse to help, but eventually he looked up at her and nodded. "Then I'll show you," he agreed. "And I'll need no payment, for Godric was good to me. There is only one place in these woods, where the sea-rose grows."

He turned to lead the way again.

"I will want you to find me some mushrooms, too," Fridgyth slipped in casually.

He looked doubtful at that. "I can show you where the sea-rose grows," he said, "but my Dad always told me that mushrooms must be our secret, for if they all know where to find them, I won't get paid no more."

"Find me the sea-rose first," Fridgyth said. "Lead on." And they set off again through the woods.

At first they followed a clear path that led up beside the rushing stream, but as the land became rocky, the pathway forked and Herrig led her through lush undergrowth and ferns. As she followed the quick movements of the boy's scratched, skinny legs, once again a vague memory from her younger days seemed to clear a little. She heard the sound of running water and realised that they were close to the stream again, though here it was narrow and close to the source. Suddenly she stopped in her tracks.

"The old woman," she murmured. "There was once an old woman who lived in a tumbledown shack, close to the spring."

Herrig turned to her, surprised. "You know it," he said. "You didn't need me to show the way, but the shack in't tumbled anymore, for the 'fay' has mended it."

Fridgyth looked at him puzzled. "The fay?" she asked.

"I call her the fay," he said. "Sometimes she's here and sometimes not and she can change her shape at will, for she's one of the fairy folk."

Fridgyth forced herself to accept what he said calmly, though his strange words set more questions flooding through her mind. They went on together and Fridgyth remembered it more and more, though some of it was wildly overgrown. At last the ancient dwelling came into view, but as Herrig said, it wasn't tumbled anymore.

He stopped and looked back at her. "There's the sea-rose, it grows all around."

The rotted thatched roof had been mended and recent wattle panels now replaced the old. Behind the hut, a spring of clear water bubbled from between the rocks, for this place marked the water source of Brigsbeck stream. The grass close by had been scythed and large clumps of rosemary grew all around.

"My mother sent me here to gather rosemary," she said dreamily. "It was a scary task, for the old woman shouted and chased us away, but then the old woman died and one day…"

"No, Herrig," told her. "She didn't die, for a fay never dies. Sometimes she is young, sometimes she is old… she told me so, herself."

Fridgyth made to move forward, but the boy caught her arm. "No," he cried. "You mustn't go near the place for you'll go blind if you see her changing shape."

When the herb-wife tried again, Herrig pulled her back more fiercely. "No," he cried. "She'll be angry with me, as well as you and she won't help me any more, but punish me instead."

Fridgyth saw genuine fear and sensed that she'd get no further if she pushed him too far. "Very well," she agreed.

"I can pick sea-rose for you," he offered. "I've picked that before for the monastery kitchens. She's never told me not to do that."

Her mind in turmoil, Fridgyth nodded. "Aye, pick me a good bunch of sea-rose," she said.

She watched for any sign of movement or life around the hut, while he picked the herbs, but she saw nothing. She thanked him when he returned to her with an armful of rosemary.

"Now we should go back," he insisted, nervously.

Fridgyth followed him, feeling fairly certain that she'd be able to find the place again herself. "What does she look like, your fay?" she asked as they wandered back through the woods.

The boy smiled. "Beautiful," he said softly.

"In what way?" Fridgyth asked.

"Like a fay should look," he said. "With long, golden hair, but as I said, she is sometimes young and sometimes old… as old as you," he said, with a flash of boldness.

"Huh! I am not so very old," Fridgyth protested.

"Sometimes she walks like this," he said and he hunched his shoulders and pulled up the hood on his ragged kirtle and hobbled along.

"I see," Fridgyth mused, frowning and wondering what that could mean. "And you said she helped you? How does she do that?"

He looked uncomfortable and gave no reply.

Fridgyth tried to carry on in a nonchalant manner. "Does she give you things?" she asked.

"She showed me something," he said. "But Father said…" and his speech trailed away.

Fridgyth struggled to sound casual. "Did the fay give you mushrooms?" she asked. "The mushrooms I'm interested in, are the ones you brought to the kitchen yesterday morning," she went on. "Did your father show you where they grew?"

Herrig relaxed a little and smiled. "No," he said. "Those were the perfect ones, the fay showed me, not Father. Do you want me to take you there?"

"Yes," she said.

The boy broke off from the faint pathway into undergrowth, where Fridgyth struggled to follow him. "Shall I pick some for you?" he asked obligingly.

She shook her head. "Just show me where they grow."

At last he stopped beneath an ancient oak tree and the herb-wife battled on after him. He pointed to a clump of perfect, white mushrooms. "See, more have come overnight," he said.

Fridgyth felt a wave of cold sweat run down her back, for she immediately understood when she saw them. "Stop! Stand back from them!" she called.

He did as she said, but looked utterly puzzled. "Don't you want them after all?"

"No," she cried. "Never touch them again! Did your father not warn you about them? Those are death caps!"

The colour fled from Herrig's cheeks. "Death caps," he murmured. "Father did warn me of death caps, but I had never seen them and these look just like perfect mushrooms, I didn't think…."

"Believe me, they are death caps," Fridgyth told him firmly.

"But… they cannot be death caps, for the fay…"

Fridgyth strode forward and kicked over the largest mushroom, so that it lay on its side, with snowy white gills exposed.

"See that," she pointed, "white gills beneath where they should be grey and if you touch them they will feel sticky."

The boy looked down at his palms, horrified. "Yes sticky… I had sticky hands when I picked them." He gasped as he realised the significance of this discovery and he stumbled as though he might faint.

Fridgyth grabbed his arm. "Steady now."

"But…" he gasped. "But… the ones I picked, they were for the Mercian Prince."

"How did you know they were for a prince?" she asked sharply.

"The food-wife ordered them, specially," he answered faintly. "She wanted them perfect and fresh on that day, and the fay…"

"You need not look so fearful. The Prince is safe. Now listen to me, did you wash your hands?"

"Yes, I washed them well, for I didn't much like the stickiness on them."

"Thank Freya for that," Fridgyth said. "Or you might be dead by now. Take me back to the path."

Herrig led her back, his face drawn with misery, though Fridgyth pressed his shoulder in concern. She tried to think quickly what was the best thing to do.

When they reached the path, the boy turned a frantic face to her. "I might as well be dead," he said. "I'll have to flee or they will hang me from the gallows tree?"

"No," Fridgyth told him firmly. "I have already persuaded the reeve to protect you, so long as you tell the truth."

"I have told the truth," he said shakily.

"I believe you," Fridgyth said. "And I think you know now that you cannot believe your fay."

"Aye," he nodded furiously.

"Be wary," she warned. "Say nothing to her, or anyone, but come to my hut and tell me if you see her again. I want to discover where and when she appears in these woods."

"I will do all you say," he said.

CHAPTER 21

HEATHER HONEY

Fridgyth and Herrig walked slowly back towards the tanners' yard, the boy's face still pale and his expression fearful. Though she'd discovered much from her mission, the herb-wife could make little sense of what he'd told her. She hated to leave him feeling so frightened and distressed and felt some responsibility towards him.

"Where do you live?" she asked.

"In the hut my parents left me," he said.

"Show me."

"It's not much," he faltered.

"But I would like to see it," she insisted. "You must miss your parents very much."

He turned away in order to hide the tears that flooded his eyes and could not answer immediately, but eventually he spoke again. "When they got the plague boils… and feared they'd die, they made me go to the tanners' hut and stay there until it was over. I didn't want to do it, but I did as they said."

"It was brave of them," Fridgyth said. "And I see that you have been very much alone. I think you know now that you cannot trust the fay, so I will help you instead. The abbess is my friend and she listens to me."

He turned to appraise her sincerity for a moment and eventually reassured, he nodded.

The shack that Herrig showed her was tiny, but the thatch had been recently mended in just the same manner as the hut in the woods. Similar work had been done to the wattle panelling.

"Did the fay help you mend your thatch?" she asked.

Herrig suddenly crowed with laughter, but his moment of mirth faded fast. "She may be powerful, but she cannot mend a thatch I think! No, Godric mended the thatch for me, and he made the frame for my new wattles and showed me how to mix the daub and slap it on."

"Ah yes," Fridgyth sighed sadly. "You said Godric was good to you. Did he mend the thatch for the fay?" she asked.

"Aye, of course he did, for he loved her."

Fridgyth blew softly, beginning to feel some distant sense of things coming together. "I see," she said. "He loved her."

His words confirmed her growing suspicions. Herrig pushed open his door to reveal a neat, clean space. The hearthstone had been swept and beside it stood a sack half full of oats, a small crock of corn and a quern for grinding, all set tidily against the wattle panelling. A wooden chest was placed beside a straw stuffed mattress half covered with a worn fur.

"You keep house well," she approved.

"Mam taught me," he said. "And the food-wife pays me for mushrooms with oats and corn, but now… she'll not want my foraging."

"So long as you promise to pick only the mushrooms your father showed you, I'll speak to her on your behalf."

"Oh I will," he agreed. "I will never touch anything else again."

"And you will get good payment from me for this day's work, for you have helped me greatly. You know where I live. Come to me tomorrow evening and I'll pay you for today with a pot of honey. Remember, *I* will help you now, not the fay."

His eyes lit up at the thought of honey.

"And I'll speak to the food-wife and set things straight for you there. Maybe I shall beg a loaf of bread too, for you."

"Thank you," he said.

And so on that more positive note, she took her leave of him.

120

Fridgyth hurried back up the hillside to the monastery, her head whirling with strange and unlikely possibilities. Her first port of call was the bustling kitchen.

Mildred threw up her hands, appalled when she understood what had happened.

"Death caps!" she cried. "We'll never take mushrooms from that lad again."

"Oh yes, you must," Fridgyth assured her. "I've made sure it can never happen again. The poor boy was ill advised and I mean to find out who by, but he needs the food you pay him with."

Sister Redburgh looked up red-faced from a steaming cauldron. "Death caps," she echoed. "We could all be dead by now!"

"It was you who brought the lad here in the first place," Mildred accused, pointing a floury finger at Redburgh. "And swore his father had taught him well."

"He did," Redburgh insisted. "That man never made a mistake, not once."

"You can stop your fretting," Fridgyth told them. "I've made sure he'll never listen to that wicked source again."

"Death caps!" Mildred murmured yet again and suddenly her eyes swam with guilty tears. "I should have examined them myself and if we'd not been so busy…"

Fridgyth waved her hand. "Don't start blaming yourself, you've had enough to do."

"But death caps? And will the Prince complain?"

"That is another matter," Fridgyth admitted. "The abbess is best placed to sort that out. Herrig works hard both for the tanner and as a forager for you and he's fearful that he will be blamed and hanged for his mistake."

Redburgh sighed and sent a pleading look to Mildred. "A reliable source of mushrooms is not easy to find," she suggested. "And he's not a bad lad at heart."

"Very well," Mildred agreed reluctantly. "And if you vouch for him herb-wife."

"I do," Fridgyth said firmly. "But I'd like to discover who was here in the kitchen when the Prince asked for mushrooms?"

Redburgh raised her eyebrows and made a wide sweep of her arm. "Why, everyone was here," she said, indicating at least ten women and girls who regularly worked there and a few more novices with rolled up sleeves, who'd been drafted in while there were visitors, to scrub pots and clean vegetables.

Mildred looked thoughtful for a moment and shrugged. "Most of the servers were here, when Wulfrun brought the order."

"Wulfrun?"

"Yes. She told us that the Mercian Prince had asked for mushroom broth on Friday, as he didn't like fish, for he's strict about his fasting. And so we sent for Herrig and gave him our orders. It was the day before and there was little time, that's how…"

"Don't fret about it," Fridgyth said. "And treat that lad with care, when he comes to you. I promised him a loaf of bread."

It was well past noon by the time Fridgyth got back to her hut.

"I must eat," she announced as she strode through the doorway.

"Have you had nothing yet?" Della asked. "Why it's almost time for supper and I wondered where you were."

"There has been too much to think about… but I'm hungry now," she admitted.

"There's bread and goats' cheese here and blackberry juice. Sit down awhile and eat. I've washed your stained gown and hung it out to dry on the gorse, in the meadow."

"Bless you, girl."

"So, what have you found out?"

"A great deal," Fridgyth said. "But it makes little sense, and Cynewise will be wanting her hands massaged again."

"And father's been looking for you," Della said.

"Yes… and I must speak to him too," Fridgyth agreed, "but I need time to think first. How would you feel about taking a turn at treating the Mercian Queen? You are good at massaging hands, you have the touch and she'll like your soothing voice I think."

Della looked shocked, but after a moment she smiled feeling a little flattered too that she should be thought capable of such a thing. "And what are you going to do?" she asked.

"I need to fetch my bees in from the heather," Fridgyth said. "And if the tide is right and I set off now, I can be back by morning. Tell Ketel that I'll speak to him then, and please explain to Queen Cynewise that I've gone to fetch an important remedy for her."

Without further ado, Fridgyth packed the bread and goats' cheese into her basket, snatched up a flask of blackberry juice and set off for the stables, lugging her panniers and linen wraps along with her. Drogo snorted and snuffled at her as she saddled him up and set the light burden on his back. She sensed that he too would be glad to be released from the stables for a while, as they were crowded and noisy with the coming and going of Ecfrid's horses and men.

"We both need a bit of peace," she said, as she led him out and through the side gate.

She set off down the hill and scrambled onto the mule's back to cross the ford, just as the deeper water began to swirl across it. They were well on their way before the light began to fade and they reached the spot where she'd left her hives as darkness fell. Her bees seemed to be contented, and she was pleased with the weight when she lifted the hives, which denoted a good haul of heather honey.

"Thank you, my darlings," she said. "I'll rest a while now and we'll set off before dawn to take you home."

Fridgyth tied up the mule, allowing him plenty of rope, so that he could graze on the lush grass that grew beside the stream. Then she ate the supper that she'd brought and sipped her blackberry juice, humming a little from time to time to reassure her bees. She mulled over the day and the discoveries she'd made. "There certainly was a woman in poor Godric's life," she told the bees. "I cannot believe in fairies, yet she comes and goes and sometimes she is young and sometimes she is old. How can that be?"

The bees buzzed contentedly at her side and with the fresh air and exertion she began to feel sleepy. She settled down on a clump of heather, having covered it with linen to make a smooth, springy pillow. As she reached for her cloak to spread over her, she stopped for a moment in thought, and then struggled to her feet again. She gathered the cloak about her and pulled up the hood and began to walk around the hives rather hunched and bent over, but then stopped and threw back the cloak to reveal her own solid, ageing body.

"But now, if I were young again," she murmured. "Yes, if I were young again."

She nodded, satisfied with a possible explanation, that had come to her and pulling her cloak around her again, she settled comfortably down on the heather. "If only I were young again," she murmured wistfully, as she fell asleep.

CHAPTER 22

A SURPRISING PILGRIMAGE

Fridgyth woke well before dawn, took a little more blackberry juice, and then struggled to her feet. While the bees were still resting inside the hives, she blocked the small entrance holes with soft linen and then wrapped the hives.

"Good lad," she murmured as she gave Drogo a gentle pat. Then she started to fasten the panniers into place. Once firmly fixed, she settled the hives into them, tucking them around with more loose linen padding, ready to set off back to Streonshalh.

The sun was just appearing over the horizon as they began the journey, always moving at the steady pace that suited the bees, herself and the mule. By the time the sun was up and climbing into the sky, she found herself at the top of the hill looking across the Usk Valley, towards the monastery.

She stopped for a moment and sighed as she contemplated the view ahead. Fridgyth had lived her whole life in this valley. Despite recent religious arguments, devastating plagues and the continued threat of warfare, this part of her life was perhaps turning out to be the happiest. As the acknowledged monastery herb-wife she felt respected and cared for.

"A beautiful spot," she murmured, "a good place to be."

Her gaze swept down from the green and purple heather strewn uplands, over the silver glint of the river and onwards past the jumbled sheds and thatched dwellings of the fishing families.

The open basin of the natural harbour with its newly built, timber quayside, stretched wide its arms towards the deep blue of the sea.

As the morning light flooded the hillside, Fridgyth moved her gaze to encompass the whole the monastery. The heather thatched roof of the Great Hall peeped over the top of the protective posts of the palisade, reaching almost as high as the preaching cross. When the abbess first arrived in Streonshalh, the elaborately patterned carved stone cross was the first thing that had been set up as a place to call the Christians to for their prayers. Since the monastery had expanded, the cross now stood in front of a substantial thatched church, the height of which topped all other buildings. But as the herb-wife contemplated this image of a peaceful, organised community, a sense of foreboding grew within her.

"But evil is moving inside those walls," she said.

She spoke the words out loud and the harshness in her voice made Drogo prick up his ears and set off, for he thought she'd given the order to move again. Fridgyth was forced to stumble forward alongside him, in order to keep control of his precious load.

Gasping a little, she started to laugh. "You are right, old friend," she agreed. "We need to get back and set about finding the rot, so that we can dig it out, for only then can Streonshalh be whole again."

They crossed the ford without difficulty, and headed up the hill back into the upper pasture, where all was still, for the cowherds had not yet arrived with their bellowing charges. The herb-wife took her time, as she carefully set up her hives again. Only then did she lead a reluctant Drogo back to the crowded stables. Where she thanked him with a bucket of oats.

She arrived back at her own hut, to find Herrig eating a breakfast of bread and honey.

"He says you promised him honey," Della said. "So I have given him bread and honey, though he seems to expect a whole pot of it."

"Fair enough, I did promise him a pot," Fridgyth said. "I didn't expect you to come so early though," she said to the boy. "And I didn't see you pass me in the upper pasture either; you must have crept by me. I've two hives heavy with the very best honey out there and I could do with some help, when I take it from the bees. Could you stay a while and assist me?"

Herrig looked uncertain. "Bees sting, don't they?"

Fridgyth laughed. "They don't sting me," she said. "And I don't want you to open the hive for me, I just need you to pass me things. I'll speak to the tanner, if you think he'd complain."

"No, I'll help you," the boy agreed.

"And how did *you* manage with the Mercian Queen?" Fridgyth turned to Della.

The girl smiled boldly. "Well… she complained a little at first, when I turned up in your place," she said. "But then she let me treat her, and when I left she said that I had gentler hands and a softer voice than you."

"Did she!" Fridgyth chuckled.

"But she also says that she must speak to you when you get back, for she says she's going home."

Fridgyth stared, greatly surprised. "What, home to Mercia?"

Della shook her head. "No, I think she meant back to Handale Head. I had the feeling that she despairs of reconciliation with her son, and these runes…"

Fridgyth nodded. "Yes… they have upset her. The abbess will be disappointed though, and she'll blame herself if Cynewise and her son leave with their differences unresolved. Aye well… so much to do, I'd better gather my honey fast. You carry these," she told Herrig, as she passed him a stack of clean clay pots and turned to gather together her special protective cloths.

Della, well practised at these tasks, lifted a wedge of glowing charcoal from the hearth with a pair of tongs and dropped it into a copper bowl. The herb-wife and the boy set off towards the pasture, laden with all the equipment they needed, just as most of the inhabitants were beginning to stir from their beds.

The excellence of the harvest of honey they gathered was rewarding. Herrig did all that the herb-wife asked of him, and she was impressed that he only ducked his head and backed away when he really needed to. It was almost noon by the time they'd finished. Herrig went back to Brigsbeck with a smile on his face and one of the smallest pots of honey, sealed with a beeswax plug, but still carried with care.

Having seen the precious, sticky haul safely back to her hut, Fridgyth paused to think what was the best thing to do next.

"I need to speak to Wulfrun," she said. "And the abbess too."

"I've brought oatcakes from the refectory," Della said. "You will wear yourself out at this rate. I can pot and seal these jars for you. Go and speak to the abbess when you have eaten, but don't forget the Mercian Queen. I promised I would give her message to you."

The herb-wife smiled at her efficient assistant and sat down obediently to eat and drink. "I won't forget," she said.

As soon as Fridgyth had finished her small meal and taken a sip or two of ale, she set off for the abbess's parlour. She found Hild, in a quiet, reflective mood and sensed the distress that lay beneath the calm exterior.

"I have heard that Cynewise wants to leave," Fridgyth told her.

"It was all too late, I fear," the abbess said sadly. "Too much distance between them. I have accepted their decision and ordered a final feast tonight."

"The failure is Oswy's, not yours," Fridgyth told her. "Why is he suddenly so bothered about reuniting them, after all?"

"He is growing old," Hild said. "As we all are, but I think he is bitterly regretting some of his most ruthless actions. After all, his decision at the Synod was made because he feared that Saint Peter would not open the gates of heaven for him, if he went with the Irish side. Another letter arrived from Bebbanburgh yesterday by boat, announcing that Oswy plans to go on a pilgrimage to Rome, to beg forgiveness of Saint Peter for his sins. Wilfrid is to go with him as escort."

Fridgyth shook her head. "To Rome? With Bishop Wilfrid? Won't they tear each other apart before they ever cross the sea? I understand it is a lengthy journey."

Hild smiled and nodded. "They may be gone a full year or more."

"Ah," said Fridgyth. "And maybe we'll all be better off without them here?"

"I didn't say that!" Hild protested, but a twitch of her lips belied the words. Fridgyth looked pensive for a moment.

"Elfled told me that her father was unwell, when she visited Bebbanburgh for the yuletide feast," Hild said. "Oswy wants to try to put things right before he dies, I think and Wilfrid plays on that fear, but I doubt very much that entrance to heaven can be bought by visits to Rome."

"Well, let them go and quarrel all the way there and back again," Fridgyth said. "Meanwhile we will do our best to live peacefully, under the new young King of Deira."

"I never thought to hear *you* say that," Hild said.

"Well... Ecfrid matures," Fridgyth said reluctantly. "He's more thoughtful as a man, and handsome too, any girl would want...."

"Yes, I can see that." Hild's sudden sharp reply was full of unspoken meaning. "We can all see it!" Fridgyth agreed.

"And while Cynewise is still here, so is Irminburgh," Hild went on. "She sits at Ecfrid's side, dressed like a queen... and I'm not blind to the fact that they cannot take their eyes off each other."

"So perhaps it is not so bad that Cynewise thinks of leaving," Fridgyth suggested.

"Yes. Irminburgh will have to go back to Handale Head with Cynewise."

"And Ecfrid, to Audrey?" Fridgyth pulled a sour face.

"Apparently Audrey has announced openly that she wishes to become a nun and it seems that Bishop Wilfrid is encouraging her. He has offered to intercede on her behalf with the Pope, when he goes to Rome."

"What is Wilfrid about?" Fridgyth asked.

Hild shook her head. "Audrey and Ecfrid should never have been married, but now they are man and wife, and well... it may be best if they all go home."

"Yes... and leave us in peace," Fridgyth agreed, "but speaking of peace, that reminds me that I came to speak of another matter, one which threatens the very security of our settlement."

"Then speak," Hild nodded.

"Yesterday I spent the morning in Brigsbeck Woods with Herrig the foraging boy, who also works in the tanners' yard. The woods, it seems, are haunted by a… a beautiful young woman, whom he calls the fay!"

"The fay… but that is one of the old names for the fairy folk," Hild said. She smiled with disbelief.

"Yes. I know it sounds strange, but believe me someone has bewitched that boy and Godric too, I fear. Whoever this person is, she persuaded the lad to pick death caps and deliver them to the kitchens for the Prince's broth."

"What!" Hild was horrified.

"Yes. Herrig was terrified when I told him what he'd done. He was ready to run, for he feared that we would string him up on the gallows tree."

"But we would not…"

"Of course… and I have promised that if he speaks the truth to us, he will be protected."

"Yes, indeed," Hild readily agreed.

"I know you have enough to worry about with your visitors, so let me talk to Ketel about these strange reports, and I would like to speak to Wulfrun too, for it was she who ordered the mushrooms for the Prince."

"Wulfrun?" Hild frowned.

"Yes. Whoever she is, this 'fay' woman knew that the Prince had requested mushrooms."

Hild frowned and looked worried. "Where will it end?" she murmured. "Wulfrun will have gone out to ride with Elfled now, but they should return at the sound of the vesper bell, which will be ringing soon. Sister Lindi might be able to help you, but she keeps silence in her hut at this time of day. I can give you permission to go into the nun's enclosure to speak to her, if you think it important."

Fridgyth hesitated. "I think I'd rather speak to Wulfrun directly," she said. "And it might be best to keep this new information quiet for a while, we don't want our foes to get wind of what we are discovering or provoke another attack. If I go to the stables now I might catch them as they return."

"Keep me informed," Hild said as they parted.

CHAPTER 23

A SHOCKING ADMISSION

No sooner had Fridgyth emerged from the abbess's house, than Irminburgh crossed the courtyard and headed towards her. She carried a parcel wrapped in plain linen, but carefully lifted her skirts to keep the dainty tablet-weave edging of her gown out of the sandy dust that swirled everywhere on the late summer breeze. A rush of rose tinted veil and sweet perfume assailed the herb-wife.

"I've found you at last," Irminburgh cried. "My mistress insists that she will return to that desolate place on the cliffs, so she needs a supply of your balm and dried herbs to take with her."

"Very well," Fridgyth agreed.

"And she also asks that you to wrap her in seaweed poultices again before we leave. I swear she'd take you with us if the abbess would allow it."

"I've other folk to care for and things to do," Fridgyth said, bridling at the very idea.

"But the Queen says…" Irminburgh began and then all at once her condescending air of self-importance seemed to ebb away, to be quickly replaced by a forlorn look of desolation.

The vesper bell began to toll.

Fridgyth found herself faintly touched by this sudden change in expression, for the young woman looked utterly dismayed. "You don't want to go," she said knowingly. "And I can well see why!"

"What would you know of such things?" Irminburgh began miserably.

131

"More than you think?" Fridgyth said. "I may be old, but that doesn't mean that I've forgotten how it feels to love a man."

Irminburgh looked surprised. "You acknowledge that it is love, then?" she said, and a faint flush touched her cheeks.

"I suppose it must be," Fridgyth admitted with a shrug. "For ambition would be much better served if you were to follow your mistress's suggestion and show willing to marry Prince Aethelred."

Irminburgh gazed into the distance for a moment, but then she nodded. "It's true, I'd rather be Ecfrid's concubine, than Aethelred's Queen," she admitted. "If only he'd have me."

"I believe you," Fridgyth said quietly, for this was a devastating admission. "And Ecfrid, will he not accept you as his mistress?"

Irminburgh simply shook her head. "He will not dishonour me by taking me as his concubine."

"Then his feelings for you must be finer than you realise," Fridgyth said. "If I were you, I'd go back to Handale Head with Cynewise and try to be content in that knowledge. Tell your mistress that I'll visit her before the feast to bring balms and simples that will suit her needs. I'll wrap her in seaweed, if that's what she wants."

Irminburgh turned sadly and wandered away, her expression thoughtful, her shoulders drooping. Fridgyth hurried on towards the stables, fearing that she'd miss the Princess, but just as she arrived she saw the two girls dismounting from their mares. Elfled rushed away, eager to dress for the final feast, before her brother left to return to York, but Wulfrun obligingly stayed behind at the herb-wife's request, and when questioned about the order for mushrooms, she frowned in thought.

"*You* don't usually order our visitor's food for them, do you?" Fridgyth asked.

"No," Wulfrun agreed. "But on that day we'd been to visit the Prince in the monastic guest house. We went with a purpose, for Elfled was to tell the Prince how sweet and lovely her sister Osthryth is and try to persuade him that she'd make a beautiful bride. The abbess sent us."

"Those were Hild's wishes?" Fridgyth asked.

132

Wulfrun shrugged. "They were King Oswy's wishes," she said emphatically. "Even the abbess can't go against our overlord."

"No, of course she can't," Fridgyth agreed. "What happened while you were there?"

"Well, Elfled did her best to speak kindly of her sister, but secretly we feared for poor Osthryth. We thought she'd have little joy were she to be married to Aethelred, for all he would talk about was fasting on Friday and how he didn't like fish, but he did like mushrooms. So as a courtesy to him, I offered to go myself to the kitchens to let them know of his preference."

"So you went there alone?"

"Yes, I did. When I heard about his terrible sickness, I felt concerned that I might somehow be blamed, but I did only what I was asked to do and did it out of politeness."

"Nobody can attach any guilt to you, over this," Fridgyth said.

Wulfrun looked somewhat relieved, but she went on rather gloomily. "Well… Elfled thinks that the Prince would make a better monk than a bridegroom. He makes it very clear that he doesn't approve of the way our Princess behaves. 'It is not appropriate,' he said 'to be riding out to hunt with the men, singing and dancing and chattering with friends, for a young girl destined to be a nun.'"

Fridgyth smiled, for she and Hild had passed many hours discussing this, and come to the conclusion that Elfled should be given as much freedom as possible, while she was still young, since a future of grave responsibility had been forced upon her.

Wulfrun pulled a miserable face. "Prince Aethelred is the one that should be given to God," she said, "then maybe Elfled could look for a prince to marry instead. What a cheerful, welcoming queen she'd make. What an excellent hostess she'd be, she'd charm all the important guests."

Fridgyth smiled and shook her head. "Marrying a king is not all dancing and entertaining," she protested. "Ask Cynewise about that. A nun can take the role of hostess too, for look at Hild, she is always entertaining guests."

"But the abbess's entertainment is nothing compared to what we've seen at the court at Bebbanburgh," Wulfrun insisted. "There are women decked in jewels who wear the richest gowns. Gold and garnets gleam everywhere, even on the men. Musicians play every night and tumblers prance and dance, they almost fly!" Her words came fast and her eyes gleamed brightly.

Fridgyth smiled at her excitement, but she forced her thoughts back to more immediate problems. "Can you remember who was there in the monastic guest house, when the Prince announced that he wanted mushrooms?" Wulfrun frowned in thought. "Elfled of course, myself, Lindi, the foster father and… oh and of course, there was Irminburgh."

"Irminburgh? What was Irminburgh doing there?"

Wulfrun smiled. "She visits Elfled almost every day and brings small gifts for us. She's very sweet to the Princess now… and she's been very sweet to me too! She says she wants to make amends and she even brings gifts for Sister Lindi. Of course we know why she tries to make friends with us, for our new King is usually there with his sister."

"Hmm, but I doubt things could ever go Irminburgh's way," Fridgyth said. "I have to admit that I have had a moment or two of almost feeling sorry for her. Now please think carefully… did anyone else overhear the Prince when he asked for mushrooms?"

"Well," she said thoughtfully. "The partitions within the monastic guest house are very thin. It is not like the royal guest house. I suppose that anyone sitting quietly in one of the other cubicles could have overheard us and not been seen. The monks move so quietly about the place."

"Yes," Fridgyth agreed. She saw that the girl was quite right about that.

The stark facilities of the monastic guest house were only too familiar to her, and she realised that almost anyone could have overheard the conversation. "Thank you," she said at last. "And there's just one more thing I need to ask and I hesitate to do so, but we need desperately to discover who is bringing death threats to our door. I saw you out in the pasture late one night, did I not… and I thought that it was Godric there at your side?"

The girl's face turned immediately sorrowful. "You did," she admitted. "But it is not what you think and poor Godric…"

"But… I thought I saw his arms about you," Fridgyth said knowingly. "Is that not so?"

Wulfrun folded her arms and looked offended. "I have told you all I can," she said, turning suddenly distant. "Either you trust me, or you do not! There was nothing between me and Godric, nothing that was improper, though I grieve for him as I would for any friend."

Fridgyth sighed. "I trust you, Wulfrun," she said quietly. "You'd best follow the Princess and get ready for the feast. Maybe when our visitors have gone, our lives can settle down again."

CHAPTER 24

AN INVITATION

Fridgyth returned to her hut to gather what she needed, and then she made her way to the royal guest house. Irminburgh was nowhere to be seen, but one of the other women recognised her and let her in. She found Cynewise unattended and pulled up a stool to sit down beside the Queen, ready to massage her knotted finger joints, but she found herself under close scrutiny.

"That girl you sent was good," Cynewise said.

"I trained her myself," Fridgyth agreed and then she added carefully. "But everyone is sad to hear that the purpose of your visit has failed, and that you wish to leave so soon."

"The journey has not been entirely without its uses," Cynewise said. "You've made me feel more comfortable. Will you come back with me to Handale Head? I'd pay you well. Oswy vowed to maintain me in the manner of a queen, and I retain my jewels and my household companions and servants. You would live in comfort at Handale Head and be my personal physician."

Fridgyth chuckled at the image that came to mind, but shook her head. "I was the Uskdale cunning-woman, long before Hild came to Streonshalh and the cunning-woman I remain. The abbess simply found an acceptable way for me to carry on my work."

"Can I offer nothing that would tempt you away from here?" Cynewise pleaded.

"No," Fridgyth said.

"Then would you come back with me, just for a while, to see me settled there?" she pleaded. "I feel so much better for your care."

"I cannot come," she said firmly. "But I can make you comfortable now. I could perhaps show Irminburgh how to mix this paste and apply the wraps? Then I could send you supplies of dried seaweed ready to be mashed and used for the purpose."

"Irminburgh? Can you see her spreading this stinking mash on me?"

They both laughed and shook their heads.

Fridgyth set about mixing the crushed seaweed to a mud-like consistency and then carefully applied it along with the wraps.

"Do you not think of returning to Mercia?" she asked. "It was after all your home."

"No," Cynewise said with a sigh. "Mercia was Penda's home, and while he lived I was determined to play my part. I bore his children, hosted his feasts, held his lands while he was away, and kept his hostages safe, but Mercia was never my home and now my sons are not my sons any more. They have both taken to this new religion…"

"Where *did* you come from?" Fridgyth asked.

"I was born far away in the south of these lands, close to where the River Solent meets the ocean. I loved living by the sea, but my father ruled the Kingdom of Wessex, and when I was seventeen I was sent to land-locked Mercia, to marry Penda as part of a peace treaty."

"You were a peace-weaver bride?"

Cynewise smiled gently. "Yes, not much peace with Penda though, but I grew to love him. He lived like a fierce wolf, the undisputed leader of the pack, but I found that I could tame him!"

"So that is why you stay at Handale Head, to be by the sea."

"Handale is nothing like the gentle sea that I knew as a girl, but you are right… I take pleasure in wandering on those high cliffs, listening to the screeching gulls, watching the silent hawks and the fierce sea eagles circling above me, while the wild waves crash below. Handale has become my home. And Ecfrid isn't far away. He is as good a friend to me, as any of my sons," she added.

"Rest now," Fridgyth advised, somewhat touched by these intimate revelations.

She covered the Queen to keep her warm, and when Cynewise shut her eyes sleepily, the herb-wife sat down to think for a while.

Her mind strayed back to Brigsbeck Woods. She wondered again what could possibly link a dangerous political act like the attempted poisoning of Prince Aethelred, with a quiet young craftsman like Godric? Could the young tanner have accidentally gained knowledge that might be feared to be dangerous? Or had he, as Cynewise had suggested, been killed simply to demonstrate that whoever was behind these threats meant business?

It was growing dark when Cynewise stirred again and the herb-wife helped her to rouse. She cleaned and dried her limbs, as the Queen tried one more time to persuade her to return with her. Just as they were finishing, Irminburgh appeared in the doorway, looking more cheerful than before.

"Where have you been?" Cynewise asked indignantly.

"Helping Sister Lindi dress the Princess for the feast," Irminburgh said. "Being a nun, she has no idea of how a princess should be garbed, but now I must go to see to my own appearance."

She turned with a swing of her skirt and was gone.

Cynewise sighed and then shook her head. "Can you see her wrapping me with seaweed?" she asked.

"No," Fridgyth agreed.

"But still I love her like a daughter," she admitted.

Fridgyth nodded, understanding well, and suddenly she relented a little. "Go back to Handale," she said, "and I'll visit you in a little while. If the abbess permits it, I'll come before the bitter months and stay a few days to see to your comfort."

"Do you promise me that?" Cynewise asked.

"I do.

Cynewise attended the feast that night, dressed like the Queen she was, in a deep red gown that glinted with gold and garnets. She appeared refreshed and more cheerful. Fridgyth was pleased that her treatments seemed to be working, though she guessed that this improvement in the Queen's demeanour also came from the knowledge that she was returning to Handale.

The food produced from the kitchens was magnificent. Platters of roast swan, trimmed with herbs and honey were served, alongside a good-sized hog baked in salt. But despite the chief guest's more cheerful mien and the appetising smells and sights, a general sense of gloom hung over the proceeding.

Ecfrid danced attendance on Cynewise, who responded with smiles and small touches that demonstrated a motherly concern for him. Though Irminburgh sat at his left hand, dressed in a stunning gold gown, he ignored her. The young woman appeared listless and distracted again, disdaining to make conversation with Aethelred, who had been placed on her other side. The Prince watched the feast with barely concealed disapproval, ate little and spoke less.

Hild, who sat between Aethelred and Siward of Dreng, tried with her usual tact and patience to soothe everyone's feelings, but Fridgyth recognised the signs of pain and exhaustion in the pallor of her skin. This particular set of visitors needed to go.

Caedmon attempted to lift their spirits with a charming hymn of praise for the fruitful harvest, but the guests clapped sporadically and it seemed that everyone was relieved when the bell rang for compline and the abbess drew proceedings to a close.

It was late when Fridgyth returned to her hut, but Ketel, freed from his burdensome duties at last, followed her there. They sat down by the hearth together and he rubbed his shoulders, complaining of stiffness.

"We are too old for this," he grumbled, "the abbess as well. Oswy asks too much of us."

"Yes," Fridgyth agreed. "Hild's reputation for wisdom brings far too many extra duties to her door... but I have another matter to talk to you about."

He shifted himself to sit more upright on his stool and waited for her to speak.

"Yesterday I went to Brigsbeck Woods with Herrig, the forager lad..."

"Della mentioned something," he said.

Fridgyth told him what she'd seen and heard. He listened carefully, alert to the significance of what she had to tell.

"So you think this 'fay', must be the woman Godric had secret assignations with?"

"Yes, I'm sure of it," Fridgyth said. "Herrig said, 'Godric loved her', but who she is remains a mystery. She comes and goes, one moment an enticing fay, the next a crone."

He yawned and his eyelids drooped again. "How can that be so?" he asked vaguely.

The herb-wife looked down at Della for a moment. The girl had settled to loll against her father's knee, enjoying a rest by the warmth of the fire, but Fridgyth leaned forwards and touched her shoulder. "Will you get up for a moment, honey?" she said. "Take my cloak from the nail and put it round your shoulders."

Father and daughter stared for a moment as though Fridgyth had gone mad.

"But I have just sat down," the girl complained.

"Humour me, sweetheart," the herb-wife begged. "I know you are tired, but this will only take a moment, and then I'll let you rest."

Shaking her head in puzzlement, Della got up and did as she was told.

"Pull the hood over your hair," Fridgyth ordered. "Yes, that's it, now hunch your shoulders and poke your head forward and hobble a little as though you have a sore foot."

Della did her best to obey and Ketel suddenly gave a grunt of understanding. "I begin to see," he said. "None would know that there was a young girl under that covering."

"Now fling off the cloak and turn to face us," Fridgyth ordered.

Enjoying the game now, Della dropped the cloak and stood straight, she turned towards them with a laugh, a vision of radiant youth, her hair glinting golden in the firelight.

"Hah!" Ketel laughed too. "I see what you mean," he said. "A young woman might appear old if she wanted to, especially from a distance."

"It's not so easy the other way round," Fridgyth commented drily.

"But what now?" Ketel wondered. He frowned deep in thought. "It seems that you have learned a great deal, but I still cannot see…"

Fridgyth shrugged. "Nor I," she admitted. "But the boy will run to tell me if he sees this mysterious 'fay' again and then…" She stopped and shook her head, for she knew it would not be easy to go running off to the woods to investigate.

"Is Godric's brother not back yet?" Ketel asked.

"No… not yet," she said.

They sat in silence for a while. Fridgyth found that once again her thoughts strayed to Ralf and his admission that he too had a lady that he wished to please. She'd given her word not to speak of it, and she took such confidences seriously, but she wondered if the time might come when she'd feel that she needed to break her promise. Godric's brother should surely have returned to Streonshalh from Gilling by now, and his absence was beginning to trouble her. An uncomfortable thought kept coming back to her, that Herrig's 'fay' might be the same woman that Ralf longed to please? Could the brothers have been rivals for the same lady's favours? But Godric was alive when Ralf set out, and she'd seen him with her own eyes heading up the hill away from Streonshalh. But that could have been an effective cover, if he'd then quietly returned to do the dreadful deed, while everyone believed him far away? She hated it when her thoughts turned that way, for murder of a brother was the foulest, saddest thing to contemplate and Ralf was a young man that she liked.

Fridgyth shook her head and got up distressed by this train of thought. "I must get to bed," she said. "My thoughts turn wild!"

"We must all get to bed," Ketel said.

CHAPTER 25

ROSEMARY AND ROPE

Having promised Cynewise that she'd visit her, Fridgyth felt little need to be amongst the dutiful crowd that waited to escort the Mercian Queen down to the quayside and the abbess's barge. Instead the herb-wife woke with fresh determination to investigate further the hut by Brigsbeck Spring.

"I'm going out for a while," she told Della.

"Don't you want to see Queen Cynewise leave?" the girl asked her.

"No. You go down to the quayside," she said. "She will like to see your sweet face amongst the crowd and be careful, for she'd take you with her, if you wanted to go, I'm sure."

Della shook her head and smiled. "I am staying here with you," she said. "You need me here."

"I certainly do," Fridgyth agreed.

Once again Fridgyth strode down the hill and up into the wooded valley. She glimpsed Herrig and Edric working together once again, but hurried past the tanners' yard, for she didn't want to explain what she was doing. The path that the boy had shown her was narrow, but clear enough, and the sun was high in the sky when she arrived at the small clearing. For a while she hovered cautiously beside the rosemary bushes, but all seemed quiet and still, save for the pleasant sounds of birdsong and small rustlings in the undergrowth. The sky grew overcast, and a few heavy raindrops pattered around her. Still she stood and watched, sheltered a little by the trees, but the leaves had begun to fall as summer faded and gradually she became cold and wet. At last she asked herself why she was standing there so foolishly when the normal thing would be to beg for shelter!

With that thought she marched boldly up to the door, knocked and waited. There came no reply, so she lifted the wooden latch and, with a thundering heart, walked in. To her relief, there was nobody there. The small space inside was clean and dry, the earthen floor recently swept. Two mugs, two bowls and a plate stood on a wooden shelf, beside which was a shallow basket of nuts.

A string of dried mushrooms hung from a nail, and suddenly her stomach lurched a little. She carefully refrained from touching them, for in their dried and shrivelled state, she could not be sure whether they were wholesome field mushrooms or the lethal death caps. A straw stuffed sack made a makeshift mattress on the floor, with a woollen rug spread over it. Fridgyth picked up one of the mugs and saw, with something of a shock, the familiar mark of the abbey potter there on the base. As she turned over the other mug and the bowls she discovered that the small stock of pots had all come from the monastery. There were provisions and comforts of a kind in the place, but somehow she doubted that someone was actually living there.

She shook her head, for with this evidence, she could no longer deny that somebody with access to the abbey kitchens, or refectory, had been here. Could it be Herrig? Her heart sank at the thought that the boy could be lying to her, but she knew that he could not be alone in this. Maybe he'd been prevailed upon to steal from the kitchens and bring these small treasures to the woods?

Fridgyth examined the meagre food-stock, nervous all the time and listening for any hint of approach. Her mind worked fast, as she struggled through a mire of muddy ideas and explanations. Eventually, she peered cautiously out from the doorway to find that the rain had eased. Should she hide herself and wait around to discover who might come? But that might take forever and she could not afford the time. A dark shape in the corner of the hut turned out to be a coiled rope and it made her shudder and glance outside again at the abundant bushes of rosemary.

The sickening sight of Godric's body came forcibly back into her mind. She could no longer doubt that whoever came and went from this place had sinister intentions. She'd be an utter fool to stay here alone. Having closed the door carefully, so that everything might appear untouched, she left and headed back through the woods.

This time she stopped at the tanners' yard and discovered Herrig there alone, attacking a freshly stretched skin with the scudding blade again. She stood still for a moment to adjust to the foul odours of the place and then strode in.

The boy worked energetically, using the sharpened bone scraper. "Shall I call Muriel?" he asked, when he looked up to find the herb-wife watching him.

"No, it's you I want to speak to," she said. "Have you seen her... your 'fay'? I went to her hut, but saw nobody there."

He shook his head. "No, she wouldn't be," he said. "Not yet. She never appears before noon."

Fridgyth frowned, wondering why that might be. "Tell me," she said. "Did she ever ask you to bring something for her?"

He stared for a moment as though he thought she was mad. "Mushrooms," he said. "I picked mushrooms for her... but I told you that before."

"Not mushrooms," Fridgyth said. "Something else... something from the monastery kitchen or refectory? I don't care whether they were stolen or not, I just need to know!"

"No," he said at once. He lowered the scraper and looked offended. "I would never... and she never asked!"

"That's fine... all I needed to know," Fridgyth assured him. "Remember to tell me as soon as you see her again."

"I will," he said earnestly.

Fridgyth went back up the hill and in through the side gate to her hut.

"They've gone," Della announced. "King Ecfrid set off to Eforwic as soon as the sun was up. He bought a fine jet-necklace from one of the monastery workshops for his wife, set in gold and with a jet carved cross in the centre. It is absolutely beautiful, he showed it to everyone and the goldsmiths are full of pride for they say it will help to market their work with other Christian, wealthy families. He thanked the abbess for her hospitality, but Irminburgh…"

"Never mind Irminburgh… what of the Mercian Queen?"

"Cynewise went off in the abbess's barge, her bed all taken apart and stacked in a smaller boat that went ahead of them. The maids and men will get it fixed for her, so that it's ready as soon as she arrives back at Handale."

"Aye, well… Oswy allows all comforts for her."

"Yes, all comforts, except for one, her favourite companion could not be found."

Fridgyth looked puzzled. "What do you mean?"

"I was trying to tell you," she said, breathlessly. "Irminburgh could not be found, when the barge was ready to leave! The Queen was upset, and then angry, but the tide was ready to turn and, in the end, she went without her."

"So Irminburgh is still here?"

Della looked at her knowingly. "Well, what do you think?" she said. "King Ecfrid set off much earlier, for he was on his way to Eforwic almost as soon as the sun was up. He was long gone by the time the boat was ready to leave for Handale, and who could ever have stopped him from taking her with him? He is our King! Even the abbess…"

Fridgyth was stunned at the news. "But Irminburgh told me he would not…" she began. "Or were those protestations subterfuge? Did she plan this all along? Has Irminburgh really gone in Ecfrid's train?"

"I think it's in everyone's mind," Della admitted, "and we suspect Queen Cynewise thinks so too. But Irminburgh's chest of clothes had been packed and stowed in the first boatload, along with the bed. Can you imagine her going away without her finery?"

Fridgyth reflected and shook her head. "But if she's gone with Ecfrid, she will soon have more."

"Yes, of course she will," Della agreed.

"This is yet another worry for the abbess," Fridgyth said, with a sigh. "If Irminburgh meant to do this, she need not have been so coy with me. Nothing shocks me these days!"

Della pulled forward a stool. "Sit down and I'll make you a brew," she said. "Not long till supper now, though we are back to plain fare, I think."

Fridgyth did as she was told, frowning as she wondered how Irminburgh's disappearance might affect the reputation of both Streonshalh and the abbess.

Later that evening, when the herb-wife entered the refectory, she sensed at once that the general mood was more relaxed. The evening meal of vegetable pottage, served with bread still warm from the oven was simple, but warming and filling. The gentle buzz of conversation put her in mind of the contented hum of bees let loose in a meadow of flowers. The scandal of Irminburgh's disappearance had sparked lively gossip, but the monastery appeared to be returning to normality.

CHAPTER 26

NEWS FROM GILLING

As Fridgyth stood watching the familiar sight of the community cheerfully eating and drinking, Sister Lindi rose briefly from the top table and beckoned to the herb-wife.

"The Princess is sad to have lost her brother's company," she whispered, when Fridgyth reached her side. "Please join us herb-wife, for Elfled refuses to eat."

The Princess overheard the quiet exchange and looked up.

"Yes, join us, Fridgyth," she said. "But I cannot eat this soggy mess, for my stomach has got used to meat and sweet cakes now. It's not just Ecfrid that has gone... it's *her* as well. Fridgyth, could you order me honey cakes? I will starve otherwise."

"I suppose by *her*, you mean Irminburgh," Fridgyth said, as she took a seat next to Wulfrun and ignored the plea for honey cakes.

"She made me begin to like her again," Elfled admitted mournfully. "But then she goes and leaves like that. At least she wasn't boring," she added with a swift, critical glance that encompassed both Wulfrun and Lindi.

"Irminburgh would have had to go anyway," Wulfrun protested. "Queen Cynewise needed her back at Handale Head."

"Nobody will say it, but we all know that she's gone with Ecfrid," Elfled said, "and no-one dare dispute it because he's Deira's King!"

None felt that they could contradict her.

One of the kitchen servers placed a bowl of steaming pottage in front of the herb-wife. She picked up a spoon and began to eat,

"Good to get back to normal, wholesome food," she said, with relish. "And it will not be so very long until Yule, and I expect you will be travelling to Bebbanburgh, Princess." This was a reference to the annual yuletide visit, that in recent years, the Princess had made to her parents.

Elfled still played with her spoon, but she also looked up thoughtfully and suddenly saw the significance of this remark. "And I will see my brother again," she said. "And it will be very interesting to see if Irminburgh appears at my father's winter feast. She would not miss that, if she could help it."

"Yes," Wulfrun agreed.

"The weather is growing chilly," Fridgyth pointed out, "and Bloodmonth will be here before you know it, and you'll be preparing for your visit."

"Yes," Wulfrun agreed, "the time will fly."

"Thank you, Fridgyth," Lindi acknowledged with a smile.

"I will write to my mother," Elfled said. "You must help me, Lindi. I want to make sure that she prepares a chamber for me next to Osthryth's – and Wulfrun must come to Bebbanburgh too."

"Permission would depend on the abbess," Lindi reminded her.

Elfled picked up a hunk of soft white bread and began to tear it apart and eat. "And you must come too, Lindi," she said, sending a mischievous look towards her young tutor. "You deserve some fun, and you and Irminburgh got on well."

Elfled's downward glance indicated a silver ring on Lindi's finger.

The young nun flushed and slipped the small but exquisite piece into her pocket. "I will consult with the abbess," Lindi said, dutifully.

Fridgyth suppressed a smile. Wulfrun had mentioned that there had been gifts from Irminburgh; who could judge a devout young woman, for accepting such a tiny touch of vanity?

As the meal was coming to an end, Hild appeared briefly in the refectory to give her usual nod to Fridgyth.

When the herb-wife arrived at the abbess's house, she found Ketel already there. They sat together in the abbess's parlour and Hild herself served them with elderberry wine. The abbess sadly mulled over recent events and especially the failure of Oswy's scheme. "And now Irminburgh," she finished. "It seems that she has vanished without taking clothes or jewels with her."

"Unlike her," Fridgyth agreed.

"But should we report her disappearance to King Oswy?" Ketel asked. "Or would it perhaps be more appropriate to inform Queen Eanfleda."

Fridgyth sighed. "Irminburgh told me pointedly that Ecfrid would not take her as his mistress," she said. "And I believed her, but I fear her words may have been intended to distract me from what she really planned. Our Deiran King is still a very young man, and the unhappiness of his marriage is no secret."

"Hmm," Hild sighed in agreement. "I fear you may be right Fridgyth," she said. "Irminburgh is second cousin to Queen Eanfleda and I worry that her powerful Kentish relations might hold us to account for her disappearance. The king of Kent is another distant cousin, and in time he's sure to enquire after her and wonder where Irminburgh has gone."

"Well he must make petition to King Ecfrid, not you," the herb-wife said frankly. "I have some sympathy for Irminburgh, for her feelings are plain to see and if Ecfrid has taken her with him, who would dare to complain about it? I think she has made her bed and must lie in it, as many others have had to do."

Hild sighed. "Only Oswy would have the power to prevent Ecfrid form taking Irminburgh as his concubine," she said. "And I don't think the purpose of peace would be served by starting such an argument up between father and son."

"No, indeed," Ketel spoke with feeling.

"The one with the greatest right to object is Cynewise," Fridgyth said. "Her lady in waiting has deserted her."

"Yes, indeed," Hild agreed, "but though she was angry when they discovered that Irminburgh was missing, Cynewise seemed to quickly accept that the girl had gone."

"What do we do now about the attempted murder of Prince Aethelred? And what about the death of Godric?" Ketel asked anxiously. "If disruption of your peace talks was intended, then they have succeeded at the cost of an innocent young life. No reunion has been achieved between the Mercian Queen and her son, and there seems to be little possibility of another marriage agreement between Northumbria and Mercia. If that was what was intended, they have won."

Hild sighed. "I expect Oswy will be angry."

Fridgyth shook her head uncertainly. "Queen Cynewise recognised that the rune of revenge linked with rosemary, meant revenge for something long remembered."

"But revenge against whom?" Hild asked.

Fridgyth had no answer. "I hated Penda. At one time the very sound of his name made me want to retch, but getting to know Cynewise has changed those feelings. She was trying to help us when she interpreted those meanings and suggested that whoever killed Godric intended it as a threat."

"Yes, I'm sure of that now," Ketel said, "for Aethelred nearly died too."

They sat in silence for a few moments, and then Hild pressed Fridgyth's hand. "I am proud of you," she said. "You treated Penda's widow with compassion."

Fridgyth smiled. "It was not the hardship I'd expected it to be."

They'd come to no conclusion when the compline bell called the abbess to her prayers and they rose to go their separate ways.

When Fridgyth returned to her hut, she found Della feeding the cat, and entertaining Herrig. The boy leapt to his feet, dropping a half-eaten oatcake, as soon as she appeared, while Wyrdkin dived through his legs and fled outside.

"You have seen her?" Fridgyth asked.

"No," he shook his head. "But there's something else. Ralf has returned from Gilling, and he is distraught to find his brother dead. He has news for the abbess too, news that will sadden and shock her."

"What?" she cried.

"They are all dead at Gilling, everyone of the monks has died of the plague, from the abbot to the youngest of the oblates. Ralf will do nothing but weep since he heard the news of Godric's death. His mother begs that you come to help to calm him. They sent me here to pass this terrible message onto the abbess and I don't know what to do!"

"Hush!" Fridgyth said. She patted his shoulder, but her own heart started beating wildly and her hands began to shake. "I'm so tired," she whispered, "but I must come with you. I have feared all along that that we hadn't seen the last of this plague. The abbess will be distraught to hear of this, but there is nothing she can do to bring the monks from Gilling back again, and allowing her a few more hours of peace makes little difference!"

Fridgyth picked up her cloak and her basket of dried herbs.

"Shall I come too?" Della asked.

"No, sweetheart, you stay here in case someone else is taken ill."

Fridgyth felt wide-awake again as she headed fast downhill to Brigsbeck Valley, for the frightening tidings had brought with them a flash of renewed energy. As she marched down the hill, she realised slowly the enormity of the news the boy had brought. Gilling had not been the only monastery destroyed by plague, for Lastingham had gone the same way, leaving only one small boy alive. The same dire sickness had taken a heavy toll in Streonshalh, leaving Herrig one amongst many children orphaned in the plague's bitter wake. Godric's death might seem small in comparison to the numbers who had died of plague, but to his family his death meant everything.

Herrig trotted at her side, relating more details of Ralf's reaction to his brother's death. "He weeps and weeps," he told her. "He mutters words so fast and low that we cannot understand what he says."

"Have you touched him?" she asked sharply, fearing that Ralf's return might bring a renewal of the pestilence to Streonshalh.

"No," he said. "But his mother has."

"You did well to fetch me," she said, aware that this boy was no stranger to death. As she hurried on the unpleasant thought crept into her mind that Ralf's dramatic reaction could possibly signify a deliberate attempt to cover guilt. She hated the very thought of it, but told herself that it was a possibility that she must not rule out. However, when she arrived at the tanners' dwelling she was convinced that the shock was genuine. Ralf was vomiting and pale, his body drenched in a cold sweat. She doubted very much that this could be faked, and worried more about the possibility of plague. His frantic parents undoubtedly feared that they might lose another son.

"Has he any boils or sores?" she demanded.

"No," Muriel said firmly, understanding well her fears. "See for yourself," she offered."

"Then he is suffering from shock," Fridgyth pronounced. She searched in her bundles for the most suitable remedy. "Honey and a tiny grain of wolfsbane in a warming drink," she proposed.

"I have water boiling ready," Muriel said.

They made a sweet drink, and Fridgyth took great care to stir into it only the tiniest fraction of the potentially dangerous plant.

"My fault, my fault," Ralf murmured over and over again.

"What is your fault?" Fridgyth could not resist asking.

"Should not have gone," he said between huge gasps. "Buried seven monks and a boy... when I should have been here... to bury my brother."

His eyes began to droop and gradually a heavy lethargy descended.

Fridgyth suppressed her desire to question him further. Now was clearly not the time. "Let him sleep," she said. "I will come back in the morning."

The tanner and his wife gently lowered their remaining son onto the straw stuffed mattress that had been set up by the hearth, and covered him with a rug. Fridgyth's mind fled back to the day they'd found his brother drowned and the similar loving care the poor parents had given to Godric's body.

Herrig stood awkwardly watching them.

"Why don't you stay here and help them?" she suggested.

"I will if they want me to," he said.

"We'd be glad of it," Muriel agreed.

CHAPTER 27

A DREADFUL DISCOVERY

Though her mind was busier than ever, by the time she'd marched back to her hut through the darkness, Fridgyth felt drained. She lay down to sleep and, despite her worries, she drifted off almost as soon as her head touched the pillow. She slept longer than she'd meant to when Della woke her at daybreak with a warm brew of sage, laced with honey.

"Sun-up," the girl said. "I'm sorry to disturb you, but I knew you wanted to speak to the abbess as soon as possible."

"Good lass," she said as she heaved herself into a sitting position, as the events of the previous evening came flooding back into her mind. The prospect of relating the terrible news from Gilling to the abbess was far from appealing, but it had to be done.

"I think I will tell Ketel first," she said. "For the abbess will need him when she hears this terrible news. Then I must hurry back to Brigsbeck to see how Ralf is. Can you manage here, honey?"

"Of course I can," Della said.

Once dressed and on her feet again, Fridgyth headed straight for the reeve's chamber, which was set behind curtains at the end of the great hall. The servants ignored her as she passed them, but winked at each other behind her back. They were used to the herb-wife visiting the reeve in his private chamber, but Fridgyth had more serious things on her mind. She found him sitting up in bed, eating a bowl of porridge.

"Get up," she ordered. "I need you to come with me, we have more disasters on our hands."

Ketel closed his eyes despondently for a moment, but then opened them again and nodded.

"What now?" he asked.

As soon as she started to explain, he put down the bowl and heaved himself out of bed.

The abbess was deeply shocked when she understood what had happened at Gilling. "I must send a priest and a party of monks to them," she said.

"No," Fridgyth insisted. "You cannot do that, you'd risk bringing the sickness here again. You must wait a while, and only then approach the place with caution. I think that Ralf and his family should be isolated for a while, for the same reason."

Hild's face furrowed with sorrow, as the enormity of the news sunk in with her.

"I fear our herb-wife is right in this," Ketel added more gently.

Hild nodded sadly as the full horror of the situation became clear. "Ah yes," she agreed. "And should the sanatorium at Gilling be burned, as you burned the one at Lastingham? I was shocked to hear of such a thing at first, but I came to understand the practical sense in it. Bishop Chad is there rebuilding the monastery now, with the help of the young boy Billfrith, and there's been no sign of plague in that place since then. I was planning to send Bossa to Lastingham to help Bishop Chad and I thought that Prince Aethelred might accompany him. He would still be under the auspices of Streonshalh there, but not reminded every day that he almost died from poisoning. I thought it might be best to get him away for a while, at least until we discover who was really behind that attempt on his life."

"That might suit the Prince very well," Ketel agreed.

"I must send a message to Oswy too," Hild said with a heavy sigh. "I cannot imagine what his reaction to this news will be. Gilling was built as penance for the wrong he did and now…"

Fridgyth felt little sympathy for their overlord. "Yes," she said. "It will be whispered that this plague is judgement on him. People will say the Christ-God has rejected Oswy's efforts to buy forgiveness. Deirans will never forget how Oswy had his much-loved cousin slaughtered in order to steal his throne."

Ketel nodded. "It will be seen as a sign, and not a good one."

"I don't believe in such things," Hild said. "But you are right... it will be whispered and we must expect unrest."

They exchanged troubled glances and a moment of silence followed. The abbess closed her eyes and clasped her hands in a rare moment of despair, while Ketel shook his head, for he could find no words of comfort.

Hild looked up at them at last, with her usual expression of determination. "I have never had faith in the idea that gold can buy forgiveness," she said. "But we must simply do our best to keep the peace, as we always do."

"Yes," Fridgyth said, somewhat relieved to have delivered her disturbing message. "And I should go back to Brigsbeck now, to see how the tanner's son fares. He was distraught to discover his brother's murder and seems to blame himself somehow. I've little fear of the plague myself, having suffered it once before and I need to talk to him and see if I can discover more from him."

"Yes, go to that poor family and do the best you can for them," Hild said, "but please be careful Fridgyth. I'll talk further with my good reeve and we'll decide what's best to be done."

Fridgyth left them to discuss further the troubling significance of this new disaster. Sister Lindi passed her as she left the abbess's house. The young nun was carrying one of the beautiful leather-bound manuscripts from the scriptorium to Elfled's schoolroom.

"Fridgyth," she cried, her face full of alarm. "It is whispered in the scriptorium that Gilling is destroyed by plague."

"I fear it's true," Fridgyth acknowledged, seeing no purpose in trying to hide the fact now. "Please pass it around that nobody must think of going there. The very fabric of the building may carry the seeds of sickness. We do not want it back here again."

"God help us, no," Lindi said, and she hurried away her face flushed and her eyes wide with horror.

Fridgyth headed back down towards the tanners' yard, apprehensive as to what she might find when she got there, but before she'd even reached the spot, Herrig came tearing along the path towards her, his face fraught with concern.

"What now?" she asked.

He grabbed her arm and started to pull her along towards the tannery.

"Gone," he cried, gasping as his breath came hard with the effort of running. "We watched him through the night, but we all fell asleep at last and woke to find that he'd dressed himself and gone. It was the sound of the door that stirred us, as he was leaving!"

"Where... where has he gone?" Fridgyth asked.

"Well... I offered to run after him and his mother called out that I was to follow him."

"And did you?"

"I did, but he leapt away like a woodland creature and besides... I knew..."

"You knew where he was heading?"

He nodded. "I thought I should run to get you!"

"Of course, to the hut by the spring?" Fridgyth guessed.

"Yes... and I'm afraid to go there by myself, you know what the fay..."

"Come. We'll go together."

They hurried on, stopping only briefly to speak to the distressed parents when they got to the tanners' yard. Edric and Muriel argued gently with each other over what to do.

"Go find the reeve," Fridgyth begged the tanner. "Tell him that I'm going to the rosemary hut... he'll remember the place, I think, but just in case you can lead him there."

The man went off at once.

"I'll come with you," Muriel cried and she reached for her cloak.

"No. You stay here at home. Your boy may come to his senses and return... he will need you when he does."

The anxious mother turned back to the rumpled mattress, imprinted still with the marks of her sleeping son. She picked up the rug that had covered him and with shaking fingers she began to fold it carefully.

"Let's go!" Fridgyth told the boy.

They hurried through the woods as fast as the herb-wife could manage, but slowed down as they approached the hut. All seemed quiet there, the door and shutters closed.

"I have to go inside and see for myself," Fridgyth said.

"No, no. The fay said…" Herrig began.

"I don't need you to come inside with me," Fridgyth said. "I want you to stay here and watch, ready to warn me if you glimpse the fay. Make a loud owl hoot, if you see her coming this way. Can you do that?"

He looked somewhat relieved, and nodded vigorously.

"And if you hear me shout for help, then run for the reeve and tell him everything!"

He nodded breathlessly and crouched down behind the rosemary bushes. Fridgyth smoothed her skirts, took a deep breath and marched once again to the door of the hut. This time she didn't knock, but simply lifted the latch and, with fast beating heart, pushed the door wide. For a moment or two she stood in thick darkness, unable to see anything, relieved at least that the place seemed empty, but then she became aware of an unpleasant smell.

A low beast-like groan came from the corner where she knew the mattress lay and she caught a slight movement in the shadows. As her eyes grew more used to the darkness she began to make out the solid shape of a body – that moved again and groaned.

"Alive," she murmured.

Moving gingerly, she edged her way to the window hole and with shaking fingers she pushed open the shutter. A shard of sharp sunlight fell inside the hut, to reveal a glimpse of long dark hair. A female form lay slumped across the mattress. Whoever it was wore the familiar un-dyed monastic robe of the nuns, though this one was badly stained. The woman's hands and feet were tied behind her back and a rag was fastened round her mouth to gag her.

"Blessed Freya!" Fridgyth gasped, as she moved cautiously towards the poor prisoner. "Who has done this to you?"

The head strained upwards and blue eyes flashed frantically in the sunlight, as the woman moaned and struggled to move.

"Hold still and I will free you," Fridgyth ordered.

She took her meat-knife from the sheath that hung from her belt and knelt down. "Keep very still!" she warned, as with shaking fingers she carefully slit the restricting rag that prevented speech. It fell away to reveal a bloodless mouth and compressed lips. Fridgyth gasped in shock, for it took her a moment or two to recognise the badly bruised face.

"Irminburgh!" she cried.

The cramped lips moved awkwardly and the tongue flicked back as Irminburgh attempted speech. "C-cut... me free," she begged.

Fridgyth rolled the young woman forward to discover how her hands were tied and the odour of stale urine rose from her body.

"Ca...careful," she cried.

"This rope is tight and strong," Fridgyth warned. "I may graze you if I push the knife in too hard."

Irminburgh's mouth worked painfully slow. "Graaaze me... then," came the desperate reply.

Fridgyth pushed the knife in and nicked the soft skin slightly, but at least the prisoner's hands came free. Fridgyth tried to rub them gently, but the girl shook her head. "My ankles," she cried.

That was easier. Fridgyth was able to slip the knife between skin and rope more easily. She quickly sliced her free.

"Don't try to stand," she warned.

But too late, Irminburgh had already struggled to her feet, only to fall again.

The herb-wife sat down beside her. "What have they done to you, honey?" she said softly.

CHAPTER 28

THIS ONE SURVIVED

Irminburgh grabbed the herb-wife and hugged her tightly. "I was never so glad to see anyone," she said and she burst into tears.

Ignoring the stale smell that hung about the young woman, Fridgyth cradled her in her arms. "You are safe, now," she said.

But Irminburgh quickly pushed her away, staring wildly about her. "No. None of us are safe," she cried. She grabbed Fridgyth's shoulders and tried once again to stand. "Help me!" she cried. "The Princess! She will kill the Princess if she can."

Fridgyth stared in horror for a moment. "The princess? Which princess? You cannot mean Elfled!"

"Yes," Irminburgh almost bellowed it. "Yes, I do mean Elfled and her wolf-girl too, they are both her intended victims. She hates and loathes Oswy and she means to kill his daughter to punish him. You cannot believe how changeable she is, she can swing from seeming kindness to the foulest evil in the space of a moment. She is utterly crazy."

"But who?" Fridgyth asked in bewilderment. "Who is this crazy woman?"

"Lindi, of course!"

Fridgyth stared aghast. "Sister Lindi?"

"She is not what she seems," Irminburgh gabbled, still rubbing at her lips and mouth as though to make them work better.

"I can't believe Lindi could…" Fridgyth began. "I have just seen her."

"I did not believe it either! I thought her a warm-hearted young woman, forced by her family to enter a monastery. I felt sorry for her and befriended her; I let her try on my gowns and jewellery. I gave her gifts… rings to wear secretly to give her pleasure."

"Yes," Fridgyth acknowledged. "I saw her with a ring and thought nothing of it."

"She showed me sympathy in return," Irminburgh went on. "I needed someone to talk to, and I foolishly confided in her and told her of my love for Ecfrid. She acted as a go-between, or said she did. She brought me to this hut, promising that he would return and meet me here. She told me that he planned to take me to Eforwic with him. And so I came!" She almost screamed the words.

"But she could not…" Fridgyth began, but then her words faded, for a shiver of ice ran down her back as she realised that Lindi had been there when the young Prince asked for mushrooms… she'd been there too in the royal guest house with the Princess just before Cynewise found the rune. "You say she is not who she seems…?" she murmured.

"I know now who she is, and that she is mad with fury! She pushed me through the door and hit me on the back of the head, with a rock I think. I must have fallen senseless, for when I revived again, I found myself trussed."

"Like Godric," Fridgyth murmured.

"Yes. She killed him too, the young tanner, she told me so. He loved her and would do almost anything she asked of him, but when he refused to help her kill the Princess… he had to go… he knew too much. The lad who came here this morning was his brother, and he knows her too. He called her by a different name and she answered him."

"You must mean Ralf?"

"Yes. He stank of the tanneries and he howled at her that she'd drowned his brother, but she laughed in his face and spoke of revenge. He told her all the monks at Gilling were dead and she laughed again… she laughed with delight. Now she's gone back to the monastery and taken my clothes and left me in this nun's smock that I have soiled and I'm so… ashamed."

Tears flooded her eyes and she turned her head away unable to speak further.

Fridgyth reached out to hug her. "No shame to you, lady... the shame is all hers," she said firmly. "But we must think fast what to do, for I begin to see that many stray threads are coiled together in this woman. You say he called her by a different name?"

"Yes. They have known each other since childhood, him and his brother both. She said they owed her loyalty."

"What was this name they used?" Fridgyth asked.

"You will understand when I say it," Irminburgh said. "He called her Hunni at first and then Hunwalda!"

"Hunwalda!" Fridgyth repeated the name, frantic that she should recognise it and then suddenly she saw the significance. "He called her Hunni... not honey! Hunwalda... Hunwald's child!"

"Yes. She means to take her revenge on Oswy!"

"But Oswy is far away in Bebbanburgh... ah no! I see! She will take her revenge on him by killing his daughter. What fools we've been," Fridgyth cried. "Cynewise knew the runes must signify revenge for something long remembered. I thought that Hunwald's family had died alongside him when the hall was burned down."

Irminburgh shook her head. "This one survived, somehow she lived!"

Fridgyth found this revelation chilling, for she could see that any surviving daughter of Hunwald, could well be crazy for revenge. "And you say that Ralf, the tanner's son knows her?"

"Yes," Irminburgh was certain of that, but then she slumped forward. "I'm... hungry!" she murmured.

"Did she not give you food?" Fridgyth asked.

"No," she said forcing herself upright again. "Those are death caps hanging there. She told me cheerfully that she'd starve me till I ate them willingly."

"You've had no food for two days?"

"No, nor drink! When the lad appeared and accused her of killing his brother she showed no remorse at all, quite the opposite she was fired with rage and went off saying that she was determined to kill the Princess now!"

"We must get out of here!" Fridgyth said with sudden urgency.

Irminburgh struggled to get up again. "Yes," she cried. "For she will kill us both without compunction if she finds you here. She has a knife and she will use it."

"Can you walk?" Fridgyth asked.

"I must."

The herb-wife hauled her to her feet and threw a supportive arm around her waist. "Walk then," she ordered.

Irminburgh managed to hobble awkwardly to the door and Herrig's head rose from the rosemary bushes as soon as they appeared.

"I'm safe," Fridgyth called. "But we need help. Run to tell the reeve to hurry, he will need more men and tell him to set a guard on Princess Elfled... that is absolutely vital. Don't forget."

He stared for a moment.

"Run!"

He leapt to his feet and started to run uphill past the hut and the spring. "No," Fridgyth cried. "That's not the way."

"Let him be," Irminburgh said. "He knows better. That is the way she comes... a quicker route."

Fridgyth frowned as she watched the boy disappear amongst the trees and undergrowth. Digging deep into her memory she saw that Irminburgh was right. "Yes," she admitted, "there *was* a footpath long ago, that led that way and up towards the ruined chieftain's hall."

"The monastery," Irminburgh cried. "It goes towards the monastery."

"I should have known," Fridgyth said fiercely. Then filled with the need for haste, she tightened her grip on Irminburgh. "Come," she said. "We will go to the tanners' yard, for you need food and drink and help."

They struggled on, clinging together, saying little for they needed all their energy to navigate the woodland path. At last they arrived in sight of the tannery.

"We've been looking in the wrong direction all the time," Fridgyth muttered, angrily.

"You were intended to look in the wrong direction," Irminburgh said. "She's crazy, but she's no fool, she's crafty as a bag of eels."

"When she left, what did Ralf do?"

"He ran after her, begging her not to harm the Princess. I'd hoped he might help me, but…"

"Say nothing in front of the mother," Fridgyth warned, as Muriel appeared in the doorway, anxious for news of her son.

"Have you found him?" she asked, staring in a bewildered way at Irminburgh.

"No," Fridgyth said truthfully. "Not yet, but we will. Can you find a little bread and milk for this lady? And a bowl of warm water for her to wash in?"

"Of course," she said and without asking more, she went purposefully back into her house.

Irminburgh lowered herself carefully down onto a bench, tearful again and ashamed of her bedraggled appearance. Muriel appeared with warm milk and bread in a wooden bowl. She offered a spoon and Irminburgh gratefully accepted.

"You must eat slowly," Fridgyth warned. "Or you'll be sick."

Muriel went back into the hut and appeared again carrying a bowl of warm water and a soft woollen cloth. "I have a clean linen gown that I keep for summer," she said tactfully. "You are welcome to wear it for as long as you wish."

More tears coursed down Irminburgh's cheeks.

Fridgyth followed Muriel into the house, for she wanted to understand how Ralf could be linked to Hunwald's daughter. "Where was it that you lived, before you came to Streonshalh?" she asked.

Muriel looked surprised. "We lived at Gilling," she said. "I thought you knew that. That's why our son has links with the monastery there. Or, he *did* have links with the monastery," she corrected herself sadly.

"Did you live near Hunwald's Hall?" Fridgyth asked.

"Yes, of course. We provided him with the leather for his saddles and his boots and his shields."

"So both your sons knew Hunwald's daughter?"

"Hunni? Oh yes, they played with her, when they were small," she said with a sorrowful smile of recollection.

"So they were friends?"

"Oh yes, but I warned my boys that they must treat her gently, for she was far above their station and must marry a lord, but then..." and an expression of horror crossed her face, "...then Oswin sought shelter there and the King's men came, that terrible day..."

"And where was Hunwald's daughter, when the hall was burned down?" Fridgyth asked.

Muriel's face crumpled with anguish as she remembered. "She was with us, poor child. She fell silent, unable to speak, once we discovered what had happened up at the hall. We couldn't hide it from her."

"What did you do with her?"

"'Kept her safe until her mother's cousin came to Gilling... she and her husband, who is a thane. They were horrified at what had happened, but afraid to complain since Oswy had become so ruthless and powerful. They took young Hunni to live with them in their hall, near Eforwic. I never saw the girl again, she must be a full grown woman by now."

Fridgyth caught her breath, for she remembered that Ecfrid had discovered revenge runes at Eforwic.

"After that, we couldn't bear to stay near Gilling," Muriel said. "So... we came to Streonshalh, where we knew the abbess was looking for craftsmen and we believed we'd be safe."

"And so you should have been," Fridgyth said with a sigh. "Rosemary... for a long remembered wrong," she murmured to herself.

Muriel pulled a woad-dyed linen gown and a woollen shawl from a wooden chest and held it up in front of her. "Will these do for the lady?" she asked.

"Yes," Fridgyth nodded, though her heart sank to her boots. She dared not tell her that the girl they spoke of had been closer than she realised, and that she believed it was Hunni who'd drowned her son and in so dreadful a manner. There would be time to do that gently, but at that moment what was needed was action. They both hurried outside again to find Irminburgh staring in confusion at the filth and muddle of the tanners yard.

"Oh, what is that?" she cried.

She jumped to her feet as though she'd run off into the woods again, for they heard the sound of hooves in the distance.

"It is the reeve... the reeve is coming," Fridgyth said and she put her arms firmly about her once again to calm her. "Now listen lady, I must get back to the monastery as fast as I can. Do you wish to come with me?"

"Of course I do," Irminburgh said almost brusquely. But then she looked down at her filthy robe and glanced at the water and clean linen that had been neatly laid out for her. "But... but, I'd like to wash myself first," she added humbly.

"Of course you may do that," Fridgyth said softly.

Muriel looked from one to the other and though she had no knowledge of the woman's ordeal, she recognised distress when she saw it. "Lady, come inside with me?" she offered. "I'm no handmaid, but I'll do my best to help you and we can be more private there."

Irminburgh's lip trembled momentarily, but she pressed her lips firmly together, took the simple tunic that was being presented to her and stood up. She laid it carefully over her arm and headed shakily toward the tanners' dwelling. Muriel picked up the bucket of water and followed her inside.

CHAPTER 29

A POISONOUS SNAKE

Fridgyth watched them go into the humble dwelling, touched for a moment by Muriel's kindness and Irminburgh's unusual meekness, but as soon as they disappeared from view, a drastic sense of urgency returned. She strode to the gate of the yard, to meet the riders.

Ketel rode into the tanners' work enclosure and Fridgyth stepped back to avoid the trampling hooves, but then as soon as she could she reached up to grab his reins.

"Give me your horse," she cried. "I must warn Hild and Wulfrun. Give me your horse!"

"Warn them of what?" he asked, still in the saddle.

"The Princess is in danger."

More armed and mounted guards arrived in the cluttered yard, along with Edric and Herrig. Fridgyth tried to explain quickly what had happened, but it was difficult, she threw her arms about, aware that she gabbled and made little sense. Two frames of stretched skins were knocked to the ground and Ketel swung down from the saddle.

"The rosemary hut," she cried and pointed frantically in the direction of the woods. "You can't have forgotten it!"

A faint, puzzled smile crossed his face. "The rosemary hut? No, of course I haven't forgotten it," he said.

But this was no time for gentle memories. "You must take them there, at once," she cried. "The hut must be watched and guarded."

"But why?" he asked. "Tell me why!"

166

A small figure flashed past her and Herrig dutifully began to right the stretching frames, while Edric helped him. Fridgyth grabbed the boy's arm. "This lad knows the way, he can take them there," she said.

Herrig nodded vigorously, stunned to find himself suddenly the focus of so much attention. Fridgyth let go of him, and instead reached up to pull Ketel towards her. "I found Irminburgh there," she whispered.

He looked astounded. "In the rosemary hut?"

"Yes. She was held prisoner... and in such a state! She's here now," she said, pointing towards the tanners' home. "But let them be, for Muriel is taking care of her. Leave two men to keep them safe for now, and escort Irminburgh back to the monastery, but only when she's ready to go."

Ketel barked out orders. "You and you... stay here and guard the tannery... Edric you should stay too, the rest of you go with the boy!"

One of the mounted guards caught Herrig's arm and hauled him up onto his saddle. The boy pointed the way and the monastery guards rode off at once into the woods, raising a cloud of dust in their wake.

Fridgyth coughed as it caught in her throat and she struggled to speak for a moment, though she was agitated that Ketel was still there. "But... hrm! But aren't you going with them? Hrm!"

"No, I'm taking you back to monastery myself, if it is so urgent... and the Princess is threatened."

"It is," she said breathlessly. "Lindi is Hunwald's daughter and she is bent on revenge. Help me up!" she cried.

Ketel's eyes widened with horror at her words, but he said no more, simply crouched to help her mount. She set her foot firmly into his cupped hands and reached up to grab the saddle pommel. With a hop and a powerful shove from the reeve, she found herself seated astride the stallion, skirts inelegantly hitched at the sides.

He hauled himself up behind her and took the reins.

"We must go fast," she begged.

"Hold tight, then!"

She gripped the stallion's rough mane as the horse sprang forward. Dust rose again as Ketel wheeled the stallion about and she closed her eyes for a moment. "Too old," she murmured. "Too old for this."

But Ketel wrapped one arm tightly about her waist. "Not yet," he whispered in her ear, "not yet!"

As they galloped back through the woods towards the main track, a touch of exhilaration came to Fridgyth. She gritted her teeth and clung tightly to the stallion's mane as they cantered up the hill to find the main gates of the monastery standing open for them. The few remaining guards were on the lookout and alert to trouble. As they trotted into the courtyard, the stable boy ran to take their reins and two lads hurried to help Fridgyth dismount.

"The Princess... first," she cried, still breathless from the ride. "We have kept a poisonous snake here in the midst of our safe haven."

"I've set a guard about the abbess's house," Ketel assured her, as he swung down from the saddle. "I did that as soon as the boy brought your message, but we didn't know what it meant."

She gave a nod of approval. "But we must see that Elfled is safe and tell Hild," she added and began to run across the courtyard.

They hurried past the refectory and the weaving sheds, towards the abbess's house, where they found Hild herself on the front steps. She was deep in conversation with three guards, who clustered about her looking troubled, as the abbess clasped and unclasped her thin hands in agitation.

"Thank goodness you are here," she cried, at their approach. "You've sent these men to guard my house, but neither they nor I know why!"

"Where is Elfled?" Fridgyth demanded.

"She is in the schoolroom," Hild said.

"I must see her for myself," Fridgyth insisted.

"Yes, this is urgent, lady," Ketel said.

Still confused, but trusting them Hild led the way across the modest hall. The schoolroom consisted of a substantial lean-to, that had been set on the southern side of the building with windows and wooden shutters that could be opened to let in the light.

Hild flung the door open to reveal the neat space inside. They saw within a table, stools, maps, books laid upon shelves, all orderly, but silent and empty.

"I don't know what has happened, they *should* be here," Hild cried.

Ketel and Fridgyth exchanged a desperate glance of concern.

"Why do you look like that?" Hild asked.

"I am so sorry," Fridgyth said, "but we fear that Lindi intends to harm our Princess. I believe her to be behind the runes and the death of Godric!"

Hild stared at her shocked. "Lindi?" she murmured. "Sister Lindi? But…"

"She is not who you think she is," Fridgyth hurried on. "She is Hunwald's daughter! Hunwalda is her true name!"

Hild looked horror struck. "No…" she murmured, for she immediately understood the significance of this disclosure. "Hunwald's child! But… I met her once, long ago… a sweet-spoken little girl, who carried the drink horn to her father's guests. I would have known her… surely? She died with the rest of her family."

Fridgyth took Hild's trembling hands in hers, for she realised how utterly devastating this revelation was. "No, she survived. She was just a girl when you knew her, she is a woman now and a clever one. She made very sure that you didn't recognise her, a nun's habit makes a good disguise. Did you see her before she took her vows?"

Hild shook her head. "No. She came from Hartlepool, with the best of commendations from Abbess Winfred. She is an excellent scribe and…"

"I think she has been planning her revenge for a very long time. When Hunwald betrayed our much-loved King on Oswy's orders, he was repaid with death! The girl's mother and siblings perished too. What would that do to even the sweetest nature? The girl is eaten up with rage, and I fear she will stop at nothing to get her revenge."

"Indeed," Hild replied darkly. "And you say she intends to harm my Elfled?"

"Dear friend," Fridgyth said urgently. "There's no time to explain this gently. I found Irminburgh imprisoned in a hut in the woods.

169

Lindi had led her there by trickery and has treated her most cruelly. There's no time to waste, Lindi's intended victim is Elfled!"

Hild's eyes flew wide with fear. "She'd harm my Elfled, to punish Oswy! Dear God, we must stop her, but how?"

"Could she have taken Elfled to her cell?"

Hild's face grew paler still, though she forced herself to remain calm. "Come," she commanded in a voice that was touched with ice.

She led them at great speed out of her house and Ketel signalled the startled guards to follow. The abbess headed for the nun's monastic enclosure. Here were the rows of small huts that housed the most dedicated women, those who chose to spend their time in prayer and silence. They ate little, and allowed themselves few comforts.

Ketel hesitated to enter this forbidden area, but Hild waved him on. "Come!" she ordered. "Bring the guards too! There are times when rules must be broken!"

Several curious heads popped out from the surrounding huts at the sound of voices. There were a few shocked expressions at the sight of their leader bringing three armed warriors into a forbidden area, though silence was still observed.

The abbess marched towards the second row and approached the first hut. She took the latch-lifter that swung from her belt and slotted it into the hole that marked the lock. Though her fingers were twisted and painful, she heaved with all her strength and lifted the interior latch. With a small click, the door swung open.

They huddled together to gape into the tiny space. It was empty too, but it was like no other cell on the monastery site, for two stunningly dyed gowns, richly braided, hung on nails, one golden, the other a soft green. A gold and garnet necklace, that Fridgyth thought she'd seen adorning Irminburgh's neck, lay on a wooden prayer stall. However, the two things that drew their eyes and filled them with utter dread were: the bundle of dried rosemary that hung from another nail, and a small stack of weaving tablets with the warning rune cut into their surfaces, which lay on the floor.

Hild clasped her hands to her veiled head. "My precious child!" she whispered.

Ketel turned as pale as Hild. "Where could they have gone?" he muttered.

Fridgyth racked her brains, trying desperately to think clearly, but then she looked up and tapped her head twice with her fist. "The rosemary hut," she cried. "Lindi doesn't know that Irminburgh has been found... surely she will take them there."

"But how would they get there?" Ketel cried. "We'd have passed them on the way! We should have asked at the stables if they'd taken horses!"

He turned and started to run back. Two of the guards followed him, while the other hesitated, concerned to do the right thing by his abbess.

Fridgyth took Hild's arm and they followed as quickly as they could.

"Ketel has sent men to watch the hut," she tried to explain to Hild. "The forager boy has gone with them to lead the way... but I fear the sight of them would have alerted Hunwald's child."

Hild shook her head frantically as they struggled on. "But would the girls go willingly?" she asked. "Wulfrun is so very protective of our Princess."

Fridgyth shook her head. "I fear she has plans for Wulfrun too, and will get rid of her by whatever means she can. Lindi persuaded Irminburgh to trust her and I'd say that's not an easy thing to do. I believe she will stop at nothing, for this woman must feel deeply wronged."

"Yes," Hild said with shudder. "If she is Hunwald's daughter she *has* reason to hate... but not to hate Elfled. I too put trust in her and she told me she was an orphan..."

"Well... in that she was not lying."

CHAPTER 30

THE OLD TROD

Ketel appeared from the stables and strode towards them, shaking his head in bewilderment. "None of the horses have been taken," he said. "But one of the lads saw the Princess earlier, walking with Wulfrun and her tutor towards the orchard. Perhaps they were heading for the southern gate."

Hild frowned. "But why would they leave that way on foot?" she asked.

"Perhaps to draw less attention?" Fridgyth surmised, though another vague possibility seemed to hover at the back of her mind, a possibility that she could not quite reach out and grasp.

"We'll go there!" Ketel said.

So, with one accord, they turned and headed for the southern gate, while the bewildered guards still followed them.

"Surely they wouldn't go this way?" Hild murmured, still troubled by the very idea of it. "Without horses they can only follow the path to Flither Bay."

The hamlet that lay to the south of Streonshalh consisted merely of a few fisherman's shacks that clung to the cliffside, where the people scraped a hard won living from the sea. Flither Bay was certainly an unlikely direction for Lindi to take. As they hurried along, the sense of something troubling at the back of Fridgyth's mind grew stronger... and suddenly she grasped it.

She tugged at Ketel's sleeve. "Not Flither Bay, but the old trod," she said. "You remember the old woman's trod! That's how Lindi comes and goes so secretly. Herrig ran this way when he came to find you."

Ketel frowned, but then nodded. "You mean the narrow path that once led up through the woods towards the remains of the chieftains hall. But that has not been used since the abbess built the monastery."

"I think it *has* been used," Fridgyth said. "Herrig knows it. I have wondered at times how he appeared so early at my door and why I did not see him coming up the hill. The tanner lads must know it too."

They rounded the scriptorium to find the southern gate standing open, as it usually did in the hours of daylight, and no sign of travellers on the road beyond the gate.

Hild spoke directly to the gatekeeper. "Who has passed this way today?"

The man bowed and began to recite a list. "The fish-seller with his cart... the salter with his mule..."

"Has Sister Lindi come this way?" Hild cut in sharply.

"No, lady."

"Nor Princess Elfled either?"

"No... but I saw the Princess and her wolf-girl in the orchard... walking with Lady Irminburgh."

Hild looked stunned. "You say Irminburgh?"

The man frowned. "I think so, lady," he said.

Fridgyth touched Hild's arm and spoke low and urgent. "Not Irminburgh... but Lindi perhaps... Hunwalda, dressed as Irminburgh."

"Yes!" Hild replied with swift understanding.

"The ladies wore cloaks... and I thought one of them was the Lady Irminburgh," the man said with less certainty.

They turned swiftly and marched back towards the orchard.

"The old path would come out somewhere near these palings," Ketel pointed out. "But how could Lindi know...?"

"Godric!" Fridgyth's answer came quickly now. "Godric and Ralf! Those boys know every pathway through the woods, and they've known Hunwald's daughter since she was a child. Herrig too... the boy was never stealing apples or honey from the orchard, he was using the loosened paling as a shortcut to get inside the monastery! Come!"

Fridgyth strode across the grass, past Sister Redburgh's hives. She began feeling her way along the palings and Ketel, seeing her purpose, did the same. It was he who suddenly sensed that one of the strong timbers might be moved and when he pushed it, it slipped quietly to the side and revealed a low opening, just wide enough for a person to slip through.

"Heavens!" Hild murmured. "And we thought we were secure!"

Beyond the loosened paling they could see a track where feet had marked a faint pathway.

"The old trod," Fridgyth said.

"I think it will lead us into the woods," Ketel said. He turned to Hild. "Lady you should stay here, the way will be rough and the trod was never wide enough to be a bridleway. We cannot even lead a mule along it."

But Hild was determined. "I'm coming with you," she said. "I'll not return without my girls… and that means Wulfrun too."

Ketel gestured the three guards to follow. One by one they squeezed through the opening and set off downhill towards the woods. At first the path was clear enough to follow and though Hild held onto Fridgyth's arm for support, they made remarkable speed. However, as Ketel predicted, once they were in the woods it became more difficult, for roots and brambles dragged at their legs. The path was narrow and overgrown, but clear enough to follow.

"I don't exactly know how, or why she did it," Fridgyth said, "but I'm sure that Lindi killed Godric."

"But how could she, a woman kill such a strong young man?" Hild gasped.

"She has the strength of anger," Fridgyth said. "Her rage and resentment has festered for years. She knocked Irminburgh unconscious and tied her up, and I think she must have done the same to Godric… you remember the wound on the back of his head? And I think he was devoted to her."

"The trouble is..." Hild said bitterly as they stumbled on, "I cannot take all of this in fast enough. If what you suspect is true, then I should have some sympathy for the girl, but to threaten my dear Elfled's life!" she stopped, gasping for breath.

"Hush now, do not think that way," Fridgyth advised, though she was breathless too.

"If only she'd gone about redress in a different way," Hild said, "I could have tried to help her, but that Elfled should pay for her father's treachery... it is unthinkable," she ended.

"We are on to her now," Fridgyth said firmly, though she spoke with a confidence she did not feel. "This pathway is hard-going, but much shorter than the outer road. We came this way when we were young, Ketel and I," she acknowledged with a glance ahead at him. "We met in the woods, and never thought then..."

"Thank God you knew of it," Hild said.

Fridgyth glanced ahead at Ketel's back, grateful that she could still rely on his strength and support, but then she saw that both he and the men were quietly turning around and moving back to them.

"They've seen something," she whispered.

Ketel lifted his hand to warn them to be quiet, and soon they caught sight of the three young women ahead of them, appearing and disappearing as they walked amongst the trees. They went arm in arm, chattering excitedly, a vision of cheerful, energetic youth, so that for a moment Fridgyth felt doubt. They appeared to be so innocent, intent only on a brief adventure.

"It's hard to tell which one is which," she whispered.

"But that is Irminburgh in the middle," Hild said, frowning in doubt. "Though we cannot see her face, it is her height, her very walk."

"No," Fridgyth said firmly and suddenly she was certain again. "I left Irminburgh hungry, distressed and wearing a stained gown, just shortly after noon. I left her in Muriel's cottage, weeping and desperately ashamed. I know that looks like Irminburgh ahead of us, but it is not."

Then Fridgyth saw Hild's expression change to one of quiet fury. "You are right," she said calmly. "One of those young women is a nun, yet none of them wear the habit. Lindi's very garb proclaims her guilt. What are they doing here? Sister Lindi should be teaching the girls to write, in the schoolroom."

As they watched, the tallest of the young women ahead of them turned momentarily, it was only a brief gesture, but it betrayed concern that they might be followed.

The watchers froze, fearful that they'd be observed. The woman's hood slipped back a little and they caught a glimpse of a beautiful, determined face, a flash of long, golden hair, unlike any Streonshalh nun. The movement was so light and brief that her companions were not aware of it, but the abbess had seen.

"That is not the woman I thought I knew," Hild whispered.

"No indeed," Fridgyth agreed.

The three girls moved on.

CHAPTER 31

THE SWEETEST CHILD

"There's no end to the wrath of bees – vexed, they'll inflame their stings with poison and, fastening to a vein, deposit darts that you can't see. Inflicting harm, they'll forfeit their own lives."

Virgil – *Georgics*. A new translation by Peter Fallon
Oxford World's Classics

"I think we should not to rush at them," Ketel said in a low voice. "We want the Princess safe, but we must be careful, for Irminburgh says that the woman has a knife. The men I sent with Herrig should be near the hut… so if we allow the three of them to move a little closer to that spot, that might be best."

"Yes," Fridgyth agreed. "We must be careful… we do not know how she might react."

Hild nodded, understanding that if Hunwalda was startled, it might provoke disaster. They went on, following the three young women as carefully and as quietly as they could, still keeping to the shelter of the trees. In a little while they came in sight of the rosemary hut and watched as the girls approached it.

"Do we allow them to go inside?" Fridgyth asked worriedly. "Once they are inside we cannot know what's happening."

Ketel frowned looking keenly about. "Where are the men I sent to guard the place? Where is the boy Herrig? We need to move closer, I think, but I'm afraid we may alert Hunwalda."

But before the young women could reach the hut, a slight figure emerged from the woodland close by and strode forward purposefully to cut across their path. It took a few moments for them to see that it was Irminburgh, for she was dressed in Muriel's pale blue gown, her lips clean of berry juice and her hair tied back in a peasant woman's knot.

Elfled was the first to recognise her. She threw back her own hood eagerly. "Is he here?" she called. "Is my brother here? But Irminburgh… why do you look so…?"

Irminburgh raised her hand to halt them in their tracks and she screamed out the words. "He isn't here! Your brother was never here!" Then she pointed to Hunwalda. "That woman has fooled you! Run, Princess… run! She means to kill you."

Ketel drew his sword and leapt headlong into the open, throwing caution to the wind. The three guards that had followed them rushed forward at his command. Elfled stared frantically from Irminburgh to her tutor and then glanced back to see the startling sight of the reeve advancing, sword in hand, with three guards close behind, weapons at the ready.

"What is happening?" she cried.

Hunwalda turned too and saw Ketel. She also glimpsed the abbess and the herb-wife, following more slowly. Her attention was dragged back to the surrounding woodland, as more and more figures emerged quietly from amongst the trees and bushes. Ralf strode forward, with Herrig at his side and, one by one, the guards that Ketel had sent to guard the hut appeared also with weapons drawn.

"Do not do it, Hunni," Ralf cried. "Beg mercy of the abbess… for you too have suffered! Make amends for what you have done and you may yet live."

As yet more men emerged from amongst the surrounding undergrowth, Hunwalda saw that she was surrounded.

"Ralf speaks with wisdom… give yourself up," Ketel cried. "Let no more harm be done!"

Hunwald's daughter turned this way and that, and then she gave a terrifying howl of mad laughter. "Do you think I am afraid to die?" she shrieked.

Then to everyone's horror she lurched towards Elfled. "I will die gladly... so long as I take Oswy's child with me!" she cried.

A knife glinted in her hand and the weapon flew towards Elfled with a powerful thrust. But Hunwalda was not the only one who carried a knife and in that same moment, Wulfrun lunged forward, pushing Elfled to the side. She placed herself between the princess and her attacker, making a fierce counter stab with the wolf-handled meat knife. Elfled screamed and the watchers gaped in horror as the two young women struggled together, then Hunwalda staggered backwards, staring down at herself in astonishment as blood spurted from her shoulder. With a small gasp, Wulfrun too fell back into Elfled's arms.

"No," Elfled howled. "She has stabbed my wolf girl."

Ketel moved fast, but Hunwalda growled with fury as she realised that she'd been foiled of her long-planned revenge. With both hands she gripped the hilt of her knife and plunged the blade back into her own body. Ketel grabbed her from behind as Ralf ran forward to help him hold her. She collapsed as she was taken.

Elfled, still clutching Wulfrun, looked desperately around. "Herb-wife!" she screamed. "Let the herb-wife through! You have to save her... Fridgyth you have to save her!"

Wulfrun turned pale and lost consciousness.

Fridgyth rushed forwards and crouched down awkwardly on the muddy ground. She pulled strips of clean, rolled, linen from her girdle. "Moss!" she cried, trying frantically to think fast. "Herrig... can you find moss!"

The boy vanished into the undergrowth.

Fridgyth took her own small meat knife from its sheath and used it to slit open the linen gown that Wulfrun wore beneath her cloak. There was a moment of uncertainty and more cutting, and blood – a good deal of blood – but then she saw something that made her smile.

"What are you doing?" Elfled cried. "If Wulfrun dies..."

"She will not die," Fridgyth said with certainty. "She is shocked and bleeding, but you are not going to lose her."

"How can you be so sure?"

"Because she is wearing a strong, protective leather jerkin beneath her gown. See for yourself."

Elfled bent down to see that Fridgyth was right. She hugged her friend. "You, did it," she cried. "You got them to make you a leather bodice and I didn't know."

"Careful now," Fridgyth warned. "She is still losing blood and I will have to cut this leather away, so that I can pack the wound."

Hild moved to where Hunwalda lay and stood looking down at the pitiful sight. The men stood guard about the young woman, but it was clear that her life was swiftly ebbing away. Ralf dropped down at her side, his face twisted with misery.

"I could not let you do it…" he began.

"Fool," she flung at him. "Just like your brother."

"Confess and ask forgiveness, Hunwald's child," Hild said. "The Christ-God is a compassionate God and even now you may be saved from damnation."

Hunwalda looked up with bitter hatred in her eyes. "No Christ-God's heaven for me…" she said. "No warrior's feasting hall. I die in battle and yet for me there is nothingness… not even revenge."

She gave a small cough, and blood trickled from the corner of her mouth. She struggled for a moment to breathe, but then fell limp, eyes open but unseeing.

Irminburgh went to stand at Hild's side.

The abbess gently took her hand in hers. "That was bravely done," she acknowledged. "I saw a noble Irminburgh today."

They watched together in solemn silence for a few moments, until Ketel bent to gently close the woman's eyes.

"Poor child," Hild murmured. "Poor Hunwald's child… she has suffered greatly and we have failed her."

Ketel turned uncertainly to the abbess. "What of burial rights…?" he asked uncertainly.

"Not Christian ones," Hild said firmly. "Tell them to build a pyre near the old chieftain's hall. They will know what to do, I think," she added after a moments thought.

"Yes," Ketel said quietly. "They will know what to do."

Then the abbess turned and walked back to where Wulfrun lay, just as Herrig reappeared with a handful of fresh green moss.

"Bless you boy," Fridgyth said. She took the moss and packed it carefully round the wound. "This will make an excellent poultice… better than anything."

Wulfrun's eyelids fluttered and opened. She groaned and immediately tried to get up.

"Stay still!" Fridgyth commanded.

"But the Princess…" she gasped.

"I'm here, unharmed," Elfled said at once.

"And our tutor…?"

"Is dead," Elfled finished for her.

Wulfrun's expression changed to one of horror. "I have killed her?"

"No," Elfled told her roundly. "She killed herself. I should have listened to you… I know that now, but…"

Wulfrun coughed as her hand went to the packed wound, where more blood seeped through the moss.

"Be still," Fridgyth warned, a finger raised. "I think this is not the time to speak, Princess," she added more gently.

Elfled nodded and crouched down beside her friend to take her hand.

Ralf too dropped down on his knees on the other side of Wulfrun, frowning with concern. "Did it work?" he asked.

"Yes," Elfled told him.

Fridgyth smiled. "I should have known that it was your handiwork," she said. "There is a wound, but it is a flesh wound and it would surely have been a death thrust, but for the protection that the leather bodice gave."

Elfled got up and moved towards the abbess. "I don't know how…" she began. "This is my fault. Sister Lindi somehow persuaded me that my brother would return to meet us all here."

"No, none of this is your fault," Hild said and she held her arms wide to her foster daughter. Elfled went to her and wept on her shoulder, while Irminburgh watched them quietly.

"What did she do to you, Irminburgh?" Elfled asked, when she at last raised her head.

"She hurt my pride, rather than my body," Irminburgh said.

"My dears," Hild murmured, as she put an arm round each of them. "This is not the fault of either of you. We must simply make sure that nothing like it can happen again."

"Help me up," Fridgyth said to Ralf.

He hauled her to her feet, as men arrived with a stretcher to carry Wulfrun back to the monastery.

A slow and sorrowful procession made its way back through the woods, past the tanners' home and back up the hill to the monastery. The abbess was offered a horse, but she refused.

Fridgyth and Ralf brought up the rear.

"I understand now," she said. "Godric measured Wulfrun for the bodice, and when I saw him doing it, I mistook it for a lovers embrace. Our wolf-girl will recover well, I think."

"The bodice had to fit exactly," Ralf said, "and yet be soft enough to make it comfortable to wear, but sturdy enough to give protection. I knew that the smell of my trade was offensive to her, for leather smells even worse than vellum from the calves and so I asked Godric..."

"And I have wondered recently if your special lady was Hunwalda," Fridgyth admitted. "I feared that you and your brother had quarrelled over her."

Ralf looked puzzled for a moment. "Ah no," he said. "Hunni was always my brother's love... though a troubled and deadly passion it turned out to be. I wanted to win the affection of a brave lass... a wolf-girl," he whispered with a worried glance ahead. "I thought that since the jeweller had gone, maybe there might be a chance, for me."

"And maybe there still will be," Fridgyth said.

Ralf's expression darkened. "As soon as I heard of Godric's death, I feared that Hunwalda had killed him... Godric would do anything she asked of him. I knew it was wrong of him to be meeting her since she'd become a nun. But he was my brother; I couldn't be disloyal to him. When I discovered that her true purpose was to kill the Princess, I followed her, determined to prevent it."

Fridgyth shook her head. "Aye, we've all discovered her plan rather late in the day," she said. "But you did well… at least Elfled is safe, for now."

"It is hard to believe it," he said sadly. "Hunni was the sweetest child, and we both adored her back then."

"I do believe it," Fridgyth said. "Who knows what it would do, to witness the father you honoured, compelled to betray his friend… and then punished for that betrayal by death… and the rest of her family too. The abbess and the reeve will have to examine it all, but don't be afraid about that; I will speak for you and the part you played. There is no blame attached to you."

The slow walk back, with Wulfrun carried carefully on the stretcher, somehow helped them all to collect their thoughts, though it would be a while before any of them came to terms with what had happened that day.

CHAPTER 32

WINTERFULLMOON

The news of what had taken place down in the wooded valley spread around the monastery. Everyone was stunned to discover that they had kept a murderer in their midst. A subdued atmosphere hung over Streonshalh as the weather turned cool. Offeringsmonth came to an end and Winterfullmoon began to turn the land silver with frost each morning. Rain and hail soon followed, making life more difficult, as the ground turned to mud. The last of the fruits were gathered in and the growing lambs and calves were prepared for slaughter. Within the sturdy monastic palisade, troubled discussions took place beside the smoking hearths, as everyone mulled over the shocking events.

Abbess Hild agonised more than most and wrote carefully worded letters, telling of the dreadful events that had taken place. Messengers were sent to carry these tidings to King Oswy at Bebbanburgh and to Ecfrid in his new timber palace at Eforwic. Prince Aethelred went willingly enough to Lastingham, with Brother Bossa as his mentor, to help rebuild the devastated community there. Fridgyth recalled a promise made in more settled times, and she appeared in the abbess's parlour, on a cold afternoon late in the month.

"I know you have much on your mind," she began, "but I made a promise and I should try to keep that promise now, I think."

Hild looked up from a vellum scroll that she was reading and Fridgyth saw that tears glistened in her eyes.

"Oh, what is wrong?" Fridgyth asked.

Hild shook her head. "No. Tell me first, what this promise is that you made."

"It was to the Mercian Queen," Fridgyth said. "I promised her that I would visit her at Handale Head. I said I'd try to make her more comfortable before the cold weather really sets in, and now that we are settling down a little here again…"

Hild looked even more distraught and a tear ran down her cheek. She let go of the vellum scroll and held both her hands up in distress, so that the vellum rolled up tightly again. "Too late, I fear," she said. "This tells me so. It is too late."

Fridgyth peered down at the scroll, but its magical markings meant nothing to her. "What do you mean?" she asked.

Hild shook her head. "This is a letter from Ecfrid, in Eforwic. Messengers reached him five days ago, from Handale Head, telling him that Cynewise had died."

"No," Fridgyth murmured.

She pulled out a chair and sat down, for her legs felt suddenly weak. "Too late to keep my promise then," she murmured.

"Yes," Hild said. "Ecfrid wants me to send a party of lay brothers to Handale to help with funeral arrangements. He wishes his foster mother to be given the burial rights due to a great and honoured queen."

"Quite right," Fridgyth said. "I surprise myself, but I think after all that she was an honourable woman."

"Yes," Hild agreed, with just the touch of a gentle smile. "I'm glad you changed your mind on that. Messengers are to be sent far and wide with invitations to gather at Handale Head for the funeral feast. If you would like to come with me, you will have your chance to say farewell to her."

"Thank you," Fridgyth said.

The herb-wife left the abbess's house and went out into the meadow to see her bees. "The Queen is dead," she announced to them. "The Queen of a distant hive is dead, and I'm deeply saddened at this news."

The bees buzzed gently around her, huddling close together as the weather turned cool. They would soon give up their foraging to settle for the winter, for the last flowers had almost gone and the tiny creatures would need to protect their Queen, in order to keep her warm through the coldest spells.

Fridgyth, now well stocked with honey-pots, would cease to steal their treasure, for the tiny creatures needed the powerful sweetness for themselves, during the harsh winter months. She'd visit them of course, to share her thoughts, and check that they were safe.

The news of Cynewise's death spread through the community, and many expressed regret, for it seemed the notion of Penda's widow as the fearful dragon-wife had altered somewhat, following her visit.

Fridgyth found Irminburgh sitting in the abbess's parlour with Hild one morning. As she entered the chamber, she immediately sensed tension in the air.

"I'll come back later," she said.

"No, wait," Hild said. "Would you feel that you could share your request with the herb-wife?" she asked turning to Irminburgh.

"They will all know soon enough," the young woman demurred.

Since her encounter with Hunwald's daughter, the Kentish noblewoman had changed hugely. Fridgyth had worried once or twice that she was looking very pale and thin. She sat down now and waited for what might come.

After a moment of silence she ventured to speak. "If there is anything that I can do, I'll be glad to help," she offered, expecting that it was the woman's health that was causing concern.

Irminburgh looked up at her with a challenging glance. "I want to be a nun," she said firmly.

Fridgyth was stunned to hear it. "But why?" she asked.

"There is nothing else left for me," Irminburgh said.

"And what does our abbess say to that?" Fridgyth asked, though she struggled to prevent herself from throwing a mocking glance towards Hild.

"I am advising a period of thoughtfulness," Hild said calmly. "It is a huge decision to make."

Fridgyth saw that Hild was right to take the matter seriously, though she couldn't think of anyone less suited to becoming a nun.

"There are other ways for a woman to live a fulfilling life," Fridgyth said. "Many thanes or noblemen would be honoured to have you as a wife, and I for one find great satisfaction in what I do."

"Would you have me cleaning up the sick?" Irminburgh asked, with a flash of her old self.

"As a nun, you might be required to do just that," Hild said.

Irminburgh bowed her head sadly. "Then I would do it," she said quietly.

"I am not saying no to you," Hild said. "Simply that you must take time to think it through."

"Thank you," Irminburgh said.

"Do you wish to come to Cynewise's funeral?" Hild asked the girl. "You do not have to come. Our young King will lead the ceremony and must take the role of host, as Cynewise was his foster mother."

She did not mention Audrey, though they all knew that this must mean that Ecfrid's wife would be expected too to take the role of hostess.

"I will go," Irminburgh said quietly. "Cynewise was my foster mother too."

She got up to leave the chamber. Only when she'd gone, did Hild and Fridgyth exchanged meaningful looks.

"What do you think of that?" Hild asked.

"I think she has been deeply hurt," Fridgyth replied. "She must feel that she's been taken for a fool. She offered herself as Ecfrid's mistress, only to discover that his acceptance of such an arrangement was yet another deceit."

Hild nodded. "The instinct to hide herself away in a monastery is very natural in such circumstances."

"But we know the real Irminburgh," Fridgyth said. "I never thought that I would say this," she added with a wry smile, "but in time, I hope the lively, ruthless Irminburgh will come back to us. Though a little more concern for others would not go amiss."

Preparations for the funeral went steadily ahead. It was rumoured that Ecfrid had ordered a special mortuary to be built, to allow the Queen's body lie in state, while many of the most powerful people in the land made arrangements to travel to Handale Head for this important day. The frost would aid the preservation of the body, but wind and rain must hinder the hazardous journeys that would need to be made over the next few weeks.

Fridgyth went into the weaving shed, one bright afternoon, with the intention of finding Cwen, only to discover that Elfled was already there, with Wulfrun, looking much recovered.

"Dark red goes with gold," Elfled was saying. "Queen Cynewise loved shining gold, set against a good strong red. Do you think you could do it?"

"Yes, Princess," Cwen said with a brief bow. "Madder with a touch of bramble juice works well and it will suit your colouring."

"No, it is not for me? It's for Wulfrun," Elfled insisted.

Wulfrun laughed at her mother's surprised look. "The Princess insists that I must have this gown," she said. "For Queen Eanfleda is to present me with a gold brooch! A letter was brought by sea, this morning!"

"And why not?" Fridgyth agreed. "You deserve it."

Ralf appeared in the doorway. "The horses are ready, Princess," he announced. "And it is a fine afternoon for a ride."

The two girls followed him out excitedly, leaving both the older women smiling quietly.

"Wulfrun looks so much better," Fridgyth commented.

"Yes, thanks to you," Cwen said.

"And a certain young tanner," Fridgyth said, nodding her head to where Ralf had appeared.

Cwen nodded. "The Princess will not let Wulfrun out of her sight," she said. "And the abbess has given the tanner permission to accompany them when they ride. He has made two new leather bodices, one for Wulfrun and one for the Princess, for the abbess had seen that these strange garments have proved their worth."

"And I see that you are overworked," Fridgyth said. " Though I too thought I might ask for your help in obtaining a new gown. I grew to respect Queen Cynewise and I'd like to look presentable at her burial rights."

Cwen looked thoughtful for a moment, but then wandered over to a wooden chest, flung open the lid and pulled out a length of cloth, newly dyed to a soft moss green.

"Ah yes," Fridgyth cried in delight. "That would be perfect for me, what a lovely shade."

"Weld, with a touch of bramble juice and iron rust," Cwen said, as she folded the soft woollen cloth into a neat bundle.

"Are you not coming with us to Handale Head?" Fridgyth asked. "Queen Eanfleda will be there, and pleased to see you. You would be treated as an honoured guest."

Cwen shook her head. "You know me too well by now to ask such things, herb-wife. I am happiest here, quietly weaving and dyeing the cloths and living peacefully, that is my joy in life."

And she put the folded cloth into Fridgyth's arms.

"Now what can I give you in exchange," Fridgyth asked.

"You have already paid for this," Cwen said. "You paid for it when you were there to save my daughter's life."

Fridgyth kissed her cheek and went away with a smile upon her face.

CHAPTER 33

HANDALE HEAD

"When their queen is safe and sound, they are all at peace. But when she dies their trust is shredded, and they take to wrecking honey halls and sacking well-wrought honeycombs."

Virgil – Georgics. A new translation by Peter Fallon.
Oxford World's Classics

On the appointed day of the funeral, a bitterly cold wind blew down from the north. Forty lay-brothers hauled on the oars of Abbess Hild's barge as it moved through the sea, heading northwest towards the towering, whale-like mass of Handale Head.

Ketel, content for an opportunity to return to one of his old skills, took the steering oar and capably swung the boat around, so that it headed landward towards the small but sturdy wharf that had been built below the cliffs. This safe landing place had been made long ago, in a suitable spot where the cliffs sloped steeply down to the Salt Skimmer's Valley.

Fridgyth sat in the centre of the barge with Caedmon at her side. He continually checked the leather bag that contained his harp, to be sure that it was undamaged and all the strings were sound.

"Leave be," Fridgyth told him, "you'll fret that instrument to pieces."

He smiled and tried to settle his nerves, for he'd been asked to sing at the funeral feast. On the other side of the herb-wife sat a quiet, much chastened Irminburgh.

"Are you ready?" Fridgyth asked gently, as the boat nosed its way towards the wharf.

"I'll never be ready, to lose my foster mother," she said sadly.

"Are you ready to meet our young King and his wife," Fridgyth said with a meaningful look, though she kept her voice low.

"I'll never be ready for that, either," Irminburgh admitted and she gave a small sigh.

Elfled stood silent and thoughtful in the prow, with Wulfrun at her side and the abbess close by. All the women were dressed in their best gowns, but covered in hoods and cloaks for warmth. For the most part, they were silent and reflective, for the burial rights of a queen were no small matter, and Penda's Queen had once been the most powerful woman in the land.

As they neared the wharf, a small ripple of anticipation passed amongst the passengers; hoods were pushed back, veils straightened, skirts smoothed and jewellery touched into place. Though they found many large boats tied up at the wharf and barely room left for them, Ketel managed deftly to manoeuvre the barge in between two smaller vessels.

Everyone knew that Cynewise's oldest son Wulfhere, now Mercia's ruler, had already arrived to attend the ceremony, along with Prince Aethelred. Even the ageing King of Wessex, had made the long and arduous journey north, to be present at the burial of his older sister. Queen Eanfleda had arrived from Bebbanburgh to represent her husband, for Oswy, overlord of all the lands north of the Humber, was too busy with preparations for his pilgrimage to Rome.

Mildred and the granary keeper from Streonshalh had travelled ahead by land with carts of grain and beasts to slaughter, along with vats of wine and ale.

The Handale reeve was there by the wharf to meet them, with mules, horses and litters, ready to carry important visitors up the steep slope. The abbess accepted a place in a litter, acknowledging that without it she'd be struggling.

"Who has arrived?" the abbess asked as she stepped inside the light, wooden construction.

"Everyone except King Ecfrid," the reeve replied. "But our outriders have seen him on the road. He should be with us soon."

"Good," Hild said, with a nod. "And I have brought John, our priest as the King requested. He will conduct the Christian part of the ceremony."

"That is good," the reeve said, with a bow; but then he added tentatively. "You know lady, that the Queen requested to be buried in her bed?"

Hild smiled faintly. "Cynewise and I came to a clear understanding," she assured him. "I respect her beliefs, as she respected mine, but I understand that some of her women have taken to the Christian religion, so we may have a Christian blessing as well. "

The man smiled with some relief. "We have accommodated your party in the hall," he said with a bow. "It will be a little cramped in there, but as it is only for one night…"

"We will manage well," Hild assured him.

"Our other royal visitors have set up tents."

Hild climbed aboard the swaying litter and glanced around her. "Fridgyth, come and sit here with me," she said.

The herb-wife consented cheerfully. Elfled invited Irminburgh to share the litter that was provided for her and Wulfrun, and she accepted the kind gesture quietly. Ketel was given a strong gelding to ride and a small procession formed, and moved forward to negotiate the steep and winding path.

Fridgyth watched for her first glimpse of the hall that Oswy had built for the widow of his most ferocious enemy. As they reached the summit of the cliffs, they began to see a high timber roof. As more came into view they perceived that the hall bore a startling pediment, carved into the shape of a dragon's head, painted gold and dark red.

Fridgyth's mouth dropped open at the sight of it.

"What do you think of Cynewise's Hall?" Hild asked, smiling gently.

"No wonder she preferred to stay here," Fridgyth said. "We called her the dragon-wife, but I never knew why!"

"I believe that was Ecfrid's suggestion," Hild said, "another small token of his respect for her, for the dragon is the symbol of Wessex, rather than the Mercian hog."

The hall was set well back from the edge of the huge cliffs, to protect it from the bitter north wind. Surrounded by many more small halls and huts, it lay at the centre of a substantial royal settlement. As they moved closer still, they saw that an astonishing spread of tents covered the fields all around, each marked with its banners, attendant warriors, horses and servants.

"Cynewise would be pleased to see this," Fridgyth said.

The litter was carried to the main entrance of the hall and set down. They climbed out and were led into the somewhat crowded accommodation of the women's bower, but nobody complained that they must share beds.

They'd had little time to take in these new surroundings, when Queen Eanfleda appeared. "Oh my darling girl," she cried, enveloping Elfled in her arms. "I am so sorry that your father couldn't come."

Elfled kissed her dutifully. "Never mind, Mother," she said calmly.

"Oh my daughter, you have grown so tall... suddenly you are a woman." Eanfleda stood back more respectfully to appraise this new, quieter, rather more poised Princess.

"Yes, Mother," Elfled said with a gentle smile. "I have grown a lot."

Fridgyth guessed that Eanfleda knew few details of the more recent traumatic events in her daughter's life, and for everyone's sake she judged it better for it to stay that way.

They set about unpacking the things they would need overnight and despite the solemn, sadness of the occasion, a sense of excitement seemed to build at the importance of the event.

Cynewise's waiting women gathered sadly around Elfled and Wulfrun, exchanging greetings. A good deal of whispering went on and a few interested glances were thrown towards Irminburgh. When she got her chance to do it, Elfled sidled up to Fridgyth.

"My brother is late," she said. "And I don't know why! They say that he and Audrey went to visit Bishop Wilfrid at Ripon and Audrey is making plans to travel to Coldingham, instead of coming here."

Fridgyth looked up with interest. "So, your brother will arrive without his wife?"

"I hope so," Elfled said with relish.

"But the abbess hasn't mentioned it," Fridgyth said.

"She doesn't know yet," Elfled said. "The messenger who brought news of the arrangements has told the women secretly."

"Mere gossip, then!" Fridgyth said.

"But it might be better for some, if Audrey didn't come!" Elfled added with a glance towards Irminburgh. "And Audrey would be likely to make a great fuss about a pagan bed-burial, she'd probably criticise my foster mother for allowing such a thing!"

"You may be right," Fridgyth agreed.

The conversation was brought to a halt by the sound of horns in the distance and everyone went out to greet the young King of Deira. Ecfrid arrived on horseback, his grandfather's eagle standard born before him and fifty or so armed warriors at his back. Though this occasion was to be solemn, still he was greeted with cheers and clapping. Seeing no sign of Queen Audrey at his side, Fridgyth searched, to no avail, amongst his followers for a lady's litter.

Eanfleda kissed her son enthusiastically, while the abbess and the Handale reeve waited to welcome him formally. Servants rushed everywhere carrying cups of mead and ale, but the pause for refreshments was brief, for the burial was to take place before sunset, and would be followed by the funeral feast. Ecfrid gave the order for the ceremony to begin.

CHAPTER 34

LAMENT FOR A DRAGON-QUEEN

Queen Eanfleda was invited to lead the procession, alongside her son, the King of Wessex, Wulfhere and Aethelred. Only then did Fridgyth feel certain that Queen Audrey was absent from the gathering. Elfled and the abbess were called forward to take their places behind the King, and Elfled insisted that Wulfrun go with her.

"Walk with me," the herb-wife said, when she saw that Irminburgh stood alone, looking miserable and awkward.

"Thank you," she murmured.

Cynewise's waiting women took their places behind the royalty, but then an unexpected call flew back down the line.

"Lady Irminburgh! Where is the Lady Irminburgh?"

"King Ecfrid has called for Irminburgh! He says the Queen's foster daughter, should be at the front."

Irminburgh turned pale, but Fridgyth smiled. "Go," she said. "Ecfrid wants you at his side."

Looking stunned, but with just the hint of a startled smile on her lips, Irminburgh went to join the most honoured guests at the front.

"So much for that," Fridgyth murmured cheerfully. "Then I shall walk by myself it seems."

But at that moment she felt a tap on her own arm.

"Walk with me?" Ketel offered.

She chuckled and allowed her hand to rest in the crook of his arm, as they joined the queue.

The sun was sinking towards the west as they set off. The site of the burial was not far from the hall, but the procession moved at a stately pace. Some of Cynewise's women wore wreathes of ivy and carried holly boughs, bright with berries. The place had been well prepared in a spot long considered to be sacred. The burial pit had been dug close to where an ancient tribe had once lived and made their round houses; near too were the stark remains of a Roman villa.

Flames rose from a fire pit that had been placed close to the wooden mortuary, the roof of it carved again into the shape of a dragon. It was substantial enough to protect the Queen's body from rain, but the sides were open to the cold. Her famous decorated bed had been placed on a plinth and the remains of Penda's wife lay inside it. Ecfrid and Eanfleda went to stand at the side of it for a moment or two.

Others gathered respectfully around in silence and Ecfrid drew Irminburgh forward to stand beside him.

"Come… she nurtured us both," he said.

Irminburgh looked as though she wanted to speak, but couldn't find the words. Instead she reached up with shaking hands to unfasten from around her neck a small, but exquisite gold and garnet pendant, shaped like a shell. She flushed awkwardly as she struggled to release it and Ecfrid gallantly helped her, then together they laid the precious jewel on Cynewise's breast. There came a gentle sigh of approval from the bystanders, though Eanfleda looked away, less impressed. Then the burial rights began.

The bed was carried respectfully on the shoulders of six elderly Mercian thanes who, along with their wives, had shared Cynewise's exile. Queen Eanfleda and Abbess Hild moved to stand with them at the front, heads bowed, alongside all the other royal Christian converts. In deference to their religion, Hild's priest declaimed the Christian burial rights. The bed was lowered into the ground and covered with a dragon painted board.

It was then that the Christians stepped back, so that the holly-bearing women could come forward. A slow, steady drumbeat began and old though most of them were, Cynewise's women danced around the burial as the sun went down.

Fridgyth's eyes filled with tears. As a young girl she'd danced like this and after a moment or two of hesitation she went to join them. Hild looked on approvingly, and lifted up her gnarled hands to clap in time to the rhythm of the drum; following her example many others joined in.

The drumming built to a crescendo and holly boughs were tossed into the burial pit, as the sun vanished.

Fridgyth returned breathless to Ketel's side. "Cynewise would have liked that," she said.

Flaming brands were lit from the fire-pit and everyone stood quietly by as lay-brothers shovelled earth into the space and then above it, to form a mound.

"I welcome you all to the Queen's funeral feast," Ecfrid cried as he turned to lead the way back to the hall.

Satisfied that Cynewise had received all honour due to her, the Mercians cheered and followed him back to the hall at a good pace, for everyone was feeling hungry.

Cynewise's feast was magnificent. Provisions had arrived not only from Streonshalh, but also from Eforwic, and sweetmeats had been brought all the way from distant Wessex. It was a rare sight to see the high table packed with so many crowned heads. The aged King of Wessex was given the seat of honour.

Fridgyth found herself comfortably seated alongside the abbess, with Ketel, Wulfrun and Irminburgh close by. At Hild's request, Caedmon sang the song that compared Cynewise to the Queen of Sheba and it was received with warm enthusiasm.

Irminburgh managed to answer courteously when anyone spoke to her and Fridgyth sensed that Ecfrid's acknowledgement of her status as Cynewise's foster daughter had done much to ease her heartache. Everyone went late to their beds, cheered and satisfied by the food and drink, so that despite the unfamiliar accommodation, they slept.

The following morning, the whole gathering made their way to the burial mound once again, where they discovered that a fine carved stone marker had been raised.

"None will doubt that a woman of great importance, lies here," Ecfrid announced.

Another horn of mead was passed around, but gradually the visiting rulers wandered back to their tents and began to make preparations for their return journeys. Tents were lowered and horses caparisoned.

Hild and her companions prepared to leave, for the tide and the weather would allow them to return to Streonshalh before it got dark. Cynewise's waiting women helped them gather their things together.

"What are you going to do?" Fridgyth asked Helga. "Will you not go back to Mercia, with Wulfhere?"

They shook their heads and smiled.

"No. Mercia is no longer our home," Helga said. "We are of one mind on this. King Ecfrid has given permission for us to stay, so we may guard our dragon-queen until our time comes too. We will be buried here with her."

Fridgyth nodded. "Your Queen inspired great loyalty," she said softly.

Irminburgh gathered together the few things she'd needed for her brief stay.

"You *could* stay here at Handale Head, with the other women," Fridgyth suggested. "These others are determined to remain here and the King has given permission."

"No," Irminburgh said determinedly. "You know what I will do."

Fridgyth shook her head and smiled. "I cannot see you as a nun," she said.

"I cannot see it, either," Elfled commented frankly. "But then I cannot quite see myself as a nun, though I will have to become one," she added with a sigh.

Irminburgh and Fridgyth smiled sympathetically, and Elfled looked up guiltily as the abbess appeared in the doorway.

"Your brother wants you, Princess," Hild said. "You too Irminburgh… and Fridgyth, I think you should come too, and Wulfrun. This is to be a private meeting, you understand?"

They all looked a little surprised.

"Does he know about Lindi?" Elfled asked, with a glance at Irminburgh.

"Yes," the abbess said. "As King of Deira, he needed to know."

Irminburgh's hands flew to cover her mouth and Hild quickly understood her fear and shame.

"No, no..." Hild assured her. "He does not know why you went with her to the hut Irminburgh... only that you were grievously mistreated by the woman."

"What does he want of us?" Elfled asked.

"I don't know," Hild said.

CHAPTER 35

A NEW QUEEN IN THE HIVE

"The more trials sent to test them, the keener they become, one and all, to throw themselves into the mending of their tumbled world."

Virgil – Georgics. A new translation by Peter Fallon.
Oxfords World's Classics

Fridgyth followed the Princess and the abbess into the luxurious private space that had once been Cynewise's parlour. Irminburgh shot a worried glance at her, and Wulfrun too gave her a rather nervous fleeting look.

The walls of the Mercian Queen's chamber were decorated with richly coloured wall hangings, set there to keep out the draughts and worked partly by the Queen's own hands. The woven images portrayed the goddess Freya in her chariot, pulled by black cats, with sheaves of corn and berries tumbling down to feed the world.

Ecfrid stood up as they came in and invited them all to sit down on the carved and painted benches that furnished the place. He stayed on his feet, looking tense and waited until the servant had closed the door, so that he could speak privately.

"My lady abbess," he began with a slight formal bow to Hild, his voice kept low to emphasise the confidential nature of his words. "I think that you and all present are aware that my wife, Queen Audrey has long wished to become a nun?"

The abbess nodded her understanding, while the others sat in silence, rather stunned that their King should choose to confide in them on this subject.

For a moment his eyes flickered over Irminburgh, then swiftly back to the abbess. "I want you to know, lady," he went on, "that my wife has made application to be divorced, so that she will be free to become a nun, and that Bishop Wilfred has agreed to support her application with the Pope."

Elfled gasped, suddenly excited at what her brother seemed to be about to announce, her hand flew up to cover her mouth. Fridgyth glanced sideways at Irminburgh and saw that she looked utterly astonished.

"The process of this divorce may take a long time," Ecfrid went on, still addressing the abbess. "But lady, I wish all present here to understand that once I am free to marry and take another woman as my queen, I will apply for the hand of Lady Irminburgh."

Elfled launched herself from her stool and threw her arms about her brother. "I am so glad.... so glad," she cried.

Hild looked quite taken aback, as did all the others. Fridgyth tried to smile reassurance at Irminburgh, but the young woman simply stared back at her in amazement, the colour drained from her face.

Ecfrid pushed Elfled gently away from him and went to bow before Irminburgh, holding out his hand. "That is, if the lady will have me."

Her cheeks still pale, she got shakily to her feet, to place her hand in his. "You know I will," she murmured.

He took both her hands in his and kissed her formally on both cheeks, but then, still holding onto her, he turned to the abbess. "I would have asked permission of Cynewise," he said, "as Irminburgh's foster mother, but now that she has gone, in her place I ask permission from you my lady abbess."

Hild smiled wryly and shook her head admonishingly, but then she held out her arms to encompass both of them. "You have my blessing," she said.

Everyone broke out into smiles and laughter as Hild went to hug them both. When they emerged from this embrace, Irminburgh appeared flushed, but happy.

"I must also now ask that Irminburgh stay with you at Streonshalh," Ecfrid said, "until the time comes when I may make this announcement openly. I know she will be safe with you there and I ask that you treat this matter with the greatest confidence."

"We will… oh yes, we will," they all agreed cheerfully.

On a bright, frosty day, towards the end of Blood-month, Fridgyth and Ketel walked together through the orchard to inspect the new south-western gateway, which was in the process of being built. The abbess had decided to reinstate the ancient trod, understanding that it afforded convenient access to the monastery for those locals who worked in the woodlands and Brigsbeck Valley. It might even improve security, as the gate would have a watchman set to guard it, and careful note could be taken of who came in and who went out.

Ketel inspected the carpenter's work with an experienced eye.

"More smoothing here and a little linseed oil," he suggested to the carpenter.

They stepped through the space newly created and followed the now clear path towards the woods.

"How is the Lady Irminburgh?" he asked, for he knew that Fridgyth had shared the high table with the royal residents the previous evening.

Fridgyth chuckled. "She is back to being Irminburgh," she said. "She noted on her recent visit to Ripon that Bishop Wilfrid possesses a very beautiful jewelled reliquary, that she thinks is rather wasted on a bishop and might make an impressive pendant for a queen. She's annoyed that Wilfrid is slow to press the Pope over this divorce, and is letting us know it."

Ketel smiled. "Yes, that sounds as though she is back to being Irminburgh again. Can we manage to keep her here a little while longer, do you think?"

"Yes. She knows that if she wants to be Queen, she must behave in a more dignified manner. I'd rather have her complaining than drooping and weeping and wanting to be a nun."

"What kind of a queen will she make, do you think?" Ketel asked.

"No worse than any other, I should say."

As they reached the woods they found more workers chopping away at brambles, to make the path wide enough for a mule to pass. Herrig, who had been employed to work with the woodcutters as a messenger, greeted them as they approached. "I've moved in with the tanners, now," he announced. "Ralf is building a lean to in the yard for me and he's taking me on as his apprentice. He's going to teach me how to stitch turnshoes."

"Like these," Fridgyth said with a smile and she raised the hem of her gown to proudly display her gleaming, new leather turnshoes.

"Yes, just like those," Herrig agreed.

"Well, I have never had anything so warm and comfortable on my feet," she admitted.

"Muriel gives me two meals a day," Herrig added cheerfully. "And they are good meals!"

"You deserve it," Fridgyth told him.

Ketel approved the work being done and he and Fridgyth continued on their way, struggling just a little as they passed through the thickest undergrowth that had not yet been cleared. At last they came in sight of the rosemary hut and both slowed down a little, as they remembered the dire circumstances that had brought them here before.

"We got there in time... but only just in time," Fridgyth murmured.

"We got there," Ketel said. "That is what matters."

"And I once had distant, dreamlike memories of this place," Fridgyth said, looking meaningfully up at him.

"I have memories too," he said with a fond sigh. "I could never forget this place. I remember that we came here after the old woman died and broke into her hut. It was our first time real time together, was it not?"

"It was," Fridgyth agreed sadly. "And now we've become so old. Those sweet memories are spoiled forever, by images of bloodshed and revenge."

"They need not be spoiled forever," Ketel said.

He reached out and took her by the hand to lead her towards the door.

"What are you doing?" Fridgyth asked.

"We are not so old that we cannot make new memories, still," he said, and he pushed the door open and waited, looking back at her.

"Go on then," she said.

And smiling, Fridgyth followed him inside.

The end.

AUTHOR'S NOTE

'*After the example of the primitive Church, no one there was rich, no one was needy, for everything was held in common, and nothing was considered to be anyone's property.*' From Bede's *History of the English Church and People* (Penguin Classic Version)

I love this quotation from Bede, which describes Hild's monastery at Streonshalh, (Whitby) and sometimes wonder if it is possibly one of the earliest ever descriptions of a kind of socialism. The picture that I present in my novels of Abbess Hild and her monastery is more – 'how I would like it to have been,' – than an attempt at accuracy, with only Bede's quotation to support this possibility.

Fridgyth the herbwife first appeared as a secondary character in *Wolf Girl* (my novel for young adults published in 2006 by Corgi – Random House.)

I also wanted to write a historical novel for adults with an Anglo-Saxon setting, so at a later date, I decided to make my ageing herbwife the main focus of a murder/mystery that became more of a 'why done it', than a 'who done it', and *A Swarming of Bees* was published in 2012 by Acorn Independent Publishers. Many readers have asked for a sequel and *Queen of a Distant Hive* is my response to those requests. I have used historical sources where they were clear, but also used my imagination freely. Irminburgh became Ecfrid's second queen, after the Pope gave permission for his divorce from his first wife (Etheldreda or Audrey), who then became a nun and eventually

Abbess of Ely (Saint Etheldreda). Irminburgh is mentioned in *The Life of Wilfrid*, by Eddius Stephanus as having quarrelled with Bishop Wilfrid and stolen his reliquary, though she too eventually became a nun in Carlisle, after Ecfrid's death. Very little else is known about Irminburgh, though her name suggests a Kentish origin, so I have taken the liberty of inventing a backstory for her that I hope is not unrealistic for the time period, as young royals were often sent away as foster children to be raised at another court – and sometimes to live there as hostages. Bede mentions that Prince Ecfrid was held hostage at the court of Queen Cynewise, at the time of Penda's death, and that he was returned to his parents at about the age of 10 years.

An Anglo-Saxon burial ground, dating to the second half of the 7th century AD, was discovered at Street House Farm near Loftus, in Cleveland, by archaeologist Steve Sherlock. The excavations revealed over a hundred graves, which were laid out roughly in a square shape, surrounding two more central graves, also dating from the 7th century and the remains of several buildings. An array of jewellery and other artefacts were found, including the jewels once worn by a high-status Anglo-Saxon woman who had been buried on a bed and covered by an earth mound. There is no indication that this woman was Cynewise, widow of Penda – that is entirely my own suggestion. The woman's identity is still unknown and likely to remain so, but the artefacts and the layout of the cemetery are similar to finds in the south and southeast of England. There are contradictory indications as to whether the occupants of the cemetery were Christian or pagan, as there were signs of both traditions present. Archaeologists have suggested that the woman, and at least some of the people buried around her may have migrated from the south, where bed burials were more common. Cynewise seemed to me to be an interesting possibility, and this idea provided much inspiration for the story. The finds were acquired by Kirkleatham Museum, Redcar in 2009 and have been on display there since 2011. The exhibition is fascinating, and well worth a visit (entrance is free). In the exhibition, the mysterious Princess is portrayed as a beautiful young woman. This makes an attractive display and also reflects the average age of death at that time, which would have been in the 20's, however, no bones were found in the Street House burial, so the actual age of the high status woman buried cannot be ascertained, and Bede records many people living well into old age. More recent excavations on the same site have revealed evidence of Iron Age, Bronze Age, Neolithic and Roman Occupation. Bede also tells the story of Oswin of Deira, and how he refused to engage in battle when challenged for his throne by Oswy. He retreated to Hunwald's Hall, but was betrayed and murdered there. It is unknown as to whether Hunwald had any children who might have survived the slaughter – that possibility is also entirely imaginary. Queen Eanfleda persuaded Oswy to build a monastery at Gilling in an effort to make amends for his treachery, but the monastery is believed to have suffered from the plague so badly, that all the monks died.

Theresa Tomlinson
Whitby – February 2017
www.theresatomlinson.com

ACKNOWLEDGEMENTS

The author would like to thank Anthea Dove for her excellent editorial help, Alan Tomlinson for drawing the maps and Steve Sherlock for his dedicated archaeology and fascinating walks and talks on the Street House excavations.

The following works have provided much information and inspiration: Bede's *History of the English Church and People* (Penguin Classic); *The Age of Bede* translated by J.F. Webb and D.H Farmer (Penguin classics); Horn and Borne's *Study of the Plan of the Monastery of St Gall* (University of California Press); John Marsden's *Northanhymbre Saga* (Kyle Cathie), Stephen Pollington's *The Mead Hall* (Anglo-Saxon Books), Kathleen Herbert's *Peace-Weavers and Shield Maidens: Women in Early English Society* (Anglo-Saxon Books), Kevin Leahy's *Anglo-Saxon Crafts,* (Tempus)

Visits to Whitby Abbey Visitor Centre, Whitby Museum, West Stow Anglo-Saxon Village and Jarrow Hall have provided further information and inspiration.

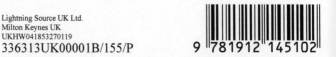